The Chaff

Joel Chafetz

The Chaff
A novel

by

Joel Chafetz

Quartet Global Books
Contact: quartetglobal@gmail.com
Cover designed by Susan Canavarro
Cover painting by Saul Chafetz
Copyright © 2013 Joel Chafetz
All rights reserved.
ISBN: 978-0-9840493-7-0 (e-book)
ISBN: 978-0-9840493-6-3 (paperback)

A
Quartet Global
Book

Dedication

This book is dedicated to my mother and her namesake, my daughter Matti, without whose lights I could not see.

ACKNOWLEDGMENTS

No work of art stands alone. These writers who worked with me over the long process of writing and revising this book are as much a part of the novel as the characters created in it. My thanks to the following people who have contributed so much there's not enough space in this volume to hold what they've done.

Nicole Blake Chafetz
Jack Remick
Robert Ray
John Emlen
Rich Cantrell

On March 13, 1881, a nihilist with a bomb assassinated Tsar Alexander II. In the days, weeks, months, and years that followed, his son, Tsar Alexander III, began both secret and overt murders called pogroms against the quarantined and unsuspecting Jews for reasons that had little or nothing to do with the death of his father.

Prologue

March 12, 1881

Toward sunset Shlomo the tailor trudged the gravel road cutting through icy unplowed fields to the shtetl of Oylaif, a village of 535 Jews who argued incessantly about the word of God. He was troubled by the constant disagreements that often turned to shouting and calling names and saying that one or the other was disloyal or unbelieving and it seemed to him that if it continued the community would tear itself apart.

Just ahead was the center square. It teemed with children kicking their rolled balls of snow to clouds, women scrubbing their clothes at the fountain, and the doors of the synagogue opening for evening prayers.

He was so lost in his thoughts that he didn't notice the men until they scrambled out of the ditch beside the road and blocked his path. They wore hoods that covered their faces, but their dark eyes glistened in the twilight and watched him.

Saying nothing, he maintained his gait and angled his passage so as to go around them.

The tallest of the men accosted him. "Where are you going, Jew?" he said.

Shlomo shook his head in a way that defined him, a man who did not look for trouble, a man who went out of his way to avoid conflict and minded his own business.

"I asked you a question, Jew."

The gang of faceless men circled about him. Their knuckles were wrapped with ragged gray cloth, the fingertips red and swollen with cold.

Shlomo lifted his palms, pressed his way to go around, but they joined shoulder-to-shoulder, making a wall of their bodies, and clenched their fists. Two others closed off Shlomo's retreat.

"What is it you want?" he asked. "I have no money."

The lingering light fell on the tallest man's angled cheek. Fair skin emerged from his hood, a pale face and an aquiline nose.

He punched Shlomo in the chest.

Staggering back, Shlomo clutched his sewing bag against the injury.

"Do you have it?" the tall man asked.

"What is it I am supposed to have?"

"The power of God."

"Only the Lord has that," Shlomo said.

"Then you are doomed."

With an eye to the woman standing up by the fountain and setting down her wet cloth, watching the events with alarm, Shlomo ducked his head and ran between two of the men. The tall man grabbed Shlomo's cloak and yanked him back. The rest of the horde descended on him.

The first punch hit Shlomo from the side and knocked the wind out of him. The second blow raised him. The third was followed by a grunting sound from inside his chest. Two from behind added their blows, and he could not cry out as time slowed and fists landed in a rhythm of one blow following another and another and another, all sensation collapsing into a nightmare of silence.

The men leaned into their punches using their weight, keeping Shlomo upright, the thumps and smacks holding him on wobbly legs. The men worked in tandem, pummeling him with businesslike patience, bludgeoning the meat about Shlomo's bones as if tenderizing him for the oven.

A blow behind his ear knocked Shlomo to the ground. One marauder kicked him in the gut and then the tormentors swarmed over him, tearing at him with their fingernails and a knife until men from the synagogue raced from the square toward the commotion.

The heedless bandits slipped into a gray mist and disappeared into the black maple forest beyond.

No one from Oylaif followed the brigands into the darkness. They gathered around the tailor, who lay half naked with his legs curled up, the cloak covering his torso in shreds.

Carved into his bleeding back was one word: *Vyĭti*. Russian. Get out.

1 . . .

From her attic garret, Usell Binah stuck her head and shoulders over the windowsill to see the commotion pour like a black river down the narrow street. Abrahim Küssel, the blacksmith, carried a bleeding man in his arms and slipped beneath the short awning at her door. He was followed by a mob of men with black beards, black suits, and black shtreimel hats, all compacting together so she could not tell one from the other. Someone pounded and the wall shook. She scurried to her attic hatch and lifted it in time to see her father flash a stay-put palm in her direction.

Propping open the hatch, she bent to the crack as Abrahim Küssel carried the bleeding man inside. Benheman Gimmel, the yarmulke and tallit maker and Rabbi Sklar followed the blacksmith. Others folded into the one room and filled the space around the hearth, pushing her father from the door to the table and demanding of him. Many voices at once.

"Do something."

"Help the poor man."

"Bandits."

"Stop his bleeding."

On the wall the shadows of three men cleared the table in front of the hearth. Abrahim Küssel laid the bleeding man down.

Her father rolled up his sleeves, washed his hands in the basin, inspected the wounds, and with cloth bandages and astringent proceeded to remove the black weave of the tailor's clothing and attack the largest of the cuts. The tailor winced as her father's ministration covered each visible wound.

The men packed into Usell's home began their questions.

"Who did this?

"Angry villagers?

"The Police?

"Peasants?"

"Nihilists?

"Was it robbers?

"What does it mean?"

"They wanted to know if I had the power of God," the tailor cried. "What did I do to them? They hid their faces. They wrapped their hands in cloth. They wrapped their hands."

The silence fell over the room. Someone murmured a prayer.

Benheman Gimmel, in addition to making tallit's and yarmulkes was treasurer of the congregation. He poked his thin face between the Rabbi and the blacksmith and asked, "What did you answer?"

On his side the tailor raised his head to see who spoke. His palm lifted and fell, as palatable as a shrug.

Chiam Flath, the saddle maker who burned his initials into each and every one he made, said, "Men cloaking themselves. Demanding answers to impossible questions. This is vendetta. It's starting again. The next thing there will be Cossacks. Khmelnytsky rising from the dead to massacre our people again."

Usell's father, bulkier and half a head taller than Rabbi Sklar raised his voice. "Everyone out. This is best left for the *Kahal,* for our leaders, to decide."

Rabbi Sklar nodded his assent.

"I have done all I can for the tailor," her father said. "Mordecai. You live alone. Make room at your home. Take this man to stay there. We will meet in the synagogue at eight. The rest of you, out. Back to your duties. Your children must be fed."

A warmth flushed Usell's chest. It was her father's way. To take charge, to calm distress. She'd seen it many times, the strong pronouncements, the logic, the reason, the practicality while others were in chaos.

Like a receding flood, black-clothed men with heavy beards and accepting shoulders departed like a gust of wind onto the street. Abrahim Küssel lifted the tailor in his arms and carried him without the help of others.

All but the rabbi left, and he sat down at the table with her father, who rubbed his forehead and reset the kippah on his head.

"Samuel," Rabbi Sklar asked. "The power of God? Why such a question?"

Her father glanced up at the attic hatch, his eyes questioning Usell's eavesdropping. Lowering his sight, he leaned his elbows on the table.

"I suspect mischief here," he said.

Rabbi Sklar worked his hands together, rolling them about each other. "Who? What were they looking to do?"

Her father stared at the crackling fire. "The tailor is not dead," her father said. "He has no broken bones. He was battered, bloodied, and bruised. Professionals beat the man. They stole nothing. If we knew motive, we would know whom? What is left? Who benefits from terrorizing us?"

"The Tsar?" the Rabbi asked.

"Or the Naradnaya Volya," her father said.

"The People's Will? What does a small political party in the Zemstvo, debating local taxes have against our people? Why would they beat a Jew?"

"They do not wish us to integrate with the empire," her father said.

"I am not so sure we should," Rabbi Sklar said.

Again her father glanced up at the crack in the attic hatch.

"Much is happening out of our control."

Firelight showered her father's cheeks. His heavy graying beard glistened with chicken fat from the meal she'd prepared. With a further glance at her he blinked. Close the hatch. Do not listen.

Usell settled the trap brace into its frame and lay down on her straw mattress. The air chilled with the setting of the sun. To beat a Jew over politics was nothing new, but this was different. Something troubled her father. He had repeatedly argued for her people not to meddle in the affairs of others. Not to be involved. Not to make enemies. But arguments in Oylaif raged with the talk of the day. Citizenship. To engage with others for the good of the state.

All sides of the issue denied the other with deaf ears: "Citizenship would steal our lives, turn us into them."

"Citizenship will give us rights, the power of the Tsar to stop the beatings, the rapes, the theft without recourse."

Striking a match and lighting her candle, she opened the leather-bound book on her straw mattress and read the last 50 pages of *Madame Bovary*, by Gustave Flaubert. She fell asleep wondering if one day she would sleep next to a man not her husband.

2 . . .

Dream fragments danced into morning light and sparkled in the roof cracks as Usell awoke. The beams had shifted over the shtetl's 105-year-old past. Her father said the building was plumb with the earth when it was built, but with age it settled to bedrock and the roof tilted to a sorcerer's hat, straining the frame and spreading cedar shingles so that they no longer touched one another enough to hold out the weather.

Shutters banged open against buildings on the street. Cold gray mist hovered over her straw bed. On the floor below her attic garret, her father's snores ended with an abrupt snort. He cleared his throat, his rope hammock stretching and the wood floor creaking with his weight. Leaden trudges guided him to the hearth, where the metal flange ached and the legs on his sturdy stool squeaked. He chopped kindling and called, "Usell, you must get up. Time is short."

The straw crackled as she snuggled beneath her heavy cloak. Winter resisted spring with a tenacity not seen in years - ice crystals furred between the wallboards and with their melt came the chilling cold.

"My daughter, come down now," her father called. "We have important things to discuss."

Important things. She snuggled into the straw warmed by her own body heat. Tsar Alexander II's edict making Jews citizens of the Russian Empire would be signed this day, but it would not affect her. Her path was set. A woman, whether in the shtetl of Oylaif or in the outer world, had one path: wife and mother to a man her father would choose. Recent word from outside the shtetl was that the Tsar's brother, the Grand Duke, had promised his daughter, Princess Ludivica Melikova, to a German for an alliance. An open royal coach carried the princess's portrait throughout the territory and was the source of rumor that the Pale would be dowry to the Germans to bind the marriage, and the Germans despised the Jews.

In shiny oils the Princess's portrait showed her wrapped in ermine, her slim beauty and iron red hair glowed against skin so white the snow faded against it. But even with all she possessed, her future, like Usell's, was set.

In the past week the *shadkhn* women had spread the word that Samuel Binah had spoken to fathers with unmarried sons.

Wrapping her hair in her snood, Usell then slipped into the felt shoes she'd stitched together from worn cloth and old leather. Removing her cloak from her bed, she swam into its oversized arms and with a glance at the volumes piled about the attic floor she set *Madame Bovary* on her bed next to *Maps of the New World.*

Lifting the squeaky hatch, she dropped the ladder and stepped down on wobbling crosspieces to the floor. Once down, she adjusted her cloak against the cold and advanced toward the candlelight that shadowed her father at the table.

He looked like the undertaker in *Oliver Twist,* only with a blue and white tallit about his shoulders and a black kippah camping on his balding scalp. On his three-legged stool with his back to the fireplace, her father scribbled figures in his ledger.

When he noted her presence, he stopped and waited for her to sit.

She folded onto the child's stool made for her before she could walk.

"This is for you," he said.

He lifted the silver mezuzah with a string through the nail hole that had held it to the doorjamb.

"It is to protect our home, Father," she said.

"It is more important that you are reminded of your heritage," he said.

"Why do I need reminding?"

"The world changes," he said. "Now turn around."

7

Usell lifted the snood off her neck. A brush of cold tickled the short hairs. Her father tied the string, and without looking at it, she slipped the silver weight beneath her garments and faced him.

"What is wrong, Father?" she asked. "What is going on?"

Clearing his throat, her father replied.

"You have finished reading *Madame Bovary*. What did you learn?"

Pausing, she assessed his somber mood and then answered.

"To rebel against convention harms those who care for you."

"Have you no sympathy for her plight?"

"Emma Bovary wished for more passion in her life, but had foolish beliefs."

"Beliefs?" he asked.

"That love would solve all her problems."

"Given her beliefs, what would you have done?" he asked.

"I do not have her beliefs nor do I have to make that choice."

"Hummm," he said. "Were the risks she took justified?"

"She broke society's rules."

"That is always the lesson," he said. "The question remains."

The wood fittings of her stool squeaked. The fire in the hearth glowed red. Rubbing her hands together in the cloth of her lap, she waited for her father's brow to unwrinkle.

"We are to our lessons this morning," he continued. "Straighten your spine to deliver with authority. Think your way through each situation. Analyze what you feel before you speak and be clinical in your logic."

"I am ready, Father," she said.

He removed the phylacteries wrapped around his head and laid them on the table.

"We begin then," he said. "*Vous êtes français, non?*"

She straightened her back and brushed a hand over the necklace before speaking. "*Oui, Monsieur. Je respire le soufflé de la liberté.*" I breathe the breath of freedom.

His second question jumped from language to the books he allowed her to read.

"Remain where thou art, proud Templar. On what fate did the speaker set herself?"

"On the precipice of the castle of Reginald Front-de-Boeuf," she answered. "Where she was taken with her father, Isaac of York, a Jew."

"What was her fate?"

"To leap from the parapets and take her own life if the Templar, Brian de Bois-Guilbert, should do what he threatened."

"What did he threaten?"

"To take her as his concubine," she said.

"Was that worth her life?"

"She loved another. She would not sacrifice it."

"Did she abide by her people's code?" her father asked.

"Her heart made the decision. Was the result not the same?"

"You answer a question with a question. What is that called?"

"Is it not Socratic dialogue?" she answered.

"Good," he said. "Take control. Seize the advantage. Have others explain themselves so that you may see their intent. Good."

She lifted her chin and a thin smile creased her lips.

"Now," he said. "What can you tell me about the Hellenes' religious beliefs?"

She folded her arms. "Thunder and lightning were the anger and warnings of unhappy Gods."

"That was the common perception of the masses. Why did the Greeks foster this belief?"

"When the Greeks conquered the land of the Hellenes," she said. "They made up stories about naiads to describe the controls the Greeks forced upon the local population."

"Examples."

"Salmacis fused with her lover. Nomia blinded hers. Zeus was surrounded with a band of golden light and demanded submission."

"How was that like what the native population saw?" he asked.

"They saw the Greeks' shiny bronze armor reflecting in the sunlight. The Greek army raped and pillaged with merciless cruelty. The myths made it all seem normal."

"What was it really about?"

"Assimilation," she said. "Smaller numbers of Greeks had to appear like Gods to their conquered populace."

"What did the Greek rulers really believe?"

"Thunder and lightning were cosmic coughs."

"What is it we believe?" he asked.

"That it is foolish to believe politicians."

Her father shook a dissatisfied head. "No. We are the chosen people. There is only one God."

Her shoulders curled. She closed her eyes and took a deep breath, readying herself for what came next.

"Summarize what you have learned from the commandments above your bed," her father said.

"Must I repeat children's lessons?"

"Ritual comforts the troubles of life."

Sitting up straight, she recited: "*Ohavei Hashem siń us ra.* If you love life, hate evil. Be clean in your heart. Do well to your fellow man. Be gentle and giving in your nature. Do not do harm with your words. Keep away from lies. Practice the way you would wish others to treat you. Hold the highest honor for your calm judgments and good behaviors. Do not give in to passions. Be a light, not a shade of darkness."

"You see," her father said. "Without studying Torah your words contain the essence of the Israelites."

"I wish to learn more than repetition."

Her father's gaze narrowed and met her for a moment. With a twitch of his eyebrows he nodded. And then he stood up. He folded his voluminous cloak, but instead of further questions he spoke in a low cushioned voice.

"I will speak with you as if you were a woman."

She took a quick gasping breath. His look was calm about the thick bristle of facial hair.

"You are old enough to participate," he said. "You are free to express your opinion."

He nodded as if the rhetoric of his teaching had not been about obligations, duties, and the sacrifices she must make; to never question the rules of living a good life with intelligence and conscience according to the laws of Moses because the force of 5,642 years of history demanded only her obedience and needed only the participation of her ears.

"I may disagree?" she asked.

Damp wood sizzled in the fireplace below the iron arms hinged into mortared stones.

"You may state your case," he said.

The long fanning beard over his chest twisted in corkscrew spirals. He smoothed his floor-length black frock down the front of his stout frame.

"You are to be married," he said.

His slow blink defined the silence.

"Have you nothing to say?"

"We will be citizens today," she said. "With rights."

Her father's thumb and forefinger rubbed the leather straps of the phylacteries still wound about his wrists.

"I have received consent," her father said. "The boy will be a rabbi. He is devout, studious, thoughtful, and hard-working - all attributes that will help make you a strong and supportive wife."

Her shoulders bowed. The stiff leather in her shoes scraped against the floor.

"Do you wish me to make breakfast?" she asked.

"Daughter. I have not been father to you these 17 years without learning something of your nature. I have not always approved, but I have stayed silent to allow you breadth of thought because you are without a mother and that is a thing that you have had to deal with. I know it has been hard, but you are smart and it is incumbent upon you to become a member of this community through your husband."

Cold air whistled into the house from the space beneath the door and sill. Candle shadows danced into a jester on the wall.

"The meydlshes do not speak with me," she said. "They cling to each other like cockleburs and speak of husbands and babies and keeping kosher. They do not read. They do not talk to me about marriage."

"Your education frightens the mothers of the maidens."

"They do not talk to me, Father."

"You have been without your mother to teach you how to become part of the community," he said. "With the changes coming, you have a second chance to become part of the whole."

She lowered her head.

"Madam Hoffman will discuss with you your cycle," he said. "In nine months from your wedding day I will have a grandson to raise to God."

She stared at her pale hands in her lap.

"I know I have not spoken to you about this," he said. "You and I have felt the strain of our situation and for that I am sorry, but I will not make excuses for myself. These are turbulent times and though you might have felt that I could have encouraged other directions, they are no longer possible. I have allowed you more freedom than most. I accept responsibility for this. Your mother left you too young, but despite all that you have had to tolerate, you have become a strong woman of spirit. May the Lord watch over you."

Usell closed her eyes.

"Please do not put on that face when I mention the Lord," he said. "You do not read Torah so you cannot understand what HE intends and you must put all that aside now because you are to become wife to a man who will be a great leader and you will bear his children."

She searched the candle flame for answers.

"You are interested in knowing whom I have chosen?" he asked.

She shook her head no.

"It is none other than the son of Benheman and Rebecca Gimmel."

She blinked three times and then stared at a tumble of ill-stacked wood in the fireplace. It collapsed and gray ash rose up the flue.

"Moshe Gimmel does not like me," she said. "He does not even look at me."

Her father frowned. "That is not an argument. He will learn to love you."

"What is love?" she asked.

Her father lifted his head.

She started to say something else, but then rose from the table and without permission headed toward the door.

"Where are you going?" he asked.

"To get water for your meal," she said.

Opening the door, she stepped outside and closed it behind her. Her father called out, "You forgot the bucket."

The cobbled street had already slipped into its daily routines. The thump-bump of wooden cartwheels and horses' hooves clattered over a few centimeters of snow, and already buyers and sellers added their banter to the clank of cow bells, goat bleats as the soft murmur of morning prayers lifting from the minions to a God that ignored all but the most accidental of wishes.

3 . . .

Breath fogged about her face. She pulled the heavy cloak up to her neck, covering as much snood and hair as a passing man might see. A merchant with a pile of buffalo skins pulling a wooden cart narrowed his eyes at her, a man from outside the shtetl. He plodded forward and hunched himself into his movement.

Her skirt twisted and whipped about her ankles and when she looked up, Yehuda, the violinmaker, his short coat buttoned to the collar, sat down in his wooden chair on the opposite side of the street. He plucked the strings of his violin to tune and lifted his thin gray beard to glance at her as if she were a fluttering crow going to branch. The expression on Yehuda's face was dour, yet to his violin he was gentle. Every day he tested his instruments and some days she would waltz in her garret when no one was home, dream she was at the grand ball, and she would dance herself into *War and Peace*. Perhaps meet Andre, someone tall, mature, sure of what he wanted, but torn inside like the rest of humanity, someone who would understand how she felt.

Yehuda tilted his head. With a squint, he raised his violin and played a vigorous Strauss waltz. No one discussed the tailor or what had happened. It had passed. And no one paid attention to the gaiety of the violin. They went about their duties as if work or obsession to do God's word were the only things in the world that mattered.

Gray clouds raced north. Few women walked the street. They did not participate in synagogue prayer and had already finished with their morning duties: sweeping the streets, tending to the meals, lactating for their children, just as God ordered it to be, just as the men wanted it to be, women doing as they were told, as a duty, an obligation, a dictate, the men choosing lives for women, fathers determining their daughters' fate, setting their paths and deciding that she should marry Moshe Gimmel.

THE CHAFF

Gimmel. She snorted. Alphabet's fourth letter. Its origins were of a man chasing another man. For what purpose? To help or to harm?

Usell knotted her arms and squeezed her knees. She'd known Moshe Gimmel most of her life and only once did he show a glint of interest. When she was a child, Madame Hoffman pointed at him. He was staring at Usell as she did the wash at the central fountain. She allowed a friendly smile, but he quickly looked away and never once caught her eye again, even though the moment was strong and their eyes had held each other.

He was a studious boy with bad skin. His prominent nose was always stuck in his prayer book. He strode through the shtetl in his too-large shoes like a skinny pea pod, kicking his cloak and hiding behind his oversized black shtreimel hat. And that distant look on his face - it was as if he were somewhere else when his eyes passed her, as if he were speaking to God and not her, seeing right through her as if she didn't exist.

"He's an intelligent boy," her father had said when the *Kahal* met to discuss the prospects of the young men for Yeshiva. She would crouch with her hatch lifted and listened.

"He has the wisdom to discuss Talmud with any scholar and he is devout," her father said.

But he never came to her house like other young men who came because her father was an educated man and would answer questions about the outside world. They would always glance up at her hatch as if they knew she watched them from above. "As a citizen," her father used to say, "you could go to University in Kyiv. There is a man, a Jew of questionable orthodoxy, who is library minister in Odessa. I could write him a letter about you if you are interested. This man could nominate those worthy to a post. There, they do not care so much about a man's interior life."

Oily rainbows ran between the round cobbles and she wondered: What kind of a father would Moshe Gimmel be? Would he be like her father and talk to his children only about duty and the laws of Moses? As far as she could see, all Moshe Gimmel cared about was God, as if he had a special relationship with Him, or was a prophet like Isaiah speaking the words told to him in sleep or like Moses questioning a burning bush. She wondered if, when Moshe Gimmel talked to God, might God ask him to prove his devotion and kill his

14

son—like Abraham—the son she might birth? Or might he be a father like Lot and offer his daughters to the citizens of Sodom to protect God's angels from the evil habits of men? And what kind of husband would he be to her? Would he ask how she wished to be loved?

She blew on her cold, cupped hands.

Across the street on the corner ten men in a minion prayed. With them was a gawky boy with a tallit draped over the back of his head, his slumped posture unmistakable. Moshe Gimmel. With phylacteries wrapped around his wrists and forehead, he davened like a bobbing bird pecking on snowy ground.

She lifted her head, glanced back at her door, and winced. Rolling clouds twisted toward the sun. Men in the busy street went about their business with sober faces.

With a quick breath she strode from her doorstep into the street filled with men in their black habits. Dodging out of their way, she slipped past them, turning aside so as not to touch, not to interrupt or unsettle her passage that might upset the customs separating men from women.

The few women on the wooden sidewalks in their babushkas, wool shawls and unsized linen dresses stopped what they were doing to watch Usell. Their faces mimicked what they said to her when there were no men around. Why are you not inside? Why are you not working for the community? Why isn't someone shielding you from the presence of men?

Prayers concluded. The old men untied their phylacteries. Moshe Gimmel talked to Levi, a younger student with reverent eyes. Moshe Gimmel waved away Levi's words with authority as Usell sliced through the traffic, slipped between the cloaks of men who kept their heads down and did not look at her. Across the street the shops and artisans set up their displays on the cracked wooden sidewalk. It creaked like a dead tree in the wind, laboring with submission. The sidewalk strained to serve more purpose than the rusted nails affixing it to the buildings. She hopped onto the planks. Gliding on the shoes she'd made herself, she headed straight for the corner with hardly a sound.

Less than ten meters away from her, Moshe Gimmel raised his voice. His face was so animated and forceful she almost stopped.

"It was Eliezer who prophesied Jehoshaphat would break his alliance with Israel and the LORD would destroy his ships. If the Cossacks come, the LORD will strike their stallions and bend their swords and if not, then we will do it." He lifted a finger to the sky.

Less than an average-sized boy, his ropy hair and black pais tickled down the stringy muscles of his pale neck. He clutched his prayer book in his right hand close to his chest; the gold silk lip of his marker dangled like a tired dog's tongue and when he took a breath and looked up, he saw her coming.

He stopped speaking. His stare solidified to a glassy brown glaze and then he spun on his worn heels and marched away with a long swing of his arm and a bounding stride into the street.

Her momentum was greater than his and she caught Moshe Gimmel under the carved wooden sign of Gerber Brothers Furniture Repairs that extended into the street from the front of their building like a flag displaying sovereignty.

"Moshe Gimmel," she said. "Stop."

Moshe Gimmel halted. He lowered his head. He did not look at her.

Madame Hoffman, who was washing the windows of the butcher shop, lifted her chin and frowned. If Moshe Gimmel had been any closer, Madame Hoffman might have interceded and chastened Usell, lectured her not to speak with a man, not in public, and certainly not in private if she wished to have the ear of the good women of the community. But that threat had faded long ago when the child Usell questioned the women preparing dinner. *Is there sense in separate dishes and silverware for meat and dairy when lye soap scrubbed both clean?*

Usell centered herself in front of Moshe Gimmel. He did not move his feet, but twisted his head as if looking for a means of escape. She spoke with a calm voice.

"Moshe Gimmel. I must speak with you."

"It . . . It's not permitted," he said.

"If you will not speak with me, I will not consent," she said.

"It is not permitted," he repeated, talking to his prayer book.

"Why not? Must someone filter our words—contain their meanings as if you were an uncontrollable bull and I a cow in heat?"

His face reddened.

"What am I to you?" she asked.

Looking down and away Moshe Gimmel trembled. "You are not a cow."

"Then speak to me."

"You are not a cow and . . . it's not permitted."

"Moshe Gimmel," she said. "If I'm to be wife, I must know what I am to you."

He lifted his pale pocked face. Something folded across his eyes as if a great cloud had cleared and rendered an articulate decision about what the heavens contained.

"We are to be married?" he asked.

His face twitched and whatever transpired, it changed his look. His eyes receded. His body leaned away.

"You do not like me?" she asked.

People in the street stared as they passed. Moshe Gimmel's head bowed under their gaze and when he looked back at her, the Moshe Gimmel who listened only to God reappeared.

"It's not permitted," he said. His tone was soft but direct, like her father's.

"All right," she said. "Is this all you have to say?"

His puzzled look confirmed nothing and then Moshe Gimmel, this studied boy, pivoted his body and marched away like a soldier, the particular thump of his passage like that of a man with no destination in mind but in a great hurry to get there.

She stood for some moments. A mule and cart bumped on cobbles. A string of bells jangled on a stick. The black-clad men made their way to their livings and duties without seeing her as anything more than an impediment to walk around.

An icy gust of wind lifted sprays off the puddles. Morning clouds thickened and shadows darkened the cobbled street. The men in their black rekels, shtreimel hats, and beards blurred to shadows as they passed.

"Mother," Usell whispered. But there was no answer. There was never any answer.

The smells of goat, hay, and a sense of coming snow quivered in the dampness, and somewhere in the shtetl, someone baked bread.

4 . . .

The sky cracked with the coming storm as Usell straightened her back, lifted the lever on the door of her house, and entered. Her father sat on his stool in his brooding slump. He frowned at her and then lifted a wheat stalk from the bowl on the table and picked his teeth.

"What is my next assignment, Father?" she asked.

"There will be none."

"My education is over?"

"From now on you must learn from your husband," he said.

"Father, I do not wish to marry Moshe Gimmel."

"Why is this?"

"He is not . . .." Despite her attempt to control her aspect, her face knotted. "I wish to go to University."

"That is not in your future."

She joined him at the table. "I have doubts. I wish to understand."

"I, too," he sighed.

And then he looked up. Something gentle and accepting cooled his face.

The fire cracked.

"Life is about choices," he said. "If history has taught us nothing else, it is that we need others' good graces in order to survive. A different belief is a burden, but it finds solace among like minds." He settled back and folded his hands at the bulge on his belly.

"I have dreams, Father," she said.

"There must be order," he said. "Dreams are fears of the mind. The world is what it is. It is beyond my power to change."

"You have taught me to think, Father, to reason, to ask for proof."

Pressing his kippah on his head, he said, "You are like your mother."

"My mother?"

"Yes. Do you remember her?"

"A little."

"Tell me what you remember."

"My mother was standing with her back to me in front of the seated men of the *Kahal*. She had long black hair, a pale blouse, and a matching skirt that showed her hips. Your beard was all black then, and you counted the knots on your tallit sitting next to me."

Her father nodded.

"It was a *mishpet,* a trial by rabbis. It was her decision to leave Oylaif."

"She did not turn around, Father. She did not look at me even at the door as she was escorted away. Even when I cried out to her."

"I had to hold you back," he said.

A careless placement of wood in the hearth crumbled into a heap of coals, red sparks, and a spray of ash.

"You may ask questions about your new life now," her father said.

"Tell me about her, Father."

"You should let this go."

"What happened to her?" Usell asked.

"I do not know. She sought things beyond our beliefs."

"Where did she go?"

The sigh he heaved reached deep inside him, the same sigh she'd heard when he didn't know she was listening.

"My daughter," he said. "You have led an isolated life. I have educated your mind and tried to educate your spirit, but you had no one to give you a center, a path to community."

"Tell me about her."

He waved his hand. "Unimportant."

"It is what I want to know."

"Have I taught you nothing about life?" he asked. "When the earth trembles beneath your feet, you do not plant the garden for the spring. One thing at a time."

"I will not leave, Father. I am not like her."

He closed his eyes for a moment and then squeezed her hand.

"When you smile, you warm the room," he said. "But you are stubborn, like her."

"Father, tell me what I really want to know."

"What is that?"

"How could she abandon me?"

His forearms spread on the surface of the table. The candle flame wavered in the hidden breeze.

"I cannot answer that," he said.

"Then tell me about her."

His chest filled and even as he was shaking his head no, he began to speak. "I was teaching the laws of banking in Tartaristan at Rodionovsky Institute for Women. Vera was a student at the school. She was only 17, but already her beauty and her fiery nature were evident. I could never tell what she was thinking."

"Where are her parents?"

"Her father was a French nobleman, the family of Figner, who emigrated to the Pale to do business. Her mother was the daughter of a wealthy Jew. Both her father and his wife were too open in their comments about the Tsar and his treatment of peasants. They disappeared, leaving their wealth to their daughter."

He grew quiet, stared into the room's dark shadows.

"What was she like?" Usell asked.

His wrinkled eyelids closed. He leaned toward her.

"She was a fuse already lit. She sparked. The temperaments of men are not made to deal with a woman of spirit. She knew what she wanted and she set out to get it. No one could tell her anything. She picked my brain. She wanted to know the workings of the police, the army, the banking system, and monetary exchange rates between nations. Books. She loved books. She wanted to know the secrets of the empire and wanted something more basic from me."

Usell turned aside. A humorous snort puffed out her father's nose.

"I was weak," he continued. "I betrayed the trust of those who trusted me to mentor. I was hired to teach but instead I fell in love. We fled the Institute to Switzerland and in Zurich she continued her studies."

"Were you happy?" Usell asked.

A smile crooked one corner of his mouth before disappearing into his beard.

"She had radical ideas. She joined a group, the Frichi, followers of a German who wrote about the conditions of the English working class. Anathema for a French aristocrat. That's what she said she was, not her mother's Jewish daughter."

Her father waved a hand in the air.

"The government persecuted the Frichi and we fled back here, where things began to fall apart. She objected to the confines of her wifely duties. You were born. Nothing was sacred to her. She challenged everything. Finally the Kahal had enough and she was pressed to stop. You paid the price for her exile. For that I am sorry."

He blew a long breath out puffed cheeks. "I told her that her words would lead to no good and that while we lived in this community, her thoughts and words between us could be her own, but she must keep them to herself outside these doors. She was the wife of a Jew in the Pale of Settlement. She said that we were fools to think that the world ended at the boundaries of Oylaif."

"I remember swimming with her, but I don't remember her," Usell said.

"Yes. You were too young. You were three, four, five, and you swam like a fish. Every day, spring through summer. She was a magnificent swimmer. She said you could swim that channel between France and England. I laughed. She got mad and said I should not make fun of her. His eyes glazed and then he looked at his hands. They cupped, and then turned over. "How could you remember?" he asked. "You were so young."

"She didn't love me?"

He set his jaw. His short fingers entwined, clenched tight.

"She had other causes," he said.

Releasing his own grip and his breath, his plump hand reached into the bowl holding the wheat stalks. Crushing a handful of the grains, a few kernels escaped his thick palm and spurted away like fleas. Tightening on the dry grain, they cracked against each other and when he opened his hand, what didn't stick there—husks, stems, broken germs—dribbled onto the table, bounced onto the floor, tumbled away. A few frail and broken skins remained on his palm. He blew on them and they fluttered by the candle flame, danced in the heat as a cold breeze from under the door lifted them into the shafts of light where they swirled like butterflies, flitted in the air, and then disappeared into shadows.

"We must hold tight to the stalk," he said. "Or like this chaff, the wind will drive us away."

The icy air seemed to shatter at the pounding on the door.

21

"Samuel. Samuel," a voice from outside shouted. "Are you there? We are being assailed. A mob, from the fields, from the river, from the countryside, from the forest. They say we will never become citizens. They approach. Make ready. Make ready. Hurry to the synagogue."

5 . . .

At the open door Usell joined her father. In the street, black-clothed men in their flyaway cloaks hurried toward the center square and the synagogue. Madame Hoffman ran to the corner and followed the path of the men. She held up the hem of her wool dress. Her chin drew down into many chins and her stern mouth tightened as she gripped a black iron frying pan like a club.

"Father, what is happening?" Usell asked.

"It is nothing," her father said. "The rabble is stirred. We will deal with it."

He glanced at the sky. Clouds stabbed across the light, mist swelling in the glow.

"Think about your future," he said. "Make plans to join our people in their struggle to fit in and still keep our ways."

He touched her cheek with his palm. The mouth buried in white beard twitched to a lopsided smile, and then he turned into the street and followed the women who gripped their children in unbroken chains, their urgencies pressing them to their homes. At the corner her father took a different direction. To the synagogue.

Coming down the street Zapora Küssel, daughter of the blacksmith, led the *meydlshes* – so many unmarried girls with children's faces and women's bodies. Their heads bobbed like whitecaps on the sea heading to the winemaker's cellar because it had the sturdiest door, the largest bolt, the only pistol in the shtetl.

Zapora, who once was her friend. Having seen Zapora with Danya Avotaynu in the alley. Their bodies were wound tight, their clothing half off. Zapora had not spoken to Usell since.

The *meydlshes* disappeared around the corner. Door bolts, windows, and shutters all around Usell's home slammed shut. She slumped at the door.

Closing it she set the latch. The room was dark and empty. Sparse. Humble. Her father's bed, a round wooden table with two stools. Fire crackled and threw long shadows on the wall. The sky above the roof rumbled, shaking the structure. Wind threw pebbled droplets against the window. She pressed the mezuzah necklace beneath her woolen dress and wondered what her mother would do.

Outside the door someone wailed, "They are so many. So many."

Usell drew her cloak tight and warmed her hands in front of the fire. She kneeled down on the hearth, chopped two alder rounds into kindling with her father's hatchet, and raised the fire. She hacked two onions to pieces, tossed a lump of chicken fat in the iron pot, and swung the trammel over the flame. When the mix caramelized, she cracked in two eggs, dumped in the remains of the previous night's kasha and noodles, and stirred it with a fractured wooden spoon, hardly touching the mix, hardly paying attention, staring at the fire, watching the crimson glow lick against the soot-blackened pot all the while clutching the mezuzah beneath her dress.

The sky rumbled. Tightening her fingers around the cloth enveloping the silver tube at her neck, she straightened her back. Pulling the trammel out, she scraped the contents of the pot into bowls and set them aside. With a thorough wiping of her hands she tied the cloak at her neck, then picked up the hatchet and left the house on the run.

Clouds had darkened the sky.

Warmed by the flush of resolve, she arrived at the synagogue with its high-pitched roof. In front of it a swarm of black rekels and shtreimel hats formed a layer of humanity.

The center fountain bubbled over the stone pond. Usell stopped behind it. The community of men stood shoulder to shoulder, those that wished a more devout population next to those that wished a wider presentation to the world.

Chiam Flath clutched a hard wood cane. The blacksmith gripped a heavy hammer. Benheman Gimmel, a staff. Madame Hoffman had her pan. Usell did not see Moshe Gimmel, but all faced the road leading into Oylaif.

The humped earth road split a mist-layered field and low-brush the meadow. Torches bobbed in the gray. Hundreds of them, like fireflies, luminescence funneling in the direction of the synagogue.

Emerging from the shadows, ragged men carrying shovels and rakes, pitchforks and bent iron, scythes and axes scrambled out of the gullies up both sides of the road, growing numbers from the fields, from the meadow, from the forest behind. Thunder cracked.

She had seen some of these men: field hands, laborers, and landless farmers who spent the winter looking for work, sometimes in Oylaif, asking for handouts, confronting her people like they were dogs. Sometimes they sat on the road and stole from Jewish farmers or merchants taking their wares to Havens, the town on the other side of the forest. A few Yeshiva boys got into fights with them. Once a young girl was taken away. She returned shaken and refused to say what had been done to her. *Ganefs,* thieves, Madame Hoffman called them, but she meant they were worse.

Usell ducked behind the wall of the fountain.

Someone in the mob yelled, *"Deyea te Zheyevees."* Death to the Jews. They took up this chant. Death to the Jews. Death to the Jews. Death to the Jews.

Usell clutched the hatchet. Angry eyes, and among them was something watching, something silent and cunning, more so than the fury passing from mouth to mouth.

Clouds rumbled and swept across a blackening sky. Someone in front of the temple shouted. "God has joined our struggle."

Out of the men of Oylaif protecting the synagogue, a large man with a robust back, marched toward the road and positioned himself in front of the fountain. He wore no hat, but a kippah camped on his bald spot.

"Father," Usell said. She lifted her head over the wall of the fountain.

Ten strides away her father put his fists on his hips with elbows wide as if he were part of a door that must be passed.

Anger from the mob spat at him.

"Get off our land." "Go away." "We don't want you here."

They headed right for the synagogue, right for her father with no hint of stopping.

A crack of thunder shook the ground and the forward edge of the mob slowed. The rolling clatter of the heavens died and her father's booming voice followed.

"Leave us before God strikes you dead."

He pointed to the heavens as if he commanded the Lord's will, and a lightning bolt ripped across the darkness.

Half the mob recoiled. Her father lifted his hands. Torches withdrew to the mist, softened to puffed yellow balls like summer dandelion heads.

With the silence her father continued. "You risk the wrath of the Lord. You challenge the Tsar. We are citizens. We are protected by the Tsar's law."

A strapping man with a knit hood, 20 years younger than her father, stepped clear of the halted men. He shook his squared fist. His loosely woven peasant coat slipped open at the waist. Beneath it was a black uniform with a silver slash over the pocket.

"Get off our land," he said.

"We are peaceful people," her father said.

The man had long yellowed hair tucked into his hood. His sharp face clenched to hard vertical lines that locked at his clamped jaw.

Her father had always said *your best opportunity is when you have the attention of one. With one you can negotiate.* Her father was known for this skill. She had seen him at it many times. He rarely lost an argument.

"We do not provoke fights," her father said.

"You are a curse," the uniformed man said.

Her father pointed to the angry heavens again. "We believe in the power of God."

Rain fell from heavy clouds and splattered on the cobbles. Like skittering rats, the mob split in half, disassembled, and scattered off the road. Those remaining carried knives and swords, not implements from the farm.

Her father spoke again.

"God is angry."

The torchlight on the road retreated to the mists of field and meadow. The man with the uniform beneath his peasant's cloak sneered at the retreating mob, but four others with rigid stances stepped right behind him. They had rifles. With bayonets. Their hands were wrapped with gray cloth. The uniformed man faced her father.

"It is our God who is angry with yours," the man said. "He demands retribution for your crimes." He lifted his hand and lightning bolts shot through the black sky. A rolling clap of thunder followed it. A cry rose from the men in the fields and meadows. The men of Oylaif shrank back. A few of the horde off the road climbed back on.

"Sh'ma Yisroël," her father's booming voice said. Hear, O Israel.

Rain became hail, splattering the cobbles and pelting the heads of all.

"I have warned you," her father said.

The uniformed man roared, "It is not your God who commands."

The hail stopped and a thick rain fell. A man with a sword in his hand waved it above his head. "Our God has defeated yours."

A raffish man in peasant garb climbed up from the field and threw a stone, hit her father on his chest, and then other stones flew and hit not only her father, but also some of the men in the front of the temple. Her father drew a thick kitchen knife from beneath his cloak and set himself.

The mob charged, absorbing him and attacking the protectors of the synagogue as the rain poured down in earnest. Men with clubs, hatchets, scythes, axes, bayonets, swords, and knives tumbled onto men with sticks, a woman with kitchenware and her father with a knife.

Usell dropped her hatchet and ran. After four strides a Jew with a black rekel coat slammed into her back and flattened her against the cobbles. His heavy weight pressed down on her and when men stomped on his back his inert body squashed against her, pressing her against stone, the edges of her mezuzah creasing her skin, her breath expressing without control. Shouts gave way to screams. Shoes blurred by. Leather soles slapped sprays of wet and the heavy body on her back squeezed down on her with the added weight of others stomping on him, compressing the air from her chest until there was nothing left.

6 . . .

Usell opened her eyes. Her cheek crushed against the cobbles. Rain splashed her face. Winking away the wet, she froze at the screams echoing through the streets. She tried to move. Weight on top of her, a chin on her hair. Wet wool smell. Not moving. Storm rain splattering the cobbles. Locking her elbows, she pressed up. Wiggling her shoulder she slid between the street and the weight and then twisted her body until the man slipped off her. Exposed to the weather, thick droplets pelted her snood. Lightning flashed.

The man lay on his side. It was Benheman Gimmel, Moshe's father. A sharpened shaft of wood stabbed through his neck.

Thunder growled. A snake of cold rippled up her back. Scrambling to her feet, she tripped backward over a body. Madame Hoffman, her heavy pan still in her hand, the back of her head missing. She lay across Levi, the first-year yeshiva student who spent hours staring at Usell as if she were a forbidden idol.

Danya Avotaynu stumbled from the dark and hobbled towards her, hesitant, reaching for her and then he fell face down, an ax buried in his back, the words on his lips unmistakable.

"Zapora."

None of the bodies around the fountain were as large as her father. Nothing moved except what the wind lifted to wet sprays off the cobbles. Hard rain. The fall of gray, charcoal, and black whipped like sheets in slanted layers, stealing whatever light was left. And then the synagogue burst into flame.

"Kill them all," a running shadow said. "Kill them all."

Usell ducked from the square down the nearest street. The buildings blurred by black rain were unrecognizable. A close scream stopped her. She hid against a wall.

A vertical mist turned from shade to shape to Chiam, the saddle maker. He cried out. A man stood behind him holding a scythe, the point in Chiam's middle. His voice disappeared into splashes and the heavy wool hem of Usell's dress slapped on her naked shins.

"Come on," a man said.

"Get them before they can hide," someone ahead yelled.

"Torch the buildings."

"Don't kill the women right away."

Fire leaped from one crooked roof to the next. Yellow swells blurred the street. Five men surrounded one ahead. The large man in the center swung heavy arms and tried in vain to land his meaty fists, but they thumped him with clubs and hammers and in the mix of black rain and yellow fire, Abrahim Küssel, the blacksmith, father of Zapora, fell down with a saber in his side. A shadow jerked the saber from Abrahim's body and the rest beat the blacksmith until he no longer moved.

Usell raced behind merchant shops, across intersections, fleeing the cries and avoiding the flames that licked out windows of broken homes. She ran through the echoes of pebble-rain on roofs. Ran in the drubbing hollow of darkness. Ran through fires consuming her village, and when she could not longer run she stumbled into a garbage alley.

Crawling over the piles of rotten cabbage, potato skins, and moldy bread, a rat skittered across her hand and she parked herself against a wall, knees drawn up, panting. The exit at the other end was filled with dark rain and quiet except for the water draining down metal pipes, splattering the overflowing barrel at the corner.

A noise from the blacker side of the garbage coiled her tight. Prayer. The sound of prayer. *"Viyish ka dal, viyish ka dash, shame rabo."*

Kaddish, prayer for the dead. A black form lifted in front of her, swelled like a terrified animal, his shade a flail of arms protecting his face as a flash of lightning dug into the alley.

"Rabbi Sklar. It's me," she said. "Samuel's daughter. "The rabbi lowered his arms. His face glistened, bareheaded, wet ropy hair, no kippah.

"No. No. Why are you not home?" he said. "You must hide. You must hide. They must not find you. Go home. Go home."

A sickening scream ricocheted down the alley. The rabbi stopped speaking, grabbed Usell's shoulders, and pushed her down on the garbage. "Hide. Stay here. They will avoid the smell. They are looking for me. Stay here."

Water dripped from his jaw and then he clambered over the garbage without looking back.

"*A Klog Iz Mir. A Klog Iz Mir*," he said before he disappeared.

A scream came from the street at the other end of the alley.

"*Blaybn avek.*" Stay away. A familiar voice, female. And then there was a shot. A pistol. Scrambling to the end of the alley Usell hid behind a rain barrel. A man lay flat on the street. At the corner a pair of torches circled a girl. One of the men slapped the pistol from her hand; the other ripped the snood from Zapora Küssel's head. She wailed when he grabbed her hair from behind, jerked her from her feet, and slammed her to the ground.

"Leave her alone," Usell shouted. Her voice hid in the rumbling thunder and she bolted from the alley right at them, slipped, hit a post and rebounded to the wooden sidewalk.

"This one is mine," a voice of authority said. "Bring her."

Usell struggled up. Horizontal lightning cracked the darkness and the man in the black uniform with silver markings kicked Zapora in her chest. Two others dragged her by the hair around the corner to a trill of her high-pitched shrieks. Zapora's cry was followed by a sound of torn cloth. Her yelp changed to shrieks, and then high-pitched, screams. Pain.

When Usell reached the corner all she could see was fire and yellow rain.

Whatever was left of Zapora's voice faded, and thunder trembled the firelight before a horse's hooves raced down the street. A stallion with a rider emerged from whipping wind and rain, galloping straight at her. She threw herself down behind a horse trough. The rider pulled to it and stopped. The large powerful figure clenched the reins. The stallion's muzzle dipped toward the water. One bulbous eye watched Usell. Arabian nostrils snorted hot breath.

She lifted her arms to hide from its bulge-eye glare. The stallion shied and in the lightning crash the stern muscled face of the rider fought to settle the animal. A long wet braid of hair swung from his crown around his back and slapped against his stallion's rump. He yanked the Arabian's head until it submitted. The sword at his hip was a shashka, a heavy double-edge blade. Cossack. The red stripe on his sleeve was an insignia recalling Khmelnitsky's uprising 200 years before, the massacre of Jews and the covenant between Cossacks and the Tsar.

29

Standing in his stirrups, the officer exhaled a low growl. Kicking his black boot heels into his stallion's flank, the black clad rider on the black horse dissolved into black rain.

Her breath was short. The rain seemed to fall upward and fire leaped roof to roof. She heard no voices, just the crackle of wood and the wet hissing in yellow flames.

She scrambled to the corner and hugged the wall on the wooden sidewalk. And then she tripped on something long and hard, something that should not have been there. She fell face down in a puddle of muddy water in the gutter.

When she tried to get up, a ragged boot kicked her arm loose and then stomped on her neck from behind, plunging her face underwater. Pushing up with all her strength, she gasped, but the foot forced her face down.

"Jewish bitch."

Fingers tore her snood and grabbed her hair, yanked her up. She choked. She coughed. A near torch flame singed her hair. A young villager – lumpy face, stained buckteeth, a pug snout – leaned close to her and sniffed.

"I got one. I got one," he shouted.

But no one answered his call. He yanked her head back.

"Pretty," he said.

With strong clawing fingers he tore the front of her cloak.

She beat her fists against blocky wooden arms.

Dropping the torch to the ground, his fist reared back and slammed into her cheek.

When she opened her eyes, she was on her back, her arms pinned above her head, the glow of the torch lying next to her, a throb in her cheek. The peasant boy lifted her blouse over her face.

She twisted one wrist loose and pushed the clothing down. She slammed the base of her palm against his neck. Pushed at his shoulder.

He kneed open her legs as his ragged fingernails raked her belly. She scratched at his face. He smacked her hand away and tore her bloomers. He laughed and rammed his hand between her legs as she pounded against his thick arms. She pushed at his gut and twisted her other hand free. Grappling her flailing punches, he pinned her wrists back over her head and ripped the blouse and undergarments from her body before he dug his calloused fingers between her legs and tried to twist his way into her.

Thunder rumbled and faded. From the darkness came a cry and a shade running in the rain, soles slapping against the cobbles, racing at Usell with long accelerating strides. A black-clothed body leaped from his feet, hitting the startled villager's side like a cannonball, knocking him off his knees and off her.

She scrambled to her feet, wrapped herself in her cloak. The villager tried to get up, but leaping on top of him was an unhatted boy with pais tangling down his stringy neck.

Lightning flashed. The thin, wiry boy, soaked to black cloth on his skeleton body, pinned the villager's arms with his knees, raised a club of smoldering black lumber and smashed it on the villager's pudgy face again and again and again.

The villager lay still. The boy stood up. Moshe Gimmel – the boy who wouldn't talk to her. He sagged there, a silhouette in the still burning torch light.

The club, too heavy for such a frail boy, dangled in his hand. Rain beat his matted hair. With his eyes looking as if they were seeing from another source, this skinny, pock-faced boy, who prayed half his day away, stepped toward her, the lumber smoking in his hand as mighty as Samson's jawbone.

In the resounding thunder he said something, something lost, but in its fading gasp the shrieks of peasants followed and a group of shadowed men raced toward Moshe Gimmel from the corner.

"There. Get them."

Without hesitation Moshe Gimmel said, "Run, Usell. Run. Run for your life."

Rotating on his gangly legs, he ran at the clutch of angry men with his club swinging, hitting the first man and knocking him off his feet. With twine-like arms Moshe Gimmel wielded his weapon and backed the peasants off so that she could flee. Despite his whirlwind the men closed on him, merging into slashing shadows. When he fell, a voice yelled, "Take him away with the others." And they dragged Moshe Gimmel into the heavy rain and she ran, ran away, ran because he told her to run, ran because she was afraid, but as she ran she could not help but think that Moshe Gimmel deserved a worthy wife.

7 . . .

Close to home the icy wind whipped the rain and bested the fires. On the creaky sidewalk in front of Yehuda's burning music shop, boys in overalls and slouch hats threw rocks at windows and laughed when they exploded. Usell hid between the butcher shop and potato warehouse.

A juvenile, too young to be out at night, pronked like a deer as his short-fingered hands choked the neck of a violin and then slammed it to splinters against a post.

Belching black smoke and yellow flames ballooned into the street. The boys cheered.

The dwellings of her neighbors collapsed in ash and dust. Across the street her father's house with its cracked foundation and crooked roof stood between flames and charring relics. The window in her garret was smashed, as was the one downstairs. No light. A black waterfall from the eaves veiled the side of the house and she slid along the wall of Ashkenazi's map workshop as the boys fled.

When there was no one else around, she burst through her half-opened door but once inside she stopped. The room was dark. The smells of burnt firewood, candle wax, kasha, onions, and chicken fat lingered. With a tentative step she bumped into something solid, wooden. A gust of icy wind fired red sparks in the hearth, caught smoldering wood, and flamed from the fireplace. Unrecognizable shadows danced the faint walls. Table overturned. Broken stool. Fractured ladder. Plates, bowls, utensils, books. Her books strewn about the wet floor.

"Father," she whispered.

Nothing.

"Father."

"Usell," her father's voice.

Lightning blanched the room and she bumped her way to the corner where he sat on the floor, his back against the wall. She knelt, pressed her cheek against his chest, and held onto him. He didn't move.

"Father," she said. "Father. There was a Cossack. They're killing everyone. You were right. Moshe Gimmel . . . Moshe Gimmel."

He lifted her torn snood over her hair.

"My daughter," he said.

A dark smear pasted her father's thinning hair against his forehead. Candlewax caught flame and ran across the floor to a man that stood next to the overturned table. She scrambled back.

"The assassin is dead," her father said.

"Assassin?"

The man's body bent at the waist, his arms hanging. A kitchen knife stabbed deep into his left side.

"Daughter," her father said.

"Don't move," she said.

"They'll be back," he said. His voice was weak.

"You're hurt."

"Listen to me."

"Let me bind your wounds," she said.

"No time. The shtetl in Havens. Go to Menahem. Warn him. Our people are betrayed. Get them on the move."

"You can tell him yourself," she said. "We'll both go."

Her father touched her cheek.

"I need to get you to a doctor."

"Hear my words," he said.

"Father, you must listen to me."

"Menahem may know where she is," he said.

Red coals sizzled in pooling water on the stone hearth.

"Who?"

"Your mother," he said.

"My mother?"

"I'm sorry, my daughter. I should have told you. It was long ago."

"I should not have defied you, Father," she said. "I should have listened to you. Moshe Gimmel would have been a good husband."

"Do not weaken," he said. He struggled to sit up. "You must subsume your heroes. Do not give in. Find a strong heart. Harden yourself to it. Trust no one. Harden yourself. Do not let them know who you are, what you are . . . .. Do not weaken."

He gripped the mezuzah dangling from her neck. "Remember," he said. And then he flopped onto his side. Usell crouched over him, held him.

"Don't leave me, Father."

"Say a Kaddish for me," he said.

And then his muscles relaxed and his presence faded away with a soft letting go, a sail in a failing wind.

How long it took for the door to blow open and bang against the wall she did not know. Standing, she kissed the top of her father's head and covered him with his blanket. Setting the chair on the table she vaulted into her garret and dressed in cotton and wool and tied her hair down with the tattered snood. At her door she took one last look, struggled into her father's heavy rekel, and slipped into the torrent of black rain.

8 . . .

Fires burned so hot the rain could not extinguish them even though it fell without restraint. Shadows thickened to shades of gray and black as unrecognizable figures hugged an eve, a porch, and any standing shelter to stave off the downpour. One hunched figure next to another held a common bond and halted the destruction.

Usell rushed through it, headed toward the back of the shtetl holding her father's heavy rekel high above her shoulders, glancing at those seeking shelter from the storm, and splashing through pools of heavy rainwater.

At the rear of the shtetl she jumped the gully into piles of refuse that were sprinkled with soaked ash and lye. Slipping and sliding in her worn leather soles, she raced over the mounds across the meadow and into the black alder forest. Once inside the dark shadows, she stopped to look back. Flames rose from Oylaif, succumbing glows licking at descending clouds dropping their black.

In the grabbing branches of bare trees and thick trunks she pushed ahead – following the line of road at the edge of the forest – her shoes so soggy and loose that her cold soaked feet seemed to bump against every rock and knotted root. In time the road widened and the leafless forest stopped her at the edge of town. Havens.

The rain lessened and light shed its black for gray. Slipping behind a building in the manufacturing district, Usell watched the road and crouched to rub the cold from her feet. A few slow-moving carriages and wagons rolled into town. No mob. No torches, no swords, no angry men.

In front of a block of factories, a man pulling an open cart stacked with wooden furniture laughed and said, "A good day's work." The two flop-hatted peasants walking beside him carried saddles and bridles with engravings in the leather.

Halfway down the block in the center of the street, a man in a peaked helmet and uniform banged the butt of his pistol on a square wooden sign. Dark epaulets fringed his cape. Russian military, a clerical staff badge on the shoulder, exactly like the charts her father had her memorize.

A factory worker in coveralls, holding his half-coat over his head, approached the soldier.

"What news?" he asked.

The soldier stepped back from the stiff parchment nailed to the wooden sign.

"Princess Ludivica Melikova proclaims," he said. "All businesses must close. The streets must be cleared. She, the soul of the Pale, will address her subjects in the market about her coming marriage. Everyone must attend."

The laborer's large nose peaked out from his jacket. "In this rain?" he asked.

The soldier's punch knocked the factory worker to the street.

"She has ordered the rain to stop," the soldier said. "Her marriage to the German will choke our enemy's gullets."

The man on the ground picked himself up and scuttled away. The soldier yelled after him, "Okhrana are here. Beware if you're a Jew. You have no rights."

With a rumble of thunder, light snowflakes began to fall in a gray brume. Usell ducked into it, but when she walked, the shoes she had so carefully cut from the best of her father's worn cloth and discarded leather were coming apart at the seams. Her toes stuck out the right foot and they were blue.

Pulling herself to a sitting ball as a man in a gray top hat crossed the street in front of her, she covered her head and coiled her fingers around the buttons of her father's baggy rekel. She clutched her toes and winced.

The sky, whether by command or natural diligence, stopped dropping its contents and the clouds fragmented. Daylight returned in rays, in streaks, and dappled on the bright wet slush. With the warmth, the people of Havens swelled from their cover and crowded into the street.

A gray-haired woman bending under her bundle of sticks spat at Usell as she passed.

"*Udają się daleko, Juden,*" she hissed. Polish. Go away, Jew.

A man removed his hat and said, "Is that Jew bothering you, old woman?"

Usell coiled into a dark alley. A policeman on a bay mare waved his arm at the pedestrians. "Move on," he said. Like the sheep with the working dog posting behind them, the citizens of Havens obeyed and picked up their pace. Within moments they were gone. The policeman pointed at a top-hatted man backing out a millinery factory across the street. The man bent over the door with a key. He fidgeted with the lock.

"Move on, now," the policeman yelled.

The flustered man pocketed his key and raced down the block. The policeman followed, did not look back. The door to the shop snapped open with a squeak.

On the storefront window painted in block letters were the words, MODERN CLOTHING FOR WOMEN. Usell lowered the collar of her father's rekel. Her hand felt around the pockets. Rubles. Her father always carried rubles. She clutched the paper money in her hand.

When both the policeman and the top-hatted man turned the corner, Usell looked both ways, saw no one, and hobbled across the street. Pressing through the unclosed door, she slipped inside. With a wrenching click she latched it tight.

An iron stove pulsed in the high-ceilinged room. Usell sat down next to it, removed the binding of her shoes, held both hands and feet to the heat. The factory smelled of bleached cloth and dried wool.

She wondered if her father would have lectured her for entering a man's business when he wasn't there. He would have her repeat the summary of God's law, but she was cold and her identity was too easily noted and this was not a safe time to be tending the garden.

Three dressed mannequins in machine-made clothing stood next to the window and stared at the curtained-off street. Cards with prices were tucked between the buttons of women's jackets. A puddle of water formed around where Usell sat. She counted her father's rubles.

Nearby cloth cuttings lay about the floor. With one of the many scissors scattered on benches and tables, Usell separated lengths of scrap cloth, selected the longer bands, and cut them to wrap her feet.

Stripping mannequin number one, Usell put on the undergarments and then the long dress and then the buttoned jacket from mannequin number two when the first was too tight. At a desk she leaned over the ledger. She entered the cost and named the clothing including the shoes. They were too large, but the smallest of the three. She counted out her father's rubles and laid them on the ledger. The price was high, but there was no one with which to haggle.

Ringing out her hair, she twisted and tied it high. Perching the hat to keep it all in place and off her neck she glanced in a small mirror at the worried face. Slipping the mezuzah beneath the garments, she inhaled, straightened her back, and looked out the door. For a moment, she considered her alien change. Sniffing, she hopped onto the sidewalk and headed for the corner.

Shuffling on the cobbles, she caught the flow of citizens melting into a wider thoroughfare and joined them. Staring straight ahead, she did not look at the policeman on the brown mare, though his eyes followed her.

9 . . .

The march of the well dressed filled the channel street. Multiple shades of beige, gray, mud, and black mixed with Usell's similar but saggy garments in a moving parade directed by the policemen's pointing arms. Soldiers with wagon-wheel insignias on their sleeves blocked cross streets so that the river of citizens had an ordered and directed flow. In the crowd Usell tried to look away from a man with a stiff back and hair hidden beneath a frumpy gray *Ushanka*. He squinted at Usell and twitched a trimmed mustache. But when she faced him, he smiled.

Arching her back, the woman next to him tilted her head, her expression curious, and then a nod as if they were familiars. Usell pressed by them, chest forward in same style, her bottom extended like a camel on hind legs.

In the middle of the block was a sign next to an alley. It read, 2K, a pointing arrow down the alley, and a yellow Star of David. Usell cut in front of the couple to the sidewalk and skipped by a policeman, who did not seem to notice her as she turned into the space between the buildings.

Breathing heavily, she leaned against one wall, pressed her hand on the mezuzah, closed her eyes, and with a quick inhale continued on her way to the other end of the alley with quick steps.

Sunlight blanched the next street. Shielding her brow, she bumped into a covered cart next to empty crates.

"Who was that?" a woman's voice across the way said.

Usell ducked behind wooden crates.

The woman stood under the awning of a gunsmith shop. Hatless, she dressed like a man in a black suit and lifted haughty black eyes at the cart and then the crates.

"It is just the wind," an older man in front of her said. He was hunchbacked and facing away from Usell. A long white fur coat hooded his head. His black cane stabbed the cobbles again and again.

"Are you prepared?" his graveled voice asked.

The woman lifted her chin. Mid-thirties, symmetry of face, seriousness set in stone. "Everything is ready," she said.

Behind the woman were an Aleut and a Mongolian, both with dangling mustaches and hand-sewn fur skins. Curved knives extruded from their waistbands and sour angry looks masked their faces. They crowded each other like two boulders.

Beside the old man two Goliaths bulged in tight sheep vests and squared the Aleut and the Mongolian.

The woman glanced up at the sky. "It's clearing," she said.

The old man poked the tip of his cane at her.

"This is necessary," he said. "We must cut the line."

"The Jews will be blamed," she said.

"When the Tsar is gone, there will be confusion enough to strike at the government's heart."

"There are no bonds that can't be severed," she said.

"You are a callous bitch," the old man said.

"Blame Alexander. He ordered the citizenship this morning."

"Once we're done they will drown the Jews in the sea."

Usell stood so quickly she crashed into the crates, knocking them over and exposing her to the street. She backed toward the alley.

Pistol barrels pointed at her from the two Goliaths.

"Don't shoot, you idiots," the woman said. "You'll ruin everything."

She nodded at the Mongolian.

With a swing of his apelike arms he turned toward Usell. She spun around and ran back down the alley. She didn't stop at the sidewalk but sliced into the forward movement of the crowd, ignoring the disturbed pinch of faces and then flowing with them, matching their strides, pressing herself ahead, slipping between shoulders and chests and backs.

The Mongolian exited the alley. He caught her eye. With a shouldering march he knocked a merchant and a gentleman aside and then pushed through the pedestrians as if they didn't exist.

Usell pressed herself sideways across the undisciplined parade. A man with a well-groomed and waxed mustache lifted bushy brows and leered at her. The Mongolian created his own path. At the cross street he paused when a policeman on horseback blew a whistle.

She hurried ahead, lifting her hem and leaning into her stride.

And then the crowd parted.

Coming from the other direction on chestnut Arabians, a troop of the Tsar's cavalry with stiff backs and blue uniforms with gold braid epaulets split the citizens to opposite sidewalks.

"Move faster," a sergeant with three blue chevrons on his sleeve, said. "The Princess Ludivica Melikova and her entourage are arriving."

The force of the crowd shoved Usell to its edge and onto the sidewalk. She compressed behind them against a faded red wall. The sign over the building's open doors said, Zebranetzski Stables. With her back against the wall and facing the street, she eased toward the dark opening in the middle of the stable.

Hollow hoof-steps clapped with precision around the corner. Soldiers in umber uniforms, Don horses from the steppe, *beshmets* low on the brows of their riders, tight *cherkesska* coats with beaver collars and cartridge belts looped across the fronts of dull leather vests. Cossacks. Shashka blades. Sour-looking men with cocks-crow braids sprouting from their scalps and flowing down their spines as they bounced in their saddles. Staring straight ahead, they reined to a stop in front of the stable.

Usell searched the crowd for the Mongolian. Nowhere in sight.

From the barn-like opening in the stable a tall, broad-backed, black-uniformed Cossack emerged. The man on horseback in Oylaif. A red captain's *kuntush* girded his waist and held a holster with a closed flap on one side and a long shashka sword in its shiny bronze sheath on the other. His long washed-out braid arched over his crown and down a muscled back to his thighs.

Usell hunched against the wall, pressed against the shoulder of the woman next to her. In a raptured voice the woman said, "Look its the princess. The princess is coming."

The captain approached the line of Cossacks and lifted his chin.

In quick order, the dozen riding Cossacks dismounted. They saluted. Another officer joined them on a white gelding. He wore black. He was younger, vertical, an aquiline nose beneath the short shiny brim of a helmet covered silky golden hair tied to a tail with a leather knot. The posture of a nobleman.

A yellow Lieutenant's *kuntush* dangled down his thigh and matched the color of the lightning bolt on his sleeve. He saluted the captain as if they were equals.

The dismounted Cossacks marched to the back of a flat open wagon pulling in behind them. They hoisted a three-step platform from the wagon and set it down in front of the captain.

"Lieutenant Yazukov," the captain said.

"We are here," the lieutenant said.

"Let's get this business over with. This can only lead to trouble."

"It is *her* wish," the lieutenant said.

"Just follow instructions, Poruchik," the captain snapped.

The lieutenant's salute sharpened and the captain returned it with military formality.

With the lieutenant's wave a procession of horses clattered around the corner.

"The princess," someone in the crowd whispered.

In the street a dozen uniformed youths in gold and cream-colored uniform with hairless faces and shiny new boots rode their pony-like Chernomors in front of three pairs of tall charcoal Friesians that pulled a covered gold and white carriage. Beside the platform the carriage came to a sudden stop. On the door of the carriage was a crest — a double heart crossed by a double sword — the Grand Duke's emblem.

Two chubby young coachmen struggled with a silvered step and placed it below the coach door. When it opened, the crowd gasped as a young woman stretched out a white boot. Taking the high step down with delicacy, she set her foot as if expecting to land on a cloud. Her face was soft and powder white. Layers of gauze hid her shoulders and accented a cone to a tulip waist. Lifting her dainty jaw, her slim neck arched as she looked around.

"Dmitriiiiii!" she screeched. "Dmitri."

She stomped up the platform. A visible stiffness gripped the soldiers. The crowd murmured. A gold comb in rusty hair glinted in the sunlight, held trembling curls from falling out of place.

The captain swept his arm in a bow, his long braid slipping off his back.

"You certainly took your time," the princess said. "Do you have it?"

"Yes, Princess," he said.

"Put it on me," she said.

"That is for your father to present at the ball," the captain said.

She jumped up and down on the stand. "I want it now."

"Princess, my orders are clear."

"You defy me? You defy me? Someday I will kill you for defying me," she said.

"Princess. The jewel is a token of your union. It will unite the empire with a powerful ally. It is your duty to honor the ritual. It is not for frivolous show."

Lt. Yazukov kicked his gelding closer to the stand.

"I will say she ordered it from you, Captain," he said.

Stomping again, the princess turned her back and lifted her dense hair off her porcelain neck.

The captain closed his eyes and exhaled. He snapped his fingers.

From the hands of a brown-clad Cossack, a coffin-shaped jewelry box extended to the captain. He opened the case and with both hands lifted a golden necklace.

Dangling in the center of the gold chain was a diamond the size of a robin's egg. Rainbows sparkled in it. The whispering crowd pressed toward the street and swelled the space around Usell so that it emptied of citizens.

She did not hesitate and slid free from the crush to the opening in the stable, keeping her eyes on the Cossack who linked the chain around the princess's neck.

The princess dropped her hair and examined the stone. After kissing it, she slipped it into the silken layers of her gown.

Usell turned into the stable only to face the Aleut from the alley. He stared at his hands as he stepped from the darkness toward the sunlight and struck a match. He lifted a heavy black ball with a finger length wick to the flame.

Sparks ignited and ran the fuse.

Usell screamed.

Stumbling two steps backward, Usell turned to face the Cossack Captain who'd drawn his shashka and glared at her.

"Bomb," Usell hollered. "Bomb." She pointed at the Aleut.

Sparks topped the black ball as the Aleut hopped two steps forward and reared back, poised to throw.

Usell crouched and covered her head.

The Aleut's next stride struck Usell's shoulder with his knee and he tumbled over her. The bomb, flying from his hand into the air, sailed over the princess and the carriage to the other side of the street.

The captain yanked the princess to the ground and covered her body with his as the bomb blast shook the air.

A fireball erupted from the detonation.

The concussion knocked Usell flat. The noise boomed to an echo and faded.

Shrapnel, torn pavement, wood splinters and fire exploded. People flew above her like loosened sheaves of paper. Smoke filled the street and rose in a thick black cloud that turned white against the blue sky. Shattered wood bounced on cobbles. Black sand, rock, and debris landed in silence. What little remained in the air fluttered in a spray of smoke and leafy particles.

Usell shook her head. She pushed up. Her hat was gone, her hair unbound. Bodies lay in mangled and twisted pieces. An organ, a liver-colored glob oozed in a pool of blood. A leg not attached to a torso of torn ribs kicked the ground. A shoulder bone, denuded of skin, was still attached to the woman in the red hat. Her mouth twisted in a scream with no sound.

The Grand Duke's carriage was shredded. Splinters fell in the fine ash and stabbed her like hot rain. The air smelled of gunpowder.

The Cossack captain, who'd covered the princess with his body, lifted off her, the back of his uniform lacerated. Rising with an angry growl, he clutched the double-edged shashka and shook it.

The Aleut, who likewise was saved by his prone position between the captain and Usell, scrambled to his feet and leaped over the dead and dying, running for the short corner just meters away.

The princess tried to rise. The captain's boot stepped on her back. Her face twisted with curses, but she did not move. The captain drew his pistol with his left hand and squeezed the trigger. A bullet hit the running Aleut in the arm. He stumbled.

A puff of smoke exited the captain pistol.

The assassin grabbed the back of his knee, twisted and fell.

The captain strode to the downed man's side. The princess pressed herself up. Her rusty hair hung over her child's face, the gold comb dangling about her ear.

The captain stomped on the Aleut's wounded knee.

The man arched his back with his mouth open, but no sound came from it. He seemed in pain.

Lifting his boot heel, the captain dropped his weight on the Aleut's temple and the fur clad man lay still.

Pale blue smoke curled in the cold breeze. The half ambulatory tottered away. A clutch of smudged-faced palace guards stumbled to the princess's side, looking like they needed her more than she needed them. Still, they helped her to her feet.

Wagons arrived with fire equipment and firemen manned a water pump. Lieutenant Yazukov pranced his gelding to the captain's side and saluted. He was untouched by the explosion.

They moved their mouths. The lieutenant saluted. The captain did not. He holstered his pistol and turned around, his searing eyes finding Usell.

In a half dozen measured strides he stood at her feet. Reaching down, he grabbed her wrist and yanked her up. Off balance, she bumped against his chest. He smelled of hickory and cordite. Jerking back, she lowered her head. He lifted her chin with a single finger and moved his lips.

"What did you say?" Usell asked.

His eyes were black and penetrating, and a straight red scar from hairline to brow pulsed on his forehead. Her ears popped.

"Did you know the assassin?" he asked. His voice was tunneled and loud. Moans mixed with cries, orders, and squawks of pain.

She shook her head no.

"Dmitri. Is that the girl who warned us? Dmitri?"

The captain's clean-shaven and weathered face clenched about the jaw. The scar whitened.

The princess lifted her hair and stabbed the comb to hold it. A few ringlets hung in her face.

"She is the one, princess," the captain said.

"Bring her over, Dmitri. I want to thank her."

The captain clasped Usell's shoulder, turning her with a stone grip. In a whisper of hazelnut breath he said,

"Listen to me, girl. If you are involved . . ."

"Dmitri. Bring the girl to me this instant," the princess snapped.

"Pray you have skills for this," he muttered. "Accept whatever is offered and say nothing."

But then the captain turned away. He released Usell. A frail-looking man came running toward him flapping a yellow paper in his hand. He wore a long white shirt banded at the elbow and cuff; a patch on his sleeve identified him as a telegraph operator. His face was pinched and pink, and he waved the message in his hand.

"The Tsar is dead," he cried. "The Tsar is dead. An assassin's bomb has killed our beloved Tsar."

The captain turned to Usell and knotted his brow.

"Dmitri, what is it?" the princess screeched.

"It's best you disappear," the captain hissed at Usell.

With a military reverse the captain marched to the princess, cupped her by the waist, lifted her to a Don horse without a rider, and set her in the saddle.

"Lieutenant Yazukov," the captain ordered. "See the princess to safety and make sure the assassin does not die."

"Protectors of the empire, join." Lieutenant Yazukov ordered the remaining soldiers.

Her pale face lost even more color when the captain told her the Tsar was dead.

"My uncle." she cried. Lowering her head, she sniffled, but when she lifted it again her expression changed. Standing in the stirrups of the Don horse she screamed, "Round up the heathens. Don't let any of the Jews escape."

10 . . .

The Cossack Captain barked orders at a detachment of soldiers as Usell hurried back to the alley marked by the Star of David. The band of conspirators was gone. Usell kept to the shadowed side of the street until the factory buildings disappeared and Yeshiva Street, the place where the boys from Oylaif were sent to study, appeared behind a quiet cemetery. Dusted snow fell and settled. Wooden one-story structures dotted the section, peaked roofs over front doors, no windows, one building then another on the straight muddy road. *Beit*

Midrash, study houses, *shtiblekh,* residences for prayer, curls of smoke from chimneys but no one out.

She had been to the section many times with her father to see her father's friend, the blind man, Menahem. He was called *Gedoylem,* wise man. A woman at a window yelled at Usell. "Get out of here, whoever you are. Get out of here."

Hurrying to the home of Menahem, she recognized the high-tilted roof. It was set between two shorter roofs, making the house appear as though on crutches. At the door Usell stopped. A gust of wind whipped her hair about her face. Pressing her crown she felt for her hat. Gone. No scarf. No snood. Wrapping a fistful of wet hair into a knot she pulled it tight. As soon as she let it go, it unraveled.

She took a quick breath, exhaled, straightened her back, and knocked twice.

A muffled voice from inside said something she couldn't make out and then the door opened with a quick yank. Standing there was a man, taller than most, the door shadow covering his face. He spoke with a calm but strained Russian accent.

"Chto vi khotitye?" What do you want?

Leaning forward, his face caught the light. Clean-shaven, late twenties, a practiced grin. His weight shifted to his hip, and when his tanned leather long coat hung open, his palm pressed on the pistol grip in an open holster tied to his leg. Foreign. A shag of dirt brown hair fell on his brow.

"Menahem," Usell said. "I must see Menahem."

The young man tapped a broad brimmed, flat-topped hat on his leg. Leaning his forearm on the doorjamb, he released a humorous snort.

"Who is it?" a coughing voice called from inside.

"A girl in too-large boots," the young man said.

She squinted at the amused glint in the man's eyes.

"My father is from Oylaif," she said into the room. "He sent me."

"Come forward," Menahem said in his scratchy voice.

Sharp bright light poured into the dark one-room house. As she passed a high reading stool below a square window, she touched its smooth wood and then navigated through crooked piles of books at different heights that reminded her of an abandoned civilization.

The meandering path of crooked towers smelled of glue, sweet wine, and age.

Menahem sat on his bed with his back against the bare wall. His milky eyes stared straight ahead. The skin about the sockets was permanently blackened. White long hair, uncombed and unkempt, dangled over his shoulders from a bony thin-skinned scalp. He was dressed in a wide-necked sleeping gown; its worn cloth draped on him like wrinkled laundry. A pale sheet covered his stretched-out bony legs.

"Who comes to my house?"

"You know me. You know my father, Samuel."

"How many children does this Samuel have?"

"You know me. I am his daughter."

"The voice is familiar. Did you get those books I sent? Did you read them? Where is my old friend? Did you come for books? Just tell me what you're looking for and I will direct you to them."

"No. I am alone," Usell said.

"You are alone? What are you doing here without your father? Where is a matron for you?"

"They are dead. They are all dead," Usell said. Her voice dropped. "My father is dead. They attacked our village. They killed. They . . ."

The tall man stepped behind her, grabbed her shoulder and spun her around. She stiffened, twisted from his grip, stepped back.

Undeterred he asked, "When?"

"An hour perhaps," she said.

"I warned you," the young man said to Menahem.

"Tell us what happened," Menahem said.

She slid sideways to the bed. The young man frowned at her, the face-hardened, the bone chiseled, the eyes inspecting, flickering with candlelight.

"They came out of the fields, from the forest, from the hills behind Oylaif," she said. "We did nothing. Everything was fine one minute and then . . ."

"That's why they won't let me send a telegraph," the young man said.

Menahem waved at the young man and aimed his milky white eyes in her direction. They were tinged with blue.

"I am sorry," he said. "Your father was a valuable friend."

47

"Was there anything different about them?" the young man asked.

"Who?" Usell said.

"The marauders."

"There were hundreds of them," she said. "They did terrible things to our people."

"Officials?" the young man asked. "Were there officials?"

"I saw a Cossack. And soldiers in black and silver."

"Okhrana," the young man said.

"Did they loot the synagogue?" Menahem asked. "What about the Torah?"

"I don't know," she said. "I don't know what happened to anyone. They destroyed everything. They burned it; the shule was on fire."

"God will punish them," Menahem said.

"I told you this could happen," the young man said. "There's no way we can conduct business with this going on."

"Father said to warn you," Usell said.

"Your father was a good man," Menahem said. "He was my friend and champion for your people. He will be missed. We will find a place for you with us."

"Protect yourselves while you still can," the young man said. "You have credits with us. You can buy guns."

"Weapons will only bring a harsher response," Menahem said. "Besides, we are not trained like you to use weapons."

"Then leave. There are other places."

"Ach. America. It's too far away. You Americans think the world is at your shores."

Usell faced him. "American. Lincoln. Poe. Emerson. Mark Twain. Fine writers, fine leader," she said in English.

His smoky eyes widened.

"How would we get there?" Menahem asked. "Do we walk? Do you think the Tsar will allow what little wealth we have to leave?"

"The Tsar is dead," Usell said.

"Yes, we heard," Menahem said. "But there is always another Tsar ready to take charge."

"You can start over if you're not dead," the American said.

"Streets paved with gold?" Menahem scoffed. "Who believes in fairy tales?"

"In three days an American ship will leave Odessa," the American said. "I'm headed there. As soon as the lines are up I'll contact my captain. It'll carry 500."

"We are many more than 500. Who would you have us leave behind? The old, the young, the infirm? And how would you transport us? We would be stopped a thousand times by the government, by the populace, by the sheer weight of our own numbers. They would send Cossacks."

The American pointed his hat at the blind man. "What about our deal? Did you contact your confederates for me? Are they interested?"

"We will consider what has been done and give you a decision before the empire responds."

The American set the broad-brimmed hat on his head and with his face shaded he said, "It'll be too late, but the offer stands. It's unsafe here."

"We have roots in Havens," Menahem said. "We will not mingle with them until this dies down. We do business with the goyim. They trust us. And to the matter of this child . . .."

He nodded in Usell's direction.

"Would you go outside and notify the first man you see that I have a female orphan who can look after Cantor Bornstein's wife?"

"I'm not an orphan," Usell said. "I have a mother."

When he sat up, Menahem's skeletal body creaked. His bones pulled the thin skin tight.

"Your mother." His voice rose. "Don't talk to me about your mother. She betrayed our people. She chose her father's aristocratic birthright over her mother's Jewish roots." He slammed his bony fist into his palm. "To betray one's own. She is an apostate."

Usell stepped back.

"Do you know where she is?" Usell asked.

"Last I heard, she joined the court in Odessa, joined the hate mongers and *traif* eaters. You cannot speak of her again."

"Odessa?"

"Yes." Menahem shook his head. "The southern palace where hate is as ever-present as lingering sunlight."

"I mean no disrespect," Usell said, "but I must find her."

"I've no word of your mother since the Grand Duchess took her own life. Thankfully, that zealot died before she could destroy us. If only her venom had died with her. No greater evil than that woman's loathing of our people."

"But the last you heard, my mother was in Odessa?" Usell asked.

"Yes."

Usell turned to the American. "I will pay you to take me to Odessa with you. I have silver."

She lifted the mezuzah from her neck and extended a fistful of her father's rubles.

The American glanced at the rubles, hefted the metal.

"Not worth much," the American said. "The paper has no value outside the empire."

Shadows wavered in the silence. Menahem's pursed his lips.

"A woman cannot be on her own," Menahem said. "You must be protected. You must abide by . . ."

"I have to find my mother," Usell said. "She's all I have left."

She turned to the American. "I need you to take me to Odessa. What do you want for it?"

"I can't be bothered with a stray," he said.

"I can be useful. It is a day and a night to Odessa. I can cook."

"No," he said.

"I will not be any trouble."

He stared down at her. "Brown eyes," he said. "You are six ways of trouble."

"Go on. Take her," Menahem said. His tone was angry. "What you owe us is cancelled. She may be useful. I have heard her beauty, like this temperament, is unapproachable. She can only be a hindrance here."

The American lifted his hat and brushed his fingers through his hair.

Menahem folded his bone-thin hands in his lap. He leaned forward before speaking. "Here is my decision. Our people will not go with you. We will see this through. We will carry on as always. And to you, daughter of my dearest friend, I offer this. If you find your mother, be forewarned, she abandoned you. She is not like us, and our people in Odessa do not follow the letter of our laws. Some of them do not even pray."

11 . . .

In her oversized shoes Usell followed the American's shadow out of the Jewish section and struggled to stay up. At Zebranetzski stables the American halted at a still smoldering storefront. Other than the remains of the fire, the smell of gunpowder, and a trickle of pink running between the cobbles in the street, there was little evidence of the tragedy remaining.

A cold wind flapped the hem of her dress. She clutched her jacket at the buttons.

"Stay here," the American said. "I'll bring a wagon."

With long-legged strides he slipped into the dark stable.

A black outline marked where the princess's platform had been. When a dark cloud shaded her from the sunlight, the cold sent shivers down her legs to her loose boots and cramping feet. Shaking her shoulders she lifted her hem and ran into the stable.

In the darkness she couldn't see and bumped against hard muscle. A whinny sprayed her face with wet hot spittle. She backed against wood. When her eyes adjusted to the dark, she discovered a stall. The American stood in the back of the barn at a doorway bathed in sunlight. The silhouette of a woman outlined the bright wall of the alley behind him. He struck a match, ignited a cigarette, blew smoke at the shadowed form in front of him.

The silhouette stepped into the light. It was the woman from the alley – the one who dressed like a man. She raked a wing of her short black hair from her eyebrow.

"You have the weapon?" she asked.

"You don't have my price, and this mess you've caused lessens the odds you'll get it."

"You play games with us?"

"You've created the risk," the American said.

"And what would you do with a marriage dowry?" the woman asked.

"You don't have it. That's all that's important."

"We have converging interests. We don't wish this alliance with the Germans."

"I just want the diamond."

"And I need your guns."

"You have three nights to get it to me," the American said.

"Or you will find other buyers?"

"The empire knows I'm here. They understand. They have an interest in new weapons."

"You play both sides," the woman said.

"Revolution is nasty business."

"Be careful, foreigner. You can't answer the Tsar's hard questions and you don't want to get mixed up with the prey."

The woman put her hand on a pistol in her waistband.

"You pull that thing, you better use it," the American said. One hand hung by his holstered weapon, the other squared his hat.

The woman looked him in the eye, grabbed him by the neck, and kissed him hard on the mouth. He backed off.

"You kiss like a rabbit," she said.

"Just so you know," he said. "I'm not getting mixed up with you, or them."

The woman patted the American's cheek.

"Meet me in Odessa," she said.

"With the jewel?" He removed her hand.

"We'll have it by tomorrow."

"And if you don't," he said.

"We told you of our alternative plan."

"Risky."

"Are you in or not?" the woman asked.

"We'll see how it goes."

"In a few days we'll control Odessa."

"They'll send an army," he said.

"They are in chaos. We have disrupted their command. The populace is distracted. With your weapon we'll be more than a match for them."

The Albanian stallion in front of Usell tried to bite the string at Usell's neck. When she jerked away, it pawed the icy straw.

The American glanced over.

Usell grabbed the Albanian's long snout and covered its eyes.

"What is it?" the woman asked.

"My horse. He's as jumpy as I am."

"We'll be at the church in the cliff," she said.

"I thought that structure had collapsed long ago."

The woman shrugged and without ceremony retreated into the sunlit alley. The American dusted the front of his long coat and strode toward the horse.

"I told you to wait outside," he said.

"I didn't like it out there," Usell said.

"If you expect to survive, you'd better do as you're told."

"You've been paid for my passage," she said.

"Trouble costs a lot more."

"Why are you helping assassins?"

"You have big ears," he said.

"They are small ears, and the Tsar would not like it if he knew your plans."

The hand at his hip flinched. "Sounds like you're trying to blackmail me."

"Who can I tell?" she said. "Would they believe me, a woman, a Jew? I can be helpful to you. I know many languages. I know Russian custom. I am as good as my word and I need you to take me to Odessa with you."

"You'd be better off staying with your people," he said.

"I must find out about my mother. My father is dead. I have no one else."

"This is not a game. One mistake . . .." He ran his finger across his throat. He threw a stirrup over the saddle of the mountain horse.

"Help me with this," he said. "I need to hook the horse to the wagon."

"You cannot draft a riding horse," Usell said.

"What do you know about horses?"

"The village blacksmith taught his daughter and me."

"Can you unsaddle him?"

"Do I have your word that you will take me to Odessa?"

He exhaled and looked up at the pitch-black roof. Rolling his eyes, he handed her the reins and walked toward a dark corner. His square shoulders cut to a smaller waist as an icy breeze blew through the open doors.

"Sure," he said. "Anything for a lady."

Usell's muscles relaxed. She leaned against the pale Albanian and patted its nose. It wrapped its neck around her back and its fat tongue licked her cheek. She hugged its snout and pressed her face to its short hairs before a ghostly chill swirled around her. Tiny pricks like needles attacked her back and before she could stop what was happening, her knees buckled and she collapsed to the ground.

12 . . .

Upon opening her eyes, golden light shimmered above her. She was on her back and jostling on rough wood and cold iron. Pressing upright, a brown wool blanket fell from her shoulders. Beneath her was metal in pieces strapped to the flooring. Blued tubes of iron, long hollow rods wrapped together like an ancient Roman *fasces*, a block mechanism with two triggers and a hinged tripod, all locked down by leather belts in the bottom of a wagon. A gun.

Bumping a rock in the road, the wagon bounced and crashed in a squeaky convergence of metal and wood and leather. Stained canvas stretched on arching metal loops and reflected the golden sunlight overhead while mountain-dry cold whistled through the bed of the wagon.

Shading her eyes she pressed through the flopping canvas at the front. The American, sitting on a high bench, flicked the reins in his hands. "Chik, chik, chik." He sucked the sound from his cheek, heading the Albanian into a high plateau.

Tying her dry hair in a knot, she buttoned her jacket and took a seat next to him. Clouds slipped beneath the blurred afternoon sun.

"I fainted."

He said nothing. The Albanian mountain horse pulled the wagon with disciplined steps.

"I've never fainted before," she said.

"Be quiet," he said.

"You do not get to tell me what to do. You have been paid for a service and I am not your inferior to treat badly."

"So you think you're better than me?" he said.

"I am certainly better mannered."

"How would you like to be left on the side of the road?"

She folded her hands in her lap as the American reined the Albanian toward the sun and followed an ancient road of made of stone blocks. Snow melted in pockets and the clop of the Albanian mixed with the bump of wooden wheels.

The American broke the silence.

"How did Menahem lose his sight?"

"Now that you wish to know something, you speak to me?"

"If you know what's good for you, you'll answer the question," the American said.

"The Grand Duke blinded Menahem. I do not understand how you know Menahem. He does not deal with guns and he is not a rebel and you are not a Jew."

His angled squint assessed her.

"Answer my question," he said.

"What question?"

"Why did the Grand Duke blind the old man?"

"Menahem refused to attend a state visit of the Tsar because it was Yom Kippur. Why is that important to you?"

The American pinched his mouth, flicked the reins. "It isn't. All I care about is getting what I want."

"The princess's diamond?"

"What do you know about it?"

"I saw it," she said. "And I saw the assassin with that woman you were talking to. They were connected. The Cossacks will find her."

"The princess wears the jewel?" he asked.

"The one you're expecting to exchange for weapons?"

"You should not repeat what you hear," he said. He snapped the reins on the Albanian's back.

"It is not right to be harsh to your horse to heal your temper," she said.

"How many Cossacks protected the jewel?"

"There must be other things of worth that would be easier to steal."

"But other things aren't magic," he said.

"A jewel is not magic."

"It has the power of God in it."

"I do not think God needs a diamond," she said.

"This jewel has a history."

"A diamond is a thing buried in the earth and polished by man."

"Then why do three cultures vie for it?" the American said. "It even has a name. Jeroboam's Jewel."

"From Solomon's kingdom?"

He snapped the reins. "Given by God to Solomon. To keep the kingdom of Israel united. When the jewel was lost, Israel and Judea split apart."

"That is fable," she said.

"Nevertheless, people believe in myth. The Assyrians had the jewel and an empire for a time. The Greeks, the Romans, the Christians after the Crusades, the Ottomans had it for a long time. The Italians lost it to the French. 30 years ago it disappeared during the Crimean War, and somehow Menahem was involved in finding it. Now it's being used to unify Russia and Europe against the British."

"A fable is not truth."

He tilted his brim back. "Who says?"

"You cannot make things up without proof."

"Oh, but I can."

"Who will believe you?" she asked.

"Those that fear my truth."

"I will find my mother and leave this circular foolishness to you."

"You'd be better off staying with friends," he said.

"I have no friends."

"Why don't you have any friends?"

"I had one. Zapora Küssel." Usell stared at her hands.

"Had?"

"I must find my mother."

"Tell me about your friend," the American said.

In the tall grass beside the road ice melted to golden crystals. A breeze swept across the field and sliced between the buttons of Usell's jacket.

"She stood up for me. When the other girls made fun of me. She said *Usell is my friend. You must not speak like that or I will not be your friend.*"

"But she's not your friend anymore?"

"I told her father what I saw. He asked me where Zapora was and I told him that she was with a boy not her husband. I didn't mean to harm her." Usell rubbed her hands in each other. "I don't wish to talk about it anymore."

"But I'm not finished asking questions," the American said.

"I do not have to answer them."

"You risk losing my help."

"I will help myself," she said.

"Then it's likely to be all the help you'll get."

She tightened her arms around her jacket and stared straight ahead.

"I am smarter than you think," she said.

"Being smart can get you killed. The difference between books and real life is the difference between a dream and this."

He grabbed her collar and pulled her face close before kissing her hard on the mouth. She broke away.

Wiping her lips, she stared at him.

"Trouble," he said. "You're a wagonload of trouble."

The sun slipped behind low clouds and on the flat the American flicked the reins on the Albanian's back and hurried the animal onto a wet dirt road dotted with pools of water.

Touching her lips, Usell moved to the far edge of the bench seat that overlooked the wheels slinging mud behind the wagon.

After a time the American poked her with his elbow, nodded in the direction ahead.

Two riders galloped towards them. The American wiped his coat sleeve across his mouth and wrapped the four reins in his left hand. He opened his coat so that the holster at his hip revealed the butt of his pistol. He drew the weapon, cocked the hammer, and set it on the bench seat.

"Lean against me," the American whispered.

"I cannot do that," she said.

"Pretend we're married." He pulled her to him, hiding the pistol.

The riders slowed their gallops to a brisk walk, riders too heavy for the short Barbs. Their restless snouts fought the tight bits.

Both men wore black uniforms with silver collars and lapels. The *shakoes* on their heads looked like black corks with white and red feathers. Shiny black brims hid their eyes.

57

The American rested his hand on the butt of his pistol as the two uniformed men stopped in front of the wagon's path. One raised his hand to halt. The American set the brake and wrapped the reins around the lever. The two riders separated around the sides of the wagon. Both aimed cocked pistols.

The American's knuckles brushed the arch of Usell's back.

The man on the American's side with a face like curdled cheese said, "What are you doing on this road? It has been cleared."

"Of what?" the American asked.

"Of Jews."

"We are not Jews," the American said.

"It is a crime to harbor Jews."

Usell lowered her head.

"The wife and I are headed to Odeska Oblast," the American said. "We're bushwhackers."

"What?"

"*Otstoyniks*," Usell said. Settlers.

Both men stared at Usell.

"Ilya," the curdle-faced man said. He nodded at Ilya and aimed right at Usell's forehead.

Ilya closed on Usell's side of the wagon.

"She is too small to work a plow," the curdle-faced man said.

"But she'll bear me many sons," the American smiled. "She has good hips, no?" He patted Usell's outer thigh.

"Look at those clothes," Ilya said. "Bourgeois." He spat next to his horse. "Not the clothes of a farmer."

"We come from the city," the American said.

"Send her down," the other rider said.

Ilya slipped his pistol in his hip holster and dismounted next to the wagon. The curdle-faced man rested his pistol on his pommel as his horse shifted weight.

"Do as they ask, my darling," the American said.

He half-lifted her to stand and whispered, "Keep your head down."

As she pressed one boot on the edge of the crib above Ilya, the American shoved and Usell flew off the wagon into Ilya's chest. He fell onto his back with her crumpling on top of him. A shot exploded. On the ground, she scrambled off Ilya's belly. He blinked at her. Her mezuzah fell from her jacket.

"She is a Jew," Ilya said. "A shape changer."

"You," the American leaned over the crib with the muzzle of his pistol pointed at Ilya's chest. He re-cocked the hammer. "Pick her up and put her back in the wagon."

The curdle-faced man was on his back with a hole through his throat. He didn't move. His horse stomped its hoof.

Ilya stood up. With a lantern jaw, tight jowls and hard hands he gripped Usell by the waist and hoisted her over the side of the wagon, where she tipped off balance.

The American grabbed her.

Ilya drew his revolver.

The American fired first. The bullet hit Ilya in the jaw and ripped it from his skull. The impact of the bullet snapped his neck.

The barrel of the American's pistol smoked under Usell's arm.

"You could have killed me," she said.

Without comment the American leaped down.

After searching their packs and pockets, the American stuffed their rubles in his belt pouch and then dragged the bodies into the snow-covered field. Reading through papers he retrieved from a pouch, he handed them up to Usell and rigged lines for the two Barbs to pull the wagon.

She read:

BY ORDER OF TSAR ALEXANDER III:

> *It is decreed that the Jews be forbidden to settle anew outside towns and boroughs.*
>
> *Jews are forbidden the issuing of mortgages and other deeds. They may not register or lease real property situated outside towns and boroughs. Any real property already owned will be disposed of.*
>
> *Jews are forbidden to transact business on Sundays and on the principal Christian holy days.*

"They can't do this. We are citizens."

"Honey," he said, "these Okhrana follow orders. You're endangering me."

She smoothed the front of her dress flat across her knees.

"You are not to touch me again," she said.

"You are awfully bossy and opinionated for someone needing so much charity."

"You will never get the princess's jewel by shooting its guards," Usell said. "There are too many."

"But the rebels almost got to the princess, didn't they?" he said. "Beside, I've got lots of bullets."

The American harnessed the two barbs, re-saddled the Albanian, and tied his reins to the wagon.

Flicking leather on the barbs' backs, he turned off the road, and they crossed the field in silence.

"Where are you going?" she asked.

"Shut up. I'm thinking."

"Thinking never sours my tongue."

"No, you do it naturally," he said. "Now be quiet."

She folded her arms tight about her chest and stared at the broad expanse following the southwestern border of the valley. Blue-black land covered by snow. Torn fields of wheat spread out on a sparsely treed plain.

"Sir," she said. "I thank you for your aid, but who are you to tell me to be quiet? You are smuggler or worse. You have no claim to character."

"Don't call me sir."

"You did not give me a name," she said.

"Cothman. Rudd Cothman."

With a slap of leather on the backs of the two barbs, he asked, "What's your name?"

He allowed his eyes to roam about the cut of her dress and something like a smile cocked in the corner of his mouth.

"I will not be charmed by a man's enthusiasm," she said. "It doesn't matter what I say my name is. The way you look at me I might as well be a wanton woman like Emma Bovary, but I assure you I am not."

"Maybe you should be," he said. "I'll call you Emma."

With the bounce of the ride she slipped her hands into the folds of the dress between her legs and stared at the white field with sprigs of dead seedless barley trembling in the icy breeze.

After a time Rudd Cothman began talking again.

"A new world's coming," he said. "Going to change everything. Steam carriages. A Frenchman, Amédée Bollée, miniaturized a furnace. He used kerosene. Distilled bituminous coal. Burns longer, burns hotter, boils water faster, no horses needed."

"A carriage without horses will not be practical," she said.

"Bollée made three prototypes. *Uttos*, he calls them. They'll make him rich."

"Is that what you want, to be rich?"

"Do you ever have something to say that doesn't challenge?" he asked.

"Do you object to my questioning your truth?"

He tilted toward her. "Do you think this conversation will end without me cutting your pretty throat?"

She leaned away.

"That is not a way to treat me."

"I choose my contacts carefully," he said.

"And I do not think you choose."

"What does that mean?"

"It means you become a friend when someone takes your side," she said.

"I'll try to remember that," he said.

The land weaved and dropped from the plateaus to lower valleys and then curled back to high rock formations scraped raw by millennia. Rudd removed his broad-brimmed hat. His sweaty hair was long at the neck, flattened like a skullcap on top.

"Bringing you with me was a mistake," he said.

"When we reach Odessa, you'll be rid of me."

"That's one choice."

"What's the other?" she asked.

He squinted at the long flat valley ahead and then shook his head. "Nah. You're just too pretty to kill."

13 . . .

Keeping a southerly direction, the wagon crossed roads heading east and west, the rough ride bouncing, straining bolts, cinching rope strappings, and slapping the covered canvas against its metal ribs.

The land was broken and inhospitable, vacant of habitants, the valley ahead in a blanket of sun-dazzled snow. Rolling hills and rounded slopes fell into each other like eggs in a nest. Shielding her brow from the sun's low angle, Usell leaned forward and pointed.

"What's that?"

Rudd removed his hat and used it as sun cover.

Black lines on several of the hills rippled on their crests.

Undulating across the snow, blurred black squiggles disappeared into creases, and then reappeared on the heights. The apparition twisted on the humps and waved with a thousand caterpillar legs, meandering like a river and linking the heights.

Rudd stood in the crib and then sat back down. He reined the barbs to the hills and stopped at the top of a bank above the twisting flow.

The marching chain cleared a hill in the haze of sundown. People, four or five wide, moved by the pressure of numbers, and trudged *en masse* with a tired determination. Golden light brushed the droplet-beading backs of men, women, and children on the move – an entire village, young, old and in-between. The men wore black, the women in cream and white, their passage a shadow on the land.

"Who are they?" Rudd asked.

"Hassidim, very religious."

Usell hopped down and stood beside the wagon. She watched the procession. Rudd joined her in silence.

Along the queue – carts push wagons, wheelbarrows, and all manner of individuals carried, nudged, pulled, and dragged what they could of life's accumulations. They lugged lamps and pots, basins and clothing, carefully wrapped parcels of their most precious possessions.

The leaders passed below the bank. At the head of the procession was the chief Rabbi. His shoulders were back. Head up, beard gray. He concentrated on his steady pace. Dressed in traditional robes of black, his brows worried as he advanced, but he swung his fists and marched, planting his feet, one then another in the ankle-deep snow.

Right behind him, four other rabbis followed two by two. Their black bearded jaws were firmed as they set an example and marked the way like the point of a spear. Tired and bent, the lumbering travelers passed over the nearest rise, an exhausted worm unwilling to stop. Their tail end whipped about in a scramble of young boys.

Usell touched her exposed wet hair, pressed a hand against the mezuzah beneath her clothes. The procession passed three meters below, steady in their parade, crunching snow, the rabbis giving the snorting barbs no more than a glance. The horses, wagon and strangers were curiosities for which the rabbi's had no time. The line following imitated their leaders.

One shawled child stared at Usell. Her mother, holding her hand, dragged her forward. Her tiny shoes dug heel first into the thin snow. She was three or four, with curls on her cheeks, bright lustrous brown eyes damp in the low sun. Usell waved, and the girl raised a cloth doll with cross-stitched eyes and a tumble of tubular dyed wool hair, a hello, even as her mother jerked her forward, a suspicious blink glancing back.

"They're on the run," Rudd said.

"They only want to observe God's laws."

"They're heading for the western border. Poland. Maybe you should join them."

"I'm going to Odessa to find my mother," she said.

Rudd spun around at the sounds coming from the rear of the refugees.

"Get in the wagon. Quick," he said. His tall frame stretched three strides, hit the wheel strut, and leaped into the crib.

"Now," he said.

Usell leaned over the bank. Toward the end of their line the Hassidim had broken. They spread like a wave along an arc from the farthest hill to closest. Black robes flew behind the men and pale skirts ballooned about the women. The line on its leading edge buckled into the crease between the mounds.

On the bald domes of snow, riders crested the hill and pressed hard on the backs of the weary travelers. Gleaming swords flashed in the light and Cossacks, dozens of them, galloped from the other side of the valley on their brown Don horses. Flying manes, tied tails and steel whipped the air.

Swords hacked at everything that moved, at every shape, every man, every woman, and every child. Sprays of blood whipped from the end of the shashkas. Sprawling clothing marked the ground.

Rudd unlaced the reins from the brake. "Come on," he said. "We need to leave."

"They'll be slaughtered."

"Get in the wagon."

A cart filled with pots and pans fell over the slope, a rag doll flew in the air and tumbled down the crease. Rudd reached down and grabbed Usell's arm. A woman shrieked. Usell twisted free.

Below the bank the mother of the young girl chased the child down the crease, calling her name. "Mara, Mara."

The child stomped round cups in the snow, heading for the rag doll that tumbled the crease between the low hills. The woman slipped on the loose gravel and slid on her bottom to a stop.

Pounding hooves rumbled around the near hill into the crease as a single rider swirled his shashka over his head, and raced his Don horse right for the child.

Usell leaped off the edge of the bank, landing on the slope. Half skiing on the leather soles of too large boots, she scrambled toward the girl, stumbling as the surface leveled, just barely catching her footing.

"Where the hell are you going?" Rudd shouted.

The rider kicked his Don horse in the flank, lifted his shashka sword above his head, and raced at them. The mother's shrill cry shivered in the icy air.

Usell ran along the edge of the slope, using the embankment for balance, skirting the rocky fold at the bottom, digging her wide boots into loose snow and grabbing at anything to keep herself upright, half erect, half gliding over the crunching ice, maintaining balance, finding a firm wedge to plant her feet as the child reached her doll and bent over for it.

Usell jumped to the bottom and grabbed the girl around the waist, turned, and raced back up the slope. Hooves pounded metal on hard rock and the sound grew louder as Usell tried to climb the embankment. Her feet slipped and the girl dropped her doll.

She cried, jerked Usell's hair.

Usell skidded down the slope with one free arm balancing like a tail. She landed with both feet, grabbed the doll, and scampered across the crease, somehow not stumbling, looking for a way out of the path of the rider as the horse's gallop pounded the earth with hollow clacks.

The rider spurred his Don and grew closer as Usell angled up the rise, but the hoof stomps grew louder and just as she reached level footing, the horse's breath blew on her neck and she threw herself down, protecting the girl, who squeaked as weight compressed her into the snow.

The rider's blade swung by in a flash. The Don horse spun around. The Cossack kicked his heels in the horse's flank and it reared before leaping to the attack.

A burst of short, repeating explosions snapped the air.

Bullets sprayed umber dirt from beneath the snow. A spew of explosions hit the Cossack with meaty thuds, kicked him off his saddle in a splash of hot blood on pristine snow. A fleece hat with its cloth-pointed peak hovered above her like a balloon. Floating.

The body crashed to the ground with a heavy grunt. The sword flew from the Cossack's hand, stabbed to the vertical and the Don stampeded away.

Usell scrambled to her feet with the girl under one arm. Running from screams and the dull thump of metal hooves Usell lifted her head. Angry riders raced over the hilltop.

The repeating blasts of machined explosions sparked the air around her. Splatters of snow and mud dug into the hill. Horses reared. The child's fingers clutched Usell's neck.

With the girl shifted to her other arm Usell changed directions and ran for the embankment beneath Rudd's wagon. It rested on the shelf with its canvas top pulled back. Rudd sat on a bicycle seat that shook with the rattle and eruptions of his firing weapon. Flashes of gunpowder burst from a long muzzle sticking out between the wagon's metal ribs, and spraying hot lead across a wide arc.

Bracing against the slope of snow, Usell covered the girl as a riderless horse fell head-over-hooves, landed on its side with its legs still running even after it was dead. Another empty-saddled horse ran back the way it had come.

Rudd glanced down and with just a flutter of his eyes he aimed the gun at more riders in the distance. The Hassidim prostrated themselves on the snow like a wave receding from the shore.

Discharged casings dropped from the bank, hot brass, melting holes.

The gun barrel smoked and shook as the muzzle swept the hills. A Cossack lost control of his spinning horse. He whipped it until it fell, crushing the rider's leg beneath its ribs. The rider kicked at the struggling horse with his one free boot. Rudd fired a short burst.

The man screamed. His chest exploded.

The child covered her ears and the horse's fearful eyes faded to a haze.

And then the fearless Cossacks turned from their charge and galloped away, horsetails and braids flying behind. Rudd's gun rattled on and a single rider jerked from his saddle, flipped over the horse's rump. And then the gunfire stopped.

Silence took a long breath and gave way to slow movement. The Hassidim rose from the ground with moaning, bawling, and howls. The wailing lifted off the hills and swirled above them.

Usell uncovered the girl and stood her up. Her blinking brown eyes were wide. She did not cry, but looked worried. Usell handed her the doll and she wrapped it tight to her chest.

"Dir bist gut?" Usell asked. You are all right?

The girl covered her mouth, but shook her head with assertive nods. She took Usell's hand and together they headed back toward the place Usell last saw the mother. Blood, torn black cloth, bodies, and black mud discolored the snow.

On a flat area where the Hassidim gathered with those needing assistance, Usell searched for the mother of the child and she appeared, fearful, the strain lining her exposed face. She reached for her daughter. *"Gebn mich. Gebn mich."* Give me. Give me.

Crushing the child to her chest and crying, the woman turned her back and hurried away.

Rudd's gun hung its head like a sleeping stork. He was gone from it and startled her when he stepped near and fingered a cut sleeve.

"Close," he said.

His voice was firm. His face was calm. He set the brim of his hat.

"Come on," he said. "These people need help."

14 . . .

With the sun barely above the horizon, a light snow fell again. Usell tended to a wrinkled old woman who kept saying, *"Der kinder, der kinder."*

There were many dead. The old woman bled from a slashed leg and would not talk to Usell even after she spoke to her in Yiddish, told her who she was. A younger woman with a lopsided babushka limped toward them and wrapped her arms around the old woman. The two cried and together they slipped away.

The Hassidim, for the most part, controlled their grief, gathered their things, and carefully wrapped the dead. A linen-wrapped child lay like a sack over a young woman's shoulder. She petted its back and cried in silence.

Rudd and Usell righted a cart and repackaged the spilled contents of phylacteries, scrolls, and other detritus of religious life. The head rabbi, his furred hat askew, approached them with a controlled stride. He raised his right hand. It was covered in blood.

"Ma shlomcha," he said to Rudd.

"Peace," Usell translated.

Rudd nodded.

The rabbi didn't look at Usell beyond a glance over his whiskered cheek. He gestured to Rudd.

"A dank dir, a dank dir." Thank you. Thank you.

Rudd grabbed the Rabbi's hand and shook it. He spoke his broken Russian. "Don't thank me. Thank this girl here. If it wasn't for her . . ."

Usell lowered her head and said, "Men of this sect don't speak directly to women not in their family."

The Rabbi folded Rudd's hand between his, held it tight.

In perfect Russian he replied, "We have been struck a great blow, but we will remember it and pass it on to those who have survived as a lesson and a memory of those who have helped us. What is your name?"

"Cothman," Rudd said. "Rudd Cothman. And this, this is Emma. What's your last name?"

Usell lowered her head. "Bovary," she said.

For just a moment the rabbi broke tradition and stared at her, a crimp in his eyes, a glance at the mezuzah dangling around her neck.

Then he said they must be on their way. They needed to find safety and time to bury their dead. With the help of a young boy to steady him, the rabbi struggled back to the main body of the gathering. "Two names," he said. "Rudd Cothman and Madame Bovary."

He raised his arms as if to call the Lord's attention to their task, and the entire village rose up, ready to move, their individual troubles and toils subservient to the caterpillar of a thousand legs and their journey toward the west.

As Rudd and Usell headed around the embankment to the wagon, the mother of the young girl ran to catch up and grabbed Usell's arm.

"Is Mara all right?" Usell asked.

She smiled at Usell. Patting her cheek, the woman said, *Mutik maydl.*" Brave girl. Her head bent aside as if she were about to turn away and then as if she couldn't control herself, she threw her arms around Usell and for a moment, held her tight, did not let go.

"Thank you," Usell said. The woman's wraps were flecked with mud, blood, and snow, but her arms were thick-pillowed, and soft.

Without saying another word, she released Usell, returned to the line of travelers, retrieved her girl, who carried her rag doll, and once again waved at Usell before becoming part of the ripple moving over the landscape.

Rudd stepped to her side.

"You saved her daughter. That's all she says? Their leader won't even talk to you. What's the matter with these people?"

"I don't expect you to understand. I really don't myself, but it's about staying pure."

"Stupid," he said. "And this was stupid of me. They'll be looking for us now that they've seen the gun."

"Why did you do it?"

He lifted the brim of his hat and placed it back on his head. "Just so you understand," he said. "All I want is the jewel."

"And all I want is to find my mother," Usell said.

15 . . .

She felt each wheel of the wagon bump the path of snow; each found its own ruts, rocks, and roots. Leaving tracks behind as they rolled by the hills, they entered a landscape of patchwork forests, cone-bearing firs, deciduous maple, and tough-leafed brush. Even with the sun down, the light hung on the land, refusing to darken. Rudd flicked the reins.

He'd been silent other than to repeat that taking her had been a mistake.

They crossed an east-west road but continued south over rolling fields.

"How far is Odessa?" she asked.

"Due south 24 hours," he said.

A mildew moon appeared through the clouds and a soaring hawk banked against the fading sky. Usell unknotted her arms.

Ahead a road cut through a section of deserted grassland. A few stacks of hay with snowcapped tops lay on one side of the road. On the other a catalpa tree stood next to a path leading to the flat gray distance.

Rudd yanked the wooden brake. Rusted metal scraped the rust from other metal. Both front wheels ached and twisted the rotating axel aside. Two barbs shook their heads and fought the leather straps straining at their mouths. The wagon jerked to a halt beside the lone catalpa. Rooted in snow, its vine-like trunk twisted from the ground like Madame Hoffman's laundry being squeezed dry. Its banding branches and long skeletal fingers framed a circular roof over its bare body, gnarled fingers gripping an egg.

"What are you doing?" Usell asked.

"We'll make camp here," he said. "You can get some sleep."

"I am not tired."

"Then stay awake. Wait here. Go find wood. Make a fire."

"Where are you going?" she asked.

"I'm going to take the Barbs to fed on the hay in the field."

He pointed at a lump on the dark flat.

"Take the Albanian with you," he said. "Hobble him beneath the tree. He doesn't need to eat."

"You do not care for him. Why?"

"Just do as I say."

"Sometimes, I do not like you, Rudd Cothman. She jumped down and slipped in the snow.

Rudd shook his head and tossed her the brown wool blanket.

Resurrecting herself and brushing off, she released the Albanian as the wagon turned. With Rudd's cheek sucking, "Chik chik," the barbs headed into the dark field and a distant mound of hay.

"Sometimes I do not like you, Rudd Cothman," she said. "Do you have matches and food?"

"Saddlebags," he said.

His hand waved the air. Dismissive. Humorous. Not even a good-bye. The wagon faded into the dark.

Leaving the Albanian hobbled at the catalpa, she gathered nearby sticks, stomped a long dead branch into pieces, and with the last of the light erected a small fire and wrapped the brown wool blanket around her shoulders. She broke a chunk of bread in half. It was hard, but she chewed until the fibers softened. Wheat, barley, peppercorn, and dried strawberries flavored the grain.

As she sat on a gnarled root, snow beginning to fall again. The fire sizzled.

After a while the night settled in. She stood up and stared in the direction Rudd had taken.

"Rudd Cothman." she shouted. "Rudd."

There was no answer. With a flaring fire stick she followed the wagon tracks to the haystack. Rudd, the wagon, and the barbs were gone. The tracks flowed into the field as the stick fire went out and she stood in the dark. She ran three steps after the tracks before she stopped.

"Rudd Cothman," she yelled. "I do not like you."

Only the wind responded.

Tramping back to the fire, she squatted down next to it. Hugging her knees, she wiped her mouth.

As sudden as the crack of a winter storm, her head sagged. Her hair curled with wet snowflakes and for a moment there was no wind, no fritter of the Albanian, no crackle of fire, only a lost sigh that sounded like the old men praying in the temple, relieving the pain. When the snow stopped, she uncovered her head from the blanket.

A clouded moon spread light onto the flat.

The mound of hay was a block of shadow and nothing moved around it. Nothing in every direction. She stood up with the blanket around her shoulders.

"I will be strong, Father," she said. "I will be strong."

16 . . .

A clatter of icy branches in the Catalpa jostled Usell awake. A brisk wind howled across the flat. The Albanian's side trembled against her cheek and the twisted trunk scraped her back. Morning. Releasing the mezuzah from her grasp, she slipped it beneath her clothing.

Light swelled over the flat land. Standing and brushing herself off, she reset the saddle and tightened the cinch. Mounting, she rode the Albanian behind the haystack and found Rudd's wagon tracks as faint shadows in the snow. Following them west, she paused at a crossroads south. A paved road.

"South to Odessa," she said. "What do you think, horse? Do you think we should trust him?"

With the pressure of her legs against the Albanian's side, she followed the wagon tracks on its wobbly path through a highland plateau where the ruts turned onto a road against a cliff. And then the wagon's shadow tracks were swallowed by wider, deeper, more recent tracks. One wheel on the right weaved over itself.

Approaching a curve against a wall of stone, she heard a deep voice order, "Kill it."

She jerked the Albanian to a stop. Dismounting, she tied the horse to a bare bush sticking out of rock. Easing around the dipping curve in the road, she peaked into the gray cold mist where shadows moved.

A rifle shot cracked the air. The echo ricocheted off the rock face and she crouched against the wall.

Two vertical shadows stood off the road.

"Get it," a deep voice ordered.

"Yes, sir." A boy's falsetto.

"Did you kill it?" A girl's voice, high pitched.

The large shadow marched past Usell and into sunlight. The shining mountainous horizon backlit the black uniformed Cossack captain. Standing in the middle of the icy road, the princess screeched at him.

"Have someone prepare it, now."

The princess swung the diamond on the end of the chain around her gloved finger.

"We must travel," the captain said.

"Kill one of the coachmen and they'll work faster."

A golden carriage sat on the edge of the road. It was tilted off balance. Next to the carriage four coachmen struggled with the broken rear wheel. Two men hunkered beneath the back axle and tried to lift the weight while two others removed the nut holding the wheel. At the end of a long iron wrench another coachmen loosened the nut from the axle. The lieutenant with his blond hair tied in a tail held white-gloved hands out to catch the nut.

"I'm hungry," the princess said.

Usell retreated to the shadow of the rock face, but the ice beneath her baggy boots cracked the brief silence.

"Do you hear that?" the captain said.

He turned toward Usell.

"You there, what are you doing?"

He strode out of the sunlight to the shadows. His shashka blade ripped from its sheath, the stern forehead furrowed across the jagged scar.

"I asked you a question," he said.

The blade extended to Usell's chest.

She lifted her face.

"You," he said.

The captain's braid looped around his neck like a shawl. One of his eyes twitched. The tip of the sword quivered before he sheathed it.

"Who is it, Dmitri?" the princess asked.

"What are you doing out here?" the captain asked under his breath.

"I am lost," Usell said. "My wagon was attacked by bandits and my driver taken."

The Albanian whinnied and the captain squinted at it.

"That is your story?" He glanced at the cut on her jacket.

"Dmitri," the princess said. "I wish these men done. You must make them work harder. Dmitri."

The captain's body stiffened. He squeezed his eyes tight. When he opened them, he looked down at Usell.

"What do you do?" the captain asked.

"Sir?" she said.

"Sprechen Sie deutsch?"

"Ja," she replied.

"Sehr Gut," he said.

"Ja. I speak five languages."

"Can you teach?" She did not answer.

"Can you?" he asked.

"I'm versed in literature, science, mathematics, history, and the Socratic dialogue."

"You cannot know that much."

"Because I am a woman?" she asked.

"Because you are young," he said.

The princess screamed, "Dmitri Rotovak, answer me. Who is that?"

Rotovak clenched his jaw, the scar of his forehead pulsed. With a long tightening of his eyes and a deep breath, Captain Rotovak spoke in clipped tones.

"It is unimportant to me what you are doing here or why you are lying, but I need you to . . . to talk to the princess. You can teach her German. You make her understand she is not the whole world. I advise you to say yes."

His hard glare carried weight. Usell nodded and looked away.

"You will be rewarded. Be attentive and obey her orders. Your warning saved her life and I give yours back to you."

"Dmitri," the princess pleaded. "I am cold."

"A ruble for every intelligent utterance."

With a slow blink he turned around.

"Princess," he said. "You are in luck. Your companion has arrived and it is the girl, the one who warned us about the assassin and then vanished in the confusion."

"Bring her to me, now."

"Well." The captain nodded at Usell. "What are you waiting for? Get started." His head jerked toward the princess.

"One thing," the captain whispered as he strode at Usell's side. "Say nothing about yourself save what I reveal. Take value in your life. Be smart. No risk will go well for you."

Aside the carriage, the princess kicked snow at the coachmen who struggled to hammer an iron fitting from the axle. She tugged her white sable stole tight about her neck as the captain halted in front of her.

Her eyes fixed on Usell. Staring first at the large shoes poking from the wet hem, and then at Usell's slim waist, bosom, and mouth, the princess met her eyes. She frowned and then poked her gloved finger in the cut on Usell's sleeve.

"What has happened to you?" she asked.

"She was attacked by the same men who threw the bomb at you," Rotovak said. "She escaped on one of their animals."

"So strange for a woman to ride these days. You ride?"

"I was taught by a blacksmith," Usell said.

The princess smiled. "I ride better. The stable-master taught me," she said. Her youthful cheeks flushed her blue-white skin. For a moment her jade eyes glowed. Sun sparkles danced with innocence.

"Princess Ludivica Melikova," Rotovak said. "This young woman is a suitable tutor and she has searched us out because of you. She believes your destinies are entwined."

The princess gasped a hand to her chest. "Destiny."

"Incorporeal," he said.

"God watches over me," she sighed. And then with a clenched jaw she asked, "Is she noble?"

"As noble as Konstantin Dmitrievich Levin and Ekaterina Alexandrovna Shcherbatskaya, a Princess like you."

"I have heard of them. Where have I heard of them?" the princess asked.

"The great writer Tolstoy has written of them," Rotovak said. "This is a woman of breeding, character, and knowledge. She can introduce you to the ways of Europeans."

"Is that true?" The princess grabbed Usell's arm and jerked her from the captain. "Go away," she said and flicked her fingers at him.

Rotovak marched to the men who struggled to raise the wagon and axle together. He kicked a coachman to the ground and set himself between coach and the wheel at end of the axle. Bracing his forearms beneath the wooden bar, he lifted it off the ground. The coachmen fit the wheel and the nut, and another man cranked the wrench. When Rotovak dropped the weight, the leather creaked, the wood squealed and metal rubbed.

His eyes found Usell. He lifted his squared chin and stared at her. She looked away. Pressing her palm against the mezuzah beneath her garments, she turned and listened to the princess, who cleared her throat.

"I will tell you who I am," the princess said. She removed her gloves and locked her fingers together. On the platform of her fitted boots she set her shoulders back, locked her knees, and began to speak with a faraway look in her eyes.

"This is a beautiful land, a perfect land, my land, the land of heroes. It's been in my family for 20 generations. It is fertile and grand and anyone who speaks against it is a traitor. My mother is dead and I have no brothers or sisters. The land will be handed to my children and I have taken an oath to God that I will never allow this territory to be possessed by Jews."

Usell trembled.

"Are you cold?"

"Russian winter is harsh," Usell said.

"Do you know my Prussian Prince?" the princess asked. "I must know. I sent him a portrait. What did he think of me?"

Rotovak blinked permission to lie.

"He believes your beauty exceeds his fondest wish," Usell said.

"Is that all?"

"He can hardly wait to see you."

"I don't think he cares at all," the princess said. "What do I call you?"

"I am . . . Emma," Usell said.

"I blame my father," the princess said. "He hardly looks at me. I can't tell what he wants. I don't think he knows who I am or cares. When we sit down to dinner, he does not even talk with me. He mutters at the servants and he pinches the girls, but I am a spirit to him, one he cannot see or hear."

"My father did not hear me, either," Usell said.

"Are you betrothed?"

Usell nodded.

"We have common cause, then," the princess said. "When I marry, I will miss my palace. I can see the valley and the sea from my bedroom. I will miss all my servants: Vyshinsky, my butler – Salem, my seamstress – Anna, my cook. But I will not miss my religious instructor, Adrianna."

"Prayer is important," Usell said.

"She carries my father's wishes to me," the princess said. "But she is a mouse. All my servants are sworn to make sure I am perfect. It is necessary for me to uphold the nobility of the empire and never give in to the weaknesses of others, but Adrianna thinks I should serve God."

The captain berated the coachmen, barked at the young man he kicked, and then smacked him across his cheeks with the back of his hand. The princess pinched Usell's arm.

"He's mean, isn't he? I told him to kill that boy, but he insists on discipline. Are you listening to me? I've been alone a long time."

"You are not alone," Usell said. "I am here."

The princess smiled.

The coachman unhooked the long wrench. At a signal, the holders of the carriage let go and the frame squeaked with leather stabilizers. One of the six unharnessed Friesians twisted his head and the long fetters on his right hoof pawed the snow.

"Your carriage is ready," Rotovak said.

The princess hooked Usell's arm and spun them both around. With an exaggerated swing in her straight hips, she ushered the two of them past Rotovak to the coach, where she waited for a servant to plant the step.

Entering the carriage first, the princess pulled Usell inside and slammed the door in Rotovak's face. After securing the bolt, the princess flopped on the bench of pillows facing where Usell sat down.

"You don't have to listen to him," the princess said.

"Who?"

"My jailer."

"The captain?" Usell asked.

Usell shivered under the princess's gaze; her posture and movements like a ground finch searching over its shoulder before pecking at a seed.

"You are cold," the princess said. She banged her knuckles on the roof. "Dmitri, bring me your coat."

The door opened and Rotovak's hand held out a black jacket with a red stripe across the shoulder. The princess grabbed it and slammed the door in his face. She handed the jacket to Usell.

"Wear this. I'll get you something better when we get to the train."

Usell slipped the heavy, rough wool over her own garments. It smelled of musk.

"You and I are friends," the princess said. "Do not worry about him. All he does is growl."

A whip cracked the air and the carriage jerked ahead, stretching leather, wood, and rolling iron wheels onto crunching snow and grinding rock. The clop of horse hooves hit the icy road in synchronous rhythm.

17 . . .

Lounging in the cushions of her carriage, the princess dug into a pouch at her waist and eased out a daguerreotype the size of a playing card.

"All I know of my betrothed is this picture," the princess said. "Can you tell me about him? What is he like?"

The boy in the picture wore a crown too large for even his bulbous head. He could not have been more than ten. He stared straight at the camera at attention. His matchstick shoulders and greasepaint face disclosed the temperament of a very grim boy with dark suspicious eyes. An oversized regal sash across his chest was so out of place it contradicted his deadly serious expression.

"He will grow up," Usell said.

"Look at him? Can't you see? How could anyone love that? He is ugly."

With her hands clasping the glass reproduction in her lap, she started to cry.

Usell hesitated before crossing benches and putting her arm around the princess. She stopped mid-sob and stared at Usell.

"You touched me."

Usell removed her hand. "I'm sorry."

"No. It's all right. It's been a long time since I've been touched."

She cuddled under Usell's arm and waited for her to replace it.

"What am I going to do?" the princess said.

A squat kerosene lantern dangled beneath the silk ceiling. The yellow glow of a short wick restrained the flame.

"I am barter," the princess said.

She pulled the long gold chain and jewel around her neck into the lemon light where the stone sparkled a thousand yellow shafts in every direction.

"I'm the vessel to carry this," she added.

"It's beautiful," Usell said. "Magic."

"Magic. Yes. I can command it to save me."

She held it up to the light.

"Princess," Usell said. "It is just a stone."

The lantern swung and the flame angled facets of multi-colored light about the carriage.

When they came to an abrupt stop in a jangle of chain and leather, there was a short rap on the door. When it swung open, an icy wind blew out the kerosene lantern. The footman, a blond boy of about 15, stood back from the step, a glance at Usell, and fluttering eyes. He stepped down and bowed his head as the princess leaned out of the carriage door.

"Come on," the princess said. She pinched the captain's jacket and pulled Usell out with her.

Rotovak jumped from the driver's crib. Snow exploded about the blond boy's boots. He scampered away.

"Where is my train, Dmitri?" the princess demanded.

"The train is late," Rotovak said.

"Make it come right away."

Rotovak snapped his fingers at the lieutenant, who, seated on his gelding, stared at the black grease on his white gloves.

When the princess marched to a wooden platform next to the water tower, Rotovak leaned close to Usell and whispered, "Do not get comfortable with her. Just see to her demands."

Steel train tracks gleamed silver in the sunlight and slashed through the long plain from the east. A light dust of snow covered the flat ground, a thousand diamonds igniting the landscape.

"Dmitri." the princess said. "Where is my seamstress, my butler, my cook?"

"They were hanged as traitors. Adrianna exposed them."

The princess squinted at the bright sunlight reflecting off the snow. "I have Emma now. We are friends. We are like sisters."

Rotovak glared at Usell.

On the track in the distance, a plume of thick black smoke boiled from a cone on the engine's snout. In a short time a whistle blew. The train squealed to a stop a few cars past the engine and a brown-clad conductor in a stiff black collar hopped off with an iron step in his hands. A metal spout lowered from the water tower. The water flowed into the engine's tank and hissing steam poured out the pistons on its sides.

The conductor set the iron step in front of the royal coach with the emblem of the Grand Duke on its side: double hearts, double swords crossing.

After helping the princess up the iron steps, Rotovak whispered in Usell's ears, "Be careful, lest you overstep your bounds."

18 . . .

Without waiting until the entourage settled, the train jerked forward.

The coach reeked of alcohol, cigar smoke, kerosene, and harlotry. Even the brocaded wallpaper – gold *fleur de lis* patterned in endless rows – reflected the antique of the Louis XVI sofa with its pastoral embroidery of young well-dressed men with naked, small–

breasted, and chubby women having a picnic in the park. Carved Bacchus figures on a cherry wood china cabinet braced against the far wall. The table in front of the sofa contained drawers and a high gloss polish of black paint. Shimmying golden tassels hung about red velvet valances on windows that ran the length of one side of the coach. The light poured through both tassel and window as the train headed south.

The princess lounged on the sofa. In the china cabinet crystal and carafes trembled and chimed with the movement of the train. Compressors hissed and iron wheels scraped against iron tracks. Usell held onto the arm of the sofa nearest the windows.

"You look ridiculous in that military jacket," the princess said. From the table drawer she pulled out a gray mink stole.

Here," she said. "Now you are like me."

Rotovak, standing nearby, bunched his brows to a knot.

"I saw that," the princess said. "It's mine to do with as I wish."

She kicked at him though he was far from her reach.

"Our Captain Rotovak here," the princess said, "sees only daggers and cares nothing for art or a woman's favors."

Rotovak did not look at her nor did he respond.

The princess gave him a smug smile, leaned close to Usell, and spoke in a loud whisper.

"All he cares about are his duties. He is not interested in us. No. Not us. We are the Tsar's expensive wine. That's all. I think they may have snipped something in him."

Rotovak did not even draw a breath.

"He saved your life," Usell said. "The bomb would surely have killed you."

"He did his duty," the princess said. Pouted duck lips.

The train accelerated. The coach rocked side to side. Wheels on rails replicated themselves in an undulating click-clack echoing beneath the floor.

A matron—a woman in her late-forties with russet hair pulled back into a bun and covered by a knit snood—entered the unbolted door at the rear and, noting Usell's presence, lowered her eyes. Clothed in black – neck to toe – her humility tightened in her shoulders at the princess's glare.

"Haven't you done enough Adrianna? What do you want?" the princess said.

"Your highness," she said. Her bow was slight and her manner submissive. "It is time for prayers."

"I don't want to pray. Now, go away."

"Your highness," Adrianna said. "God needs his tithes."

"God didn't stop that Jew from hurling my mother off the palace to her death, and I'll never forgive you for it."

Adrianna seemed to shrink.

Rotovak pressed his palm to his forehead and brushed it over his scalp.

"You highness," Usell said. "Kindness to one's servants has virtue."

The princess mashed her lips together. "Oh, all right."

"I know it wasn't your fault, Adrianna," the princess said. "But you should have been more careful with the friends you chose for my mother."

"When you are ready," Adrianna said. The twitch in her cheek disappeared as she left through the front end of the coach.

"What friends were those?" Usell asked.

"One friend. A French aristocrat. I don't know. The stories of my mother and her friend and the suicide are fables. They say she was unhappy and the whore was her only companion."

Usell straightened her back.

"The woman that was her companion, French?"

"She was rumored to be a Jew and she disappeared after my mother died. I think she threw my mother over the palace walls into the sea. It's what a Jew would do."

Usell clutched the back of the sofa.

"Adrianna knew her?" Usell asked.

"All Adrianna knows are rules," the princess said. "I hate her. Dmitri, get me some sherry."

The rumble from Rotovak's deep breath ended with a glance at Usell.

"No," Usell said. "I shall get it for you. The captain's duties are too important."

She unfastened a crystal goblet from the cabinet, poured sherry from a carafe, and handed it to the princess.

The princess swallowed two gulps before waving for more. "Adrianna thinks because she was my mother's governess that there is something between us, but there is nothing."

"How long has she been with you?" Usell asked.

"Since before my mother died. I was young. They say my mother tried to fly to heaven. I don't know why."

"My mother left me when I was very young," Usell said.

The princess folded her hands over her heart. "We are like one. Destiny has brought our souls together."

"I would like to pray with Adrianna," Usell said.

"When we get to the palace. I don't like praying. It never gets me anything. Don't look at me like that, Dmitri."

Rotovak stared out the windows at the long morning shadows.

"Do you know any American Barons?" the princess asked. "I hear they will charm the blush to your face."

Usell glanced at Rotovak, but he did not look at her.

"Princess," Usell said. "You could charm any American."

Rotovak's head pivoted to look at Usell. His gaze demanded attention, obedience, but to the princess it meant nothing at all and Usell pretended not to notice.

"I do believe the captain likes you," the princess said.

She pressed herself up from her lounging position. She gulped down the rest of her goblet and refilled it herself.

A hard rap on the door at the forward end of the coach caused the princess to spill her sherry.

"Have the intruder flogged," the princess said.

Rotovak opened the door. His lieutenant saluted.

"What is it, Poruchik?"

"We have word from Odessa."

"I will deal with it later," Rotovak said.

"There are new orders from the Tsar."

"Later, Lieutenant."

"Sir, the new Tsar."

He glanced over at the princess tilting her third goblet and then squinted at Usell.

"Lieutenant," Rotovak said.

"Our troops have a heathen in custody," the lieutenant said. "Alexander III wants answers. There are many spies."

"What's this? A spy?" the princess said.

Rotovak lifted his chin.

"Our men in 9th company have him in the forward car," the lieutenant said. "He is a Jew. He was caught at the telegraph office in Havens."

Usell flinched.

"I will attend to it, Princess," Rotovak said.

"We'll see about that." The princess stood up. With a quick smile at Usell she said, "I will interrogate this prisoner."

Rotovak's black eyes faded like an eclipsed sun.

"Let us deal with the pawns, Princess," he said. "We will question him."

"You, Lieutenant," the princess said. "Bring this man in here so that I might get answers you have not."

"That's not a good idea," Rotovak said.

The princess threw her crystal goblet at his head. It missed by a finger-length. He did not flinch, even as it smashed against the door. Standing with her fists on her hips, she stomped her heel.

"Bring the prisoner to me," she said.

"You heard the princess," Rotovak said. "Bring him in."

The lieutenant reversed and Rotovak closed the door.

"Princess," he said. His tone trembled with impatience. "We may yet be able to turn this prisoner. The young are malleable. Please be careful. It is a delicate matter better left to professionals. If he is to be foiled, perhaps even turned, it will be necessary to break him slowly, a thing not to be trifled with by amateurs."

"Piffle, piffle, piffle," she said. "I will get some of Doctor Pasteur's powder to disinfect myself later."

"It is a military matter, Princess," he said.

"Soldiers. You think your maneuvers are all important."

Rotovak braced himself but didn't respond.

The snowy landscape flew by so fast that mountain shadow, white snow, and dark forest melded to rivers of gray.

There was a short rap on the door.

"Enter," Rotovak said.

The door opened and a body dressed in a bloodied, torn rekel hurled inside and tumbled against the floor in a rattle of chains. A young man with wet straggling black hair and pais rose up on his hands and knees like a cornered animal. He was manacled wrist to ankles. When he lifted his cringing head, he looked right at Usell.

The bruised face swallowed and lost whatever courage struggled against abuse. Moshe Gimmel. His top lip was split, cheeks red, right eye swollen. He ducked his head before the lieutenant kicked him in the side.

"He refuses to say anything," Lieutenant Yazukov said. He closed the door behind him. Grabbing Moshe Gimmel's neck, he twisted him to face Ludivica. "Tell us what you know, rebel. Name your confederates who burned down the telegraph office."

Moshe Gimmel said nothing.

The lieutenant yanked his hair.

"Leave him alone," Usell said.

She stepped to the lieutenant and looked him in the eye.

Moshe Gimmel squinted up at her behind his broken mask.

Rotovak, the lieutenant, and the princess stared.

"I'm trying to educate the princess in the ways of civilization," Usell said. She turned to the princess. "Please. This is not right. Not good for you."

The lieutenant looked at the captain, who stared at Ludivica.

"But he is nothing," Ludivica said. "He is a dog. He is rabid."

"I see a young man," Usell said. "I see no dog."

"But he—is—a . . ."

"Princess," Usell interrupted. "The people in the new Europe would not approve of this. And you must not participate if you are to be a member of a civilized society."

The lieutenant tightened his grip on Moshe Gimmel, and he winced in pain.

"Stop it," Usell said. She spun around, slammed her closed palms against the lieutenant's arm, but it did nothing to stop the pain on Moshe Gimmel's face. Rotovak snarled. His smooth features distorted, the symmetry torqued.

"Emma," the princess said. She approached behind Usell and touched her arm. "You must be strong, Emma. We cannot let our emotions dictate kindness to our enemies."

"This is not for him," Usell said. "It is for you, princess. You are soon to be wife of a man on the throne of a powerful empire. This is not a thing a woman with such power must do to prepare herself. If you abide in cruelty, you will be unable to control others. The people depend on you."

Her gray jade eyes shined.

"Princess," Usell said. "Trust me. This is wrong. You do not want to go into your position with an impure conscience."

The princess swelled to her full height. "Leave him alone," she said.

With a nod from Rotovak, the lieutenant released Moshe Gimmel. He slipped to the floor.

Moshe Gimmel's hand brushed the edge of Usell's boot.

The princess blinked a tear and then threw her bony arms around Usell.

"I am so happy to have a friend," The princess said. "I have never had anyone care so much about me."

"I will help you, princess," Usell said.

The princess released Usell, sniffled, and with her hand brushing everyone away like flies, the princess said, "Take the Jew from us."

"And leave him alone," Usell said.

Rotovak nodded at the lieutenant. "Tend to his wounds, Yevgeny. Add him with those we take to the docks. Do not disturb him otherwise."

The lieutenant saluted longer than he should have. Stiffer. He clutched Moshe Gimmel beneath the arm and jerked him toward the door.

Just before he disappeared, Moshe Gimmel caught Usell's eye and she lost the tension in her cheeks and the muscles in her abdomen fluttered.

"I really don't understand why you defended him," the Princess said.

"Let justice decide his fate," Usell said.

Ludivica squeezed her fingers around her jewel. "God's mercy is for all of us," she said. "I'm so glad you believe in me. Just this once I shall consider charity, but only because you have asked me for it."

19 . . .

The black train snaked up the Carpathians to highlands of cliff rock and black spruce forests. After two more glasses of sherry, the princess slept on her sofa. Usell stood next to it, kept her head down, eyes avoiding Rotovak, who growled and paced as if arguing with himself. The train swayed less on long curves where the landscape disclosed only crags of icy brown rock rushing toward the sky like steeples.

"Women. You are as impertinent as she," Rotovak said.

His eyes were dark, penetrating.

"What do you wish from Adrianna?"

Usell did not look up. "Why, prayer, of course."

"Your answers have tentacles."

"I don't know what you mean."

"What interests you about the dead Duchess?" Rotovak asked.

"The princess is my interest, as you desired. A mother forms a child."

"Yet, you say you lost yours."

"I feel the princess's pain," Usell said.

"You feel your own pain."

"I am human."

"I think you hide the truth," he said.

"You are mistaken."

"I am not fooled. I have warned you."

"I look for facts," Usell said.

"She doesn't care about facts," Rotovak said. "She wants. She wants."

"I have wants, too."

"What is it you want?"

"I want my family. I want to be free to make my own choices."

His eyes narrowed. The dark braid rising from his shaved scalp slid off his shoulder.

"Everyone wants," he said. "All right. When this is over, you may do as you wish."

He faced the window and found a distant focus in the passing forest.

"Thank you for helping me," she said.

"I am as immune to gratitude as I am to lies," he said.

"Then you shall receive neither from me," she said. She folded her arms and turned away from him.

A knock on the door sent him to it. He yanked it open.

Yazukov entered, spoke in hushed tones, moved with Rotovak to the corner. Rotovak listened to the Lieutenant, his eyes straying to Usell as the lieutenant raised his voice.

"Three coaches of men on the train might not be enough if there is another attack on her."

The princess slept, lifeless except for a rising rib cage and rocking on her side to the sway of the train as it angled down and then tilted on a long curve coming out of the snowy pass. The bottles and crystal in the liquor cabinets, even bolted to the floor, chimed against themselves. Flaxen light flickered through mountain shadows changing from night to bright day and back to shadows.

Around the descending curve the engine, a half a dozen cars ahead, chugged toward a dark tunnel, its black mane of smoke following the stack. The princess stretched as she woke.

"What is it like to be married?" she asked.

"I have never been married."

"That's not what I meant."

The train tilted on an angle along the curve. Usell grabbed the arm of the sofa and flattened her boots against the floor.

"Why can't they make these tracks all straight?" the princess complained.

The captain steadied himself without an anchor, but his narrowed gaze seemed to smolder.

"There's trouble in Odessa," the lieutenant said. "Word of rebels appearing openly in the streets, cheers of happiness over the death of Alexander and they carry weapons."

The captain seemed not to hear his Lieutenant's words.

"What I know of marriage comes from books," Usell said.

"Then how can you prepare me to become a wife?"

A cliff rose on one side of the curve as the train headed into a black tunnel. In front of it was a billowing bonfire on the tracks. Usell gripped the sofa. Outside the windows a snow-covered meadow spread to a thick forest of evergreens. A flash of light exploded from the tree shadows.

The boom that erupted shook the coach, the blast exploding outside the windows, throwing a clod of earth at the shaking train. The wheels rocked off one track, canted at a severe angle for a moment, and then collapsed back with a loud bang of metal on metal. The china cabinet against the wall smashed on the floor in a spray of wine, liquor, and shattered glass.

A hole, revealing clouds above, dropped splintered wood from the open roof. The train whistled a long blast. Brakes squealed and the collision of coaches crunched into each other in a series of domino concussions, throwing all forward. The princess hurtled against Usell and they fell to the floor.

"Emma, Emma, help me," the princess said. Usell locked her hand to her wrist.

Gunpowder smell and smoke tumbled into the coach. The train stopped with a squealing gasp. Weight shifted forward and steadied. Steam and smoke whipped through shattered openings as reversing wheels screeched and pushed back against the slope of the mountain.

A second explosion ignited a fire outside the wooden walls and whipped flames about the hole in the roof. The train convulsed. Metal screamed in a twisted agony. The cars crunched again, backward, upending Usell and untangling the princess, tossing her over the sofa.

In three strides Rotovak pressed Usell down and bent over her. Wood cracked, metal pinged, and a shower of bullets shattered windows and punctured the coach. The heat of metal buzzed through the wall and out the opposite side. The princess tried to stand.

"Stay down," Rotovak ordered. In a crouch he lifted Usell by the back of her stole, pulled her to the princess, and flattened them both to the floor.

Lieutenant Yazukov scrambled to the windows and with his pistol drawn he fired into the faraway trees. The train lurched upward and back. Flaring discharges fired from the forest. Pistons strained as crackling flames and choking smoke swirled about the coach. The boom of cannon was followed by the scream of a projectile. The explosion seared the air, blew the smoke out of the coach, and threw a rain of dirt and rock on top of them.

Standing, Rotovak dripped debris. He yanked Usell upright along with the princess. Bullets pinged against the iron wheels and pelted the wooden walls. The train picked up speed. The princess grabbed Usell and shielded herself.

"Heathens," she said. "I should have killed that Jew."

"Rebels," Lieutenant Yazukov yelled. "Nihilists."

Bullets popped through wood.

"In the trees," Lieutenant Yazukov said. "They must know the princess is aboard."

"Go to your men, Lieutenant. Rapid fire return."

The lieutenant ducked through the forward door.

The captain lifted the princess up as fire swirled in the coach. "Out," he said, "toward the caboose."

He pushed the princess toward the rear. With his hand under Usell's arm he said, "Come." He pushed her ahead of the princess. "You lead, stay low," he said.

Usell pushed open the small door of one carriage, stumbled across the wayward and shifting landing and through the next door.

A dozen Cossacks kneeling at the windows fired their rifles into the trees. Usell ducked. She ran hunched, down the aisle between the double rows of seats. Puffs of smoke and flashes erupted from forest shadows where the rebel guns hid. Cossacks fired and reloaded a bullet at a time. Lead hit wood and glass as the kneeling Cossacks took their turns and fired back. A body jerked with recoil and fell into the aisle.

Stepping over the dead Cossack, Usell ran bowed, hastening toward the next door. The train rocked as the speed increased. The princess's fingers pulled at the back of Usell's jacket.

"Stay close," the princess said.

"Next coach," Rotovak said.

Passing through the door to the landing between the Cossack's coach and the caboose, the princess slipped backward, releasing Usell, who wobbled above the couplings between cars. Steadying herself, Usell saw the fiery blast out of the corner of her eye before hearing the cannon boom.

The explosion hit the caboose and flung Usell off the train. She flew, arms extended like wings. The exchange of fire crossed the meadow as she sailed over on her back, downward. Hitting, she tumbled head over heels on a snowy slope and rolled like a spinning ball, down a long grade, bouncing, jolting, and skimming at an angle so fast she hardly touched the ground. On leveling ground the last few rotations in a pillow of white came to a quick stop. Her head pitched forward between her legs and rebounded back into the snow.

A violet sky darkened in the east and filled the arc with sunlight. In front of Usell was a shadow surrounded by a bright haze. The shadow leaned over her, upside-down.

A curious face cocked her head to the side. Black eyes. Dark unblemished skin. A wine-colored handkerchief tied about the forehead. Long, black silky hair bordered an angry face. Gypsy. Itinerant travelers, who visited Oylaif with wares to sell, a gypsy girl, like the young women who swayed through Oylaif's market offering trinkets of buttons, shells, beads, and smiles that drew blushes from the meydlshes and caused the boys to crowd around and stare. All the boys but one—the boy who kept his nose in his books.

A rifle muzzle poked in Usell's face as the sky turned from gold to black and vanished into oblivion.

20 . . .

When Usell awoke it was night. Low campfires perched like burning bushes on lumpy, snow-covered ground. A howl of wind blew flames to swirls. Sparks popped in a fire nearby. Three large men hunched by it.

She tried to rise, but as she struggled up, a bulk of fur, smelling like bear and rendered fat, sealed her to the ground. She pushed the poorly tanned fur away and pressed her hand against her throbbing forehead. Icy breezes snipped like gnats at her bare skin. She wore only undergarments. Pulling up the greasy fur, she shivered against the cold.

Wincing when she sat up, she touched her arm, her knee, and her bruised bottom. Struggling to her feet, she hefted the bear fur around her shoulders.

The three squatting men at the fire argued.

"Petra chased away the pests."

"Rats. You can never get rid of all the rats."

"He was an obedient dog."

"You are manipulated by the charms of animals."

"Stop complaining and eat your meat."

A spit skewered a headless animal – anus to neck – above the fire. A man dressed in stitched skins turned to Usell. Two unkempt strings of black hair dangled from his upper lips. The Mongolian from Havens. He squinted slit-black eyes.

"She is awake," he grunted.

"Good." A woman with impatience in her voice burst from the darkness past the fire and strode right at Usell. Small hard mouth, short hair wings on her forehead tucked behind her ears. The princess's stole fluttered in the cold wind about the woman's shoulders. She carried her left fist clenched and crossed the space between the men and Usell with long strides.

"Why is a Jew dressed like a bourgeois and wearing this?" She pinched the mink.

Usell closed the bearskin about her neck.

"What were you doing on the Tsar's train?"

The woman's nostrils flared.

"Where am I?" Usell asked.

A slap spun Usell's head. The woman leaned closer.

"I advise you to answer," she said.

"You struck me," Usell said.

The back of the woman's hand smacked Usell's other cheek.

"Answer me or I'll cut your throat."

Usell crossed her arms with fur. "What do you want?" she asked.

The woman unclenched her fist, exposing the mezuzah.

"What is a Jew doing with the empire?"

Usell grabbed for the icon. The woman snatched it away. She slipped the tube in the pocket of her trousers. "Now. What were you doing on the Tsar's train?"

Usell said nothing.

"Arragos," the woman said. She flipped her hair off her brow.

The broad Mongolian dressed in sealskins rose from his squat before the fire. His trunk-like arms hung parallel to the thin drooping mustache above a sour mouth. The woman twitched her face into a frown.

Usell took a step back.

"Persuade the girl to speak."

In three quick, lumbering strides he was over Usell. He ripped the bearskin off her back, snatched her wrist, and yanked it up behind her like a stick he was attempting to snap from a tree.

Usell screamed. Her body bent over.

"Arragos enjoys hurting people," the woman said. "Now tell us what we wish to know."

At a nod from the woman the Mongolian increased the strain on her arm.

"An accident," Usell said. "It was an accident."

The woman nodded.

The Mongolian released her wrist. Recoiling, Usell rubbed her shoulder and angled away from him. Retrieving the bear fur, she wrapped against a swirl of wind.

"What is your name?"

"Emma," Usell said.

"Emma what?"

"Bovary."

"Arragos."

"It is the name I have," Usell said.

The woman waved him back. The Mongolian's block chin lifted.

"What were you doing on the Tsar's train?"

"I was captured," Usell said.

"Where did you get this?" The woman clutched the stole.

"The princess gave it to me."

"Explain what were you doing on the train."

"I was told to handmaid the princess," Usell said.

"What is the princess to you?"

"Nothing."

"That's not an answer," the woman said.

"I don't know what you want to know."

"Tell me how you got on the train."

"They knew me from Havens."

The woman's smooth oval face crimped at her brow. "I saw you spying on me from an alley."

"An accident," Usell said.

"Was it also an accident that you foiled the Ahnah's throw?"

"I will cut her throat," the Mongolian growled. He removed a scimitar from the sash about his waist.

"I didn't mean anything. The bomber startled me. He tripped over me."

The woman lifted an open palm and Arragos slipped his long knife back into its metal sleeve.

"You warned them," the woman said.

"It wasn't my fault," Usell said.

The meat cooking on the skew hung heavy in the middle.

"Did the Princess have the jewel on the train?"

"Why do you want to kill her?"

"I ask the questions," the woman said. "What were your duties with the princess?"

"Teaching her," Usell said.

"Are you a teacher?"

"My father was a teacher," Usell said. "He taught me."

"Taught you what?"

"Languages. Literature. Argument."

The woman threw her head back with her hands on her hips and erupted in a full guffaw.

"Who trains a Jew like that?"

"My father," Usell said.

"You talk in circles," the woman said.

A greasy forearm broke from the carcass above the fire and crashed into the flames. The woman pinched her fleshy nose. The fire flared as the meat inside the flame sizzled.

"Who gave you this job to teach a princess?" the woman asked.

"The officer."

"What officer?"

"A captain," Usell said.

"Why did he hire you?"

"I think he was displeased with the princess. Maybe he thought she . . ."

"She what?" the woman asked.

"She might learn from me."

"What could a princess learn from a Jew?"

Usell set her shoulders. "The officer could not know who I was. He made up a lie and said to keep my mouth shut."

"Why would he do that?" the woman said.

"I don't know."

The Mongolian growled.

Usell rubbed her shoulder. Bubbling juice from the meat dripped into the fire in a string of hisses. The woman set her boot on an exposed rock. She wiped her lips. "How did you end up on the train?"

"I ran away from Havens. It snowed. I got lost. On the road the Cossack . . ."

"Cossack?"

"The captain."

"A big man with a scar?" She drew a line with her finger down her forehead.

"Yes."

"Rotovak," she said. "Continue."

"He found me on the road in the snow. He recognized me from the bombing. And he just said I was to tend to the princess. He insisted on it."

The woman walked around Usell with slow deliberate steps.

"This Cossack Captain . . . Rotovak. We know him. He is no longer a member of the Second Chancery. He has no friends there now that Alexander is dead. He was not given duties commensurate with his service or record. Alexi doesn't trust him. Which creates the puzzle. He does not need trouble. So the question is, why would he make it for himself by bringing a stranger on board so soon after an attack on the princess? A stranger involved in the episode."

"The princess is difficult for him to handle," Usell said.

"But he is Cossack. He doesn't risk the nobility. The Cossack is indifferent to snow, sun, or wind."

"I don't know why he did it," Usell said.

"There you were on the train with the princess and a Cossack. You know what Cossacks do to Jews? You know what the princess thinks of Jews?"

"She believes what she has been taught. Don't you?" Usell asked.

"Maybe, but you don't get to ask the questions here. Perhaps this Cossack likes you."

The woman examined Usell, pinched her jaw, and turned her head to profile.

"Clearly, something about you haunts him. Stand up."

"What?"

She jerked the fur from Usell. "Yes. He would like you. Tell me more."

"What do you want to know?"

"Never mind. What else did the Cossack say to you?"

"He implied I was as impudent as the princess," Usell said.

"What else?"

"He saved me from your bullets."

"Tell me about that," the woman said.

"You shot at us. He knocked me to the floor and held me down."

"What was the princess doing?"

"Screaming about Jews," Usell said.

"He wasn't protecting her?"

"He did, right after me."

"Right after you . . . .." The woman strode to the fire and thrust her hands in her pockets, stared at the flames. Lifting her head, she said, "You can be useful to us."

"I'm headed to Odessa to find my mother."

The woman stared, said nothing. A bone with flaring meat broke from the carcass and fell into the fire. Burnt skin held the dog to the spit. Usell covered herself with the fur.

"Are you hungry?" the woman asked.

"I do not eat dog."

"You would eat it if you were hungry enough."

"I would like to go now," Usell said. "Can you point me toward Odessa?"

"You have a fine sense of humor," the woman said.

"Please, now. I've answered your questions."

"Didn't you hear me when I said you can be useful?" the woman said.

"Can I have my mezuzah back?" Usell asked.

"What kind of shtetl girl are you?"

"I don't know what you mean."

95

The woman brushed her hair off her brow. "You are taught to withhold, show respect, and not question. Jewish children do not challenge their elders."

"I am not a child," Usell said.

"Your women do not dispute decisions made by men."

"I do not always agree."

The woman knelt to the fire. "If you wish to stay alive, you will practice what your people taught and keep your opinions to yourself."

"And if I refuse?"

"You will not live to see the dawn, and the night will be very hard on you."

Usell sagged beneath the bear skin. "What is it you wish me to do?" she asked.

"We will talk about it after you eat. In the meantime . . .."

The woman rose and joined Usell, clasped her shoulders.

The woman's eyes sparkled with firelight.

"Welcome to the Naradnaya Volya. I am Nikolayevna Fillipova, and you have now joined the fight for the People's Will."

21 . . .

Nikolayevna Fillipova shouted her orders. The rebels broke camp and a caravan of work wagons followed a gray ridge to the rendezvous with the rest of her troops.

In a wagon with Arragos, Usell kept warm under the bearskin until they arrived at an abandoned cathedral sculpted into a chalk white cliff.

"Leave that," Arragos said and tore skin from her back.

He led her up broad steps carrying a heavy steamer trunk on his back. At an entryway below the spires the interior of the cathedral echoed their footsteps through the disfigured statues strewn about the vast antechamber. When they stopped, a hollow silence pulsed the empty nave. Keystones dripped dust from vaulted arches.

Splintered pews crushed against each other in jagged piles and crumbling blocks of carved stone friezes lay where they'd fallen.

The flutter of a dove in the clerestory reverberated from a fractured dome as spears of moonlight angled to the floor. From narthex to chancel, phantoms prayed in the shadows and Nikolayevna waved for them to hurry.

She ignited a torch, kicked open a panel behind the altar and lead the way into the dark, stone stairs leading down. Arragos struggled with the steamer trunk bringing up the rear.

At the bottom a low ceiling and a wet stone floor flickered waves of torchlight. Recessed in the walls, ossuaries tunneled into the stone of the catacomb. It smelled of mold, moisture, and something faintly sweet.

Arragos dropped the load on his back. With a squeak of tight belts and the snap of metal clips, he opened the steamer trunk.

"Heat," Usell said. "I feel heat."

Pointing the torch, Nikolayevna lighted faint ghosts of steam above a bubbling pool.

"God's bathwaters," Nikolayevna said.

Arragos pulled drawers from the trunk, lit candles, lay blankets and towels, and unfolded a sturdy wooden stool. Nikolayevna seated herself and waited until he finished. When he backed away from the trunk toward the stairs, he said, "Make her into a gypsy. She has their nose for trouble." He disappeared up the stairs.

"You have done well, my brother," Nikolayevna said to the darkness. "And you, you filthy Jew . . . Your cleansing awaits."

Embarrassed by her nakedness, Usell coiled under the large towel. Nikolayevna tore the towel off and shoved her into the pool. Bending to a knee, Nikolayevna plunged Usell's head beneath the hot spring water. Usell splashed, grasped for handholds and hit Nikolayevna's arms until she let go.

Usell gulped air at the surface. Her hip hit a stone ledge. Kneeling on it, she caught her breath as wavelets splashed the smooth rock slope.

"Think of this as cleansing your past," Nikolayevna said.

Usell wiped a veil of hair from her face.

"We must remake you, purify you, if you are to become a noble," Nikolayevna said.

"You cannot make me something I'm not."

Nikolayevna reached down and shoved Usell off the ledge and underwater again. Usell twisted free and fought to right herself on the shelf.

"You are what I say you are," Nikolayevna said. "Get used to it. Come closer. Turn around."

Nikolayevna's hands worked Usell's hair with oils and combs. She soothed scrapes with creams and cloth, and Usell's color changed from soft pink to bright red in the heated pool.

"Your beauty is a weapon," Nikolayevna said.

Usell shook free of her grip. "I don't need a weapon."

"If you're going to manipulate your captain, beauty can only be half your power."

"He's not my captain," Usell said.

Nikolayevna laughed. "You do have a sense of humor."

She plunged Usell's head beneath the water and held her down until her struggling slowed. Usell came up, frog-kicked to the side, and glared at Nikolayevna.

"Your past is an illusion," Nikolayevna said. "All your learning. Language, literature, your rhetoric . . . mean nothing. You had no life. You have none now. You are a vessel stuffed with air and I'm filling you with meaning and power. You must present yourself to the world as a Goddess and I am giving you a chance to participate in something noble, something great, where a person of substance can dominate weak minds, bend others to their will."

Usell brushed the long strands of hair from her face. "You do not know who I am."

"And yet I shape you with ideas," Nikolayevna said. "I understand your fear. I was forced to marry a man much older, but I freed myself."

Usell lifted her arms out of the water. The cool air swirled about her.

"How?" she asked.

Nikolayevna smiled. Faint lines bracketed her mouth like fissures in granite.

"You are either a woman to be used by men or a woman to bend them to your will."

"I don't wish to be used or to use," Usell said.

"Look. I need strong beautiful women in my ranks. Take power. Do something for yourself. Control. I am giving you a chance. Do you want it?"

"I want to find my mother," Usell said.

"A mother is for a child. Do you wish to be a child forever?"

"I can't put myself in the hands of that Cossack again."

"Does he frighten you?" Nikolayevna asked.

"He is a wolf leading a pack."

"And yet he protected you."

"I don't know why," Usell said.

"Your beauty protects you. He is no threat. You can bend him like a bow and shoot his arrows as if they were yours."

With one hand on the crown of Usell's head, Nikolayevna dunked her under water again. This time Usell sank to the bottom of the pool and watched the hand in the light above poking through, hurried, digging deeper.

Usell leaped off the stone bottom, clasped Nikolayevna's wrists, braced against the ledge, and yanked Nikolayevna into the water.

In a swirl of kicking bodies Usell rose and waited until Nikolayevna bobbed to the surface. With an exasperated choke, she looked at Usell, brushed the short hair to one side, wiped her face, rotated in the water, and pulled herself up to the floor of the chamber. Setting herself on firm rock, she reached down and extended her hand.

"Come on up," she said. "Maybe there was something in all that learning after all."

Nikolayevna removed her own clothing and tossed them aside. In a lower drawer on one side of the trunk, she removed garments and laid them on towels.

"Some of these undergarments will fit you. Dry yourself and put them on."

She looked over her shoulder at Usell. "Come on."

Usell dressed in undergarments as the taut muscled body of Nikolayevna slipped into men's clothing that did not detract from her femininity and sure movements. When redressed in fresh trousers and blouse, Nikolayevna seated herself on the stool.

"You have a spirit in there," she said. "You will need it. You are going to the princess's betrothal ball. And if you cannot take command of your powers, the Cossack will see through your charade and you will not live through tomorrow."

"Are you trying to frighten me?" Usell asked.

"I'm telling you the truth of your situation. The captain is a powerful and dangerous man, but with his heart occupied he may not think. You can do whatever you want and he will not interfere."

"And what is it you want me to do?" Usell asked.

"The princess. He guards her. Separate the Cossack from her and we can get her alone."

"Kill her?"

"Take the jewel," Nikolayevna said. "Trying to kill her was a mistake. We don't need her dead. We must stop the alliance and the power it gives the new Tsar."

"What happens to me afterwards?" Usell asked.

"The Cossack will protect you," Nikolayevna said.

"So I can be his concubine?"

"A simple walk will suffice. Get him alone. We will do the rest."

"I am bait?" Usell asked.

"You catch on slowly." Nikolayevna smiled. She picked up a coral comb. "Turn your back. This will unsnarl your hair."

Adding an ivory brush Nikolayevna untangled and curried Usell's hair smooth and straight.

"Where did you learn to do this?" Usell asked.

The grip on Usell's hair tightened.

"I am of noble birth," she said. "I understand the life of privilege, but I choose to learn what I can use."

"How do you know the customs of my people?" Usell asked.

"You are looking for answers in the wrong place."

"Why won't you tell me?"

"A woman passes through many curtains," Nikolayevna said.

"You wish to steal the princess's jewel. I am not a thief."

"Let me ask you a question."

Usell's bare shoulders twitched a shrug.

"Those clothes you were wearing . . . They are not your people's clothes," Nikolayevna said. "Where did you get them?"

"I bought them."

"They were too large for you. You looked disconnected, irregular."

"I am the same person who put them on and paid for them," Usell said.

"How much did you pay?"

"I don't know. Thirty rubles."

"And where did you get the rubles?" Nikolayevna asked.

"From my father's coat pocket. He was dead. They were mine from him."

"No one would sell Jews clothes like that for thirty rubles. No milliner would fit you so poorly."

"I paid a fair price," Usell said.

"A Jew does not get a fair price."

"I paid the amount on the tag."

"The price is lower for the bourgeoisie," Nikolayevna said. "Much higher for the Jew."

"The price is the price," Usell said.

"You did not pay the price the shopkeeper wanted; therefore, you stole."

"I would not to be cheated."

"My reasoning exactly," Nikolayevna said. "It is sometimes all right to steal. Now about this hair."

With a pitcher of hot water Nikolayevna washed Usell's hair with a soap smelling of Neem seed oil. With the hair slippery, Nikolayevna scissored, combed, and shortened its length. Pouring a cherry scented liquid on a cloth, she rubbed it across Usell's neck. With a softer voice she said, "We have intelligencers in the palace that will advantage the situation. We wish you to be the lone actress on the stage. The trick is to define you in a way your captain can accept. We will make you stand out so that he will have no choice. That will favor your odds of success. Just get him alone."

"So you can kill him?" Usell asked.

"Inquisitiveness will also get *you* killed. Just do as you're told. Now squat down."

Wrapping Usell's towel around her shoulders, Nikolayevna proceeded to decorate Usell's hair, worked it from behind, pulling strands, brushing, smoothing, and wrapping the lengths and silky thickness to a swirl at the top of her head.

A woman with girth, layers of bland clothing, and sexagenarian years appeared from the darkness. Beneath her white cloth bonnet a bulbous nose twitched and dark beady eyes glistened in torchlight.

"Black silk," Nikolayevna said. "Bare shoulders. Accentuate the long neck. And you." She pointed at Usell. "Stand on that rock."

On the smooth half-exposed lump of black rock beneath a torch plugged into the stone wall, Usell held still while the woman scented her skin with sweet pea oils and patched her into a gown meant for a larger woman. She pulled and tugged and then with movements like a rolling ball, circled around Usell. Her short arms and tiny hands stitched with quick strokes and sharp front teeth. She exacted the most from needles and thread. Pinching cloth tight and stretching silk to fit the contours of Usell's body, the seamstress, said,

"Don't move."

Dressing and undressing Usell, the woman tailored the gown and fit the material to her worried mannequin. With stitching and cross-stitching the woman said, "Lift your arm. Bend. Do not bend. Lift your leg. Don't move. Move. Take a breath." Working the cloth onto her live cushion, she then removed the gown and hunched over the sleek black creation like a vulture gorging itself on live prey.

Nikolayevna sat on the stool a few meters away watching the process out of some humor that only she digested with snorting laughs and coughing chuckles.

The seamstress removed a pin from the side of her mouth, released a pinch of cloth, and hid her face beneath her deflated bonnet.

Finishing her stitching, she redressed Usell, tugged at sheer ribbon, aligned the seams, twisted and snipped before smoothing her hands over the lines about the bodice, the waist, hips, and legs.

"She is ready for the royal court," the seamstress said.

With her straw basket under her arm, she disappeared up the steps with heavy hipped trudges.

When she was gone, Usell said, "I don't know how to act with the aristocracy. I'll be found out in a moment."

"Ignore courtly manners," Nikolayevna said. "The wealthy are so full of idle intrigues and so involved with themselves, they won't notice your awkwardness; and when you waltz, they will see their dreams. Do you waltz?"

"Yes," Usell said. "But I cannot waltz with a man not my husband."

"Don't be ridiculous," Nikolayevna said. "When your captain focuses on you, put all your attention into his eyes. Sink into him. Nothing else matters."

"Did you hear me? I cannot dance with a man. It's not permitted."

"You really don't know who you are, do you?" Nikolayevna said.

She removed two hand mirrors from the trunk. One she gave to Usell and the other she held behind Usell's back.

"I am almost naked," Usell said.

Her back defined slim shoulders, thin waist, and sloping hips. A faint glint of spine rippled down the mirror. Chestnut hair rose off a long neck and twined into a swirling bun at the top of her head. Nikolayevna dabbed a powdered cloth over a bruise on Usell's shoulder.

"This is not me," Usell said.

"Being you has landed you here. It is time to move on. Think less. Depend upon your looks to define who you are. Look at your face. When men look at you, they'll be driven by desire. Beauty controls their will."

Usell stared at her reflection. The plain girl's face was gone. In her place was a smooth oval, the hair gone from the forehead. Tiny pink ears. Teardrop eyes tilted against round cheeks, the nose compact and straight, and the mouth open.

"This is not me," Usell said.

"You can change who you are. The dress, the style are façade; how you look gives you an edge, but it is the will inside you that has the power to control."

Nikolayevna removed a silk black choker from a shallow drawer at the top of the trunk. She buttoned it around Usell's neck.

"At the ball you will discover your power and you will conquer men's hearts."

22 . . .

Behind Nikolayevna's rising torchlight and dressed in silky black cloth, Usell lifted the hem of her gown and climbed the steps in velvet slippers. Hundreds of rebels stood in the nave. When Nikolyevna entered it filled with murmurs, but they grew silent as Usell exited the panel. The chilled air bit at her neck and shoulders.

Arragos joined them. He held out the mink stole.

Taking it Nikolayevna said, "Here. This is for you."

Torchlight blazed the high clerestory windows and mirrored the shine onto the army of rebels stretching from narthex to sacristy, transept to transept. Nikolayevna marched through them and the men bowed their heads. The gypsy girl tightened one side of her face and spit.

They were all armed. Pistols in their waistbands. Knives in their boots. Long swords in their hands pointing at the shattered floor in salute. Through the vestibule hallway Usell followed Nikolayevna to the antechamber where she seated herself on a block of stone and pointed to an arch projecting from a disintegrated wall mural.

"You stand there and wait for your escort," Nikolayevna said.

"Escort?"

"I want to see his reaction to you. Someone has to take you to the ball. Just stand there. Try to look demure."

"I cannot do this," Usell said. "I am not prepared."

"That has little to do with it," Nikolayevna said. "The beggar and the ruler are natural enemies who feed off each other. Only beauty stands alone."

"A piece of meat thrown into the lion's den," Usell said.

"You are not a woman chosen for a man. You choose. Play a lyre, become the siren, and turn the predator's head."

"This is not me," Usell said.

"It is everyone. Strike a blow for vengeance. You've heard what they've done to your people. Don't you care? Help us cut off the head. The body will die. And then you can be who you want to be."

"What you want me to be?"

"Look," Nikolayevna said. "We are at the crossroads of history. With the right people and organization we make things better. It will not be perfect, but it will be better."

"Every dictator says the same thing," Usell said.

Nikolayevna tossed her head back and laughed. It was the laugh of a woman who did not laugh much, but someone who found guilt in its expansion, stupidity in its waste, and loss at its conclusion. For a moment she dropped her guard and stared at Usell.

"What is so funny?"

"You remind me of me," she said. "Don't worry about the future. Your innocence protects your present. Fate has decided your steps. Just do as you are told."

"I don't believe in chance."

"No, you wouldn't," Nikolayevna said.

Footsteps echoed through the antechamber.

"Your escort has arrived," Nikolayevna said.

The flickering of torchlight played tricks with shadows moving on the other side of the arches. Boot steps at an easy pace. The figure cut through arches and stopped when he saw Usell standing in front of the broken mural.

"What the hell is this?" Rudd Cothman said. He was dressed in a black tuxedo, a black tie, and stiff white shirt.

"I want you to meet Mademoiselle Emma Bovary."

"And who am I supposed to be, her seducer or her escort?"

"Take your choice," Nikolayevna laughed.

Ignoring Usell, Rudd strode to Nikolayevna and the two of them growled at each other as they moved away.

"She's too young," he said.

"Isn't youth what we want?" Nikolayevna said. "Look at her. She's perfect."

He glanced at Usell and when she met his eyes, she blurted out, "Rudd Cothman is a scoundrel and a cad. He is not to be trusted."

"Oh, stop it," he said. "Even a blind man could follow wagon tracks. You had the horse, the blanket, and a fire. I knew you'd find someone else to annoy."

Nikolayevna interrupted. "I didn't know there was anything between you, but it makes no difference. You are our soldiers and there's no time to change the plan."

Rudd folded his arms across his chest. "It won't work with her."

"Rotovak protects her," Nikolayevna said. "That means you may be able to get closer to the princess. She wears the jewel tonight to show the rich the strength of the empire's resilience. Emma will help. She will distract the Cossack."

"It's too dangerous," he said. He marched to Usell. "I don't know how you got mixed up in this, but this is not a game for amateurs. Do you know what happens if we're caught?"

"She'll be fine," Nikolayevna said. "She's smarter than you think."

He took Nikolayevna's arm and turned her away, muttered in her ear. She shook him off. "Look at her," Nikolayevna said. "Who could see beyond that innocence?"

In an empty corner they spoke at each other with gestures and raised voices. Nikolayevna smiled. She lifted a hand and stroked his cheek. He balked. With a short sticky kiss on his mouth she left him standing there and walked back to Usell.

"I'm glad you know your escort," Nikolayevna said. "It will make things easier."

Rudd folded his arms across his chest.

"What is he to you?" Usell asked.

"Forget your thoughts," Nikolayevna said. "It's dangerous for a Jew to lend her heart. Stay in your head, especially when you're with the Cossack."

Nikolayevna stood at the entrance to the cathedral and waved goodbye as Rudd Cothman led Usell down the broad steps. He gripped her arm as if she might tip off balance.

"I don't like the way you're walking," he said.

"You left me. You just left me in the middle of nowhere."

"Too tentative. Walk like this," he said.

He walked like a horse with a measured prance. "Walk like the earth beneath your feet was put there just for you."

"I'll walk the way I please," Usell said. "You broke your word to me."

"I don't have time for children's games."

"You abandoned me."

"You were better off on your own," he said.

"Do you know what happened to me? People tried to kill me. I've been coerced into doing this. With you."

"How would I know Nikolayevna would take a shine to you? She has expressed distaste for your people. Why would I put you in their hands? No. I thought you were better off finding someone else to take you south."

"You took a coward's way. You did not know I would be all right. You could have explained. I am reasonable and I have a right to choose my own destiny."

Exhaling and in a quieter tone, he said, "Okay. You've earned that. But I'm not against you. Do you think Menahem would do business with me if he didn't trust me?"

Usell slowed her pace and set the soft slippers down with an easier step.

"That's better," he said.

"I'm not trained for this," she said.

"Honey," he said, "the way you look, I feel sorry for all mankind."

She watched his eyes examine her.

"My father would not approve of your looking at me like that."

"But he'd understand why," Rudd said.

The broad steps out of the cathedral led to the wide exterior courtyard where a ring of torchlights circled the stone patio. Standing alone inside the circle was a machine. It puffed smoke from a brass stack sitting on the back of a wagon bed. In front of the stack was a black cab with doors on each side and a rectangular metal snout extending from its center. There were two large wheels on the back, two smaller ones in front, no horses. Pistons compressed, chains rattled, and the whole thing trembled and chuffed. The smell of kerosene fumes filled the air.

"What is that?"

"Welcome to the next century," Rudd said.

"What is it? What does it do?"

"Takes you where you want to go."

"A carriage?"

"Steam-powered, no horses. Remember, the Frenchman? Calls it *Utto*."

"We're going to ride in it?" Usell asked.

"It will attract attention to itself and to you instead of me. The government knows who I am and this is sleight-of-hand. Pick their pockets while they are distracted. That's the plan, isn't it? You, the machine, magician's tricks."

"So you can get the jewel," she said.

"Yes. That's all I want." His tone was sarcastic.

Inside the cab she sat on a bench seat cushioned with mahogany-dyed leather. Behind a glass windscreen the enclosed space was boxy and high above the frame. Rudd hopped inside the opposite door, pushed a button on the forward panel, and flipped the switch next to it. He tapped a gauge next to that before grabbing one of three levers sticking up from the floor between their seated positions. When he moved the farthest lever back, the structure trembled to life. It vibrated. With the middle lever, a chain locked to a gear. On the forward panel below the windshield, Rudd turned a knob and lanterns affixed to the snout glowed yellow and shined ahead. With the engagement of the third lever, the carriage rolled forward and the machine fled the church onto the cliff, leaving balls of steam in its wake.

With a single tiller, a rod between his legs, Rudd steered on a radius of 180 degrees. The machine gained speed down the cliff, and Arragos on an Azerbaijan gray beat the horse with a whip to keep up.

By following the crest of the cliff, they rode the plateau to the gleaming white palace spread out on the height. It overlooked the city of Odessa. A barrier of jagged mountains to the west protected the land and from their view, the metropolis spread out in a bowl. Moonlight flickered on minarets, spires, onion domes, and the sprawl of the Black Sea.

They drove across snow-covered grounds stretching over a broad flat lea. A Macadam road of crushed marble crystals reflected the pale moonshine and led to a vast terrace in front of a wide marble staircase.

Up the steps an emblazoned palace – six stories, two wings shooting out like welcoming arms – ignited the darkness.

As they rolled into the vast curving driveway, Usell folded her hands in her lap and bowed her head.

Rudd rubbed his lips.

"Look," he said. "If by some chance you make it out of the palace alive and I'm not with you, get to the harbor. There's an American ship. It sails midnight tomorrow on the tide. Get to it. Give them my name. Tell them I said to take you. And then just get the hell out of this place."

"I have to find my mother," she said.

"Still kicking that dead horse?"

Sitting back against the smooth leather, he manipulated the levers and gears controlling direction with the tiller between his legs.

"This machine is not so complicated," Usell said. "I see how you do it. It is not magic."

With a glance he said, "Brown eyes, all that matters is the way you look."

23 . . .

Usell leaned her head out the hinged window on her side. Dozens of carriages lined up waiting for footmen, short stature men who rushed to the doors of the carriages, dropped the silver steps, and snapped to attention in their red and black uniforms, their eyes with no hint of interest.

Rudd pushed his tiller in the direction of the curb across three lines of carriages waiting in order to be waved to the center of the stairs. With his grip pulling back the second lever, *Utto* released clouds of steam across the paths of well-groomed horses. Some reared. Some frittered. Carriages compressed against the animals and curses raged from high-hatted drivers in their cribs.

Utto chuffed to the curb. Hit by steam, a woman screamed. A man with a white silk shawl raised his cane. Arragos dismounted his Azerbaijan gray as an upset uniformed attendant raced toward them to protest the unprecedented intrusion. The attendant backed away when Arragos growled.

Releasing the levers in reverse order, Rudd set the machine still. A final exhaust of compressors ended in a rattle of chains.

"Wait for them to open the door for you," Rudd said.

"I can get out myself."

"Just do as you're told. This is a dirty business and not a game for obstreperous children."

"I'm not playing games," Usell said.

"I'm here for the princess's jewel, honey. I don't care about anything else. Do your part. Don't foul it up."

He exited his door and slammed it shut.

A middle-aged attendant, standing like a rooster with a nose to match, opened the carriage door and set a silver step beneath the edge. He stood back, his black and red raiments beading dew and complementing the drip of sweat down his sweating temple. His eyes, though glazed with torchlight and staring straight ahead, blinked three times as Usell hopped down.

Groups of couples, top-hatted men and high-coiffed women, circled *Utto* as if trying to decide whether the dragon was friend or foe.

Rudd slipped beside Usell, offered her his arm. She clasped the bend at his elbow as the chattering crowd closed and muted to a hush.

"Look them in the eye and smile," Rudd said.

Usell swallowed and stared straight ahead, not focused, just ahead, but when she met their powdered faces and confronted their matted frowns, she grasped Rudd's arm tighter.

"I can't do this," she said.

"Stand up straight."

"They're staring at me."

"You aren't like them," he said. "You are foreign, mysterious, a fairy charming a zephyr."

"They look alarmed."

Arragos, dressed in the faded gold fur of his people, slid behind Usell. The crowd abandoned their interest.

"Pigs," Arragos said. "They think they are Gods, but they are pigs."

"Leave your stole with Arragos," Rudd said. "Arragos, you stay here and guard the machine."

"I was told not to let you out of sight," Arragos said.

"My tickets are only for two," Rudd said.

With concern in his brow, Arragos stopped. He jerked the stole from Usell's shoulder.

"It's freezing," Usell said.

Rudd grappled Usell's elbow and ushered her up the steps.

"You're delicious," he said.

When she tugged away from him, he whispered, "Play your part."

The eyes of guests frittered about Usell's uncovered skin. When a young officer tripped on a step and swore, Rudd smiled.

"See," he said.

"Such boldness," a man with a trimmed white mustached said.

"I think it's disgusting," an elder woman with a foxtail about her neck said.

Rudd put his arm and cape about Usell's shoulder and at the height of the broad steps torchlight glowed and welcomed the guests at six sets of black oak, double-high, double doors leading inside to a white, wishbone staircase in the grand style.

At the entry door an officious man in a red vest fingered Rudd's invitation.

"Title," he said.

"Arch Baron. New York," he replied.

The pinched man in the red vest twitched the black pencil mustache lining his upper lip. "Up the stairs to mezzanine. Wait until you are presented before you enter the grand ballroom." He handed the invitation back.

"Why didn't you make yourself a Grand Duke so you could be first in line?" she whispered as they walked away.

"Because I'd be shot as an impersonator. Barons are like cousins. There are so many relations, no one knows which second cousin has a brother."

"Lies catch the dog's tail," she said.

"Just walk slow and look pretty."

The marble steps followed the silvery railing two flights up to a pitched ceiling at the landing where an esplanade led through grand arches to a broad mezzanine. On the mezzanine, embellished in finely stitched clothes, the invitees mingled. Men and women of the upper classes - those of privilege, business and industry, military, and commoners of wealth - mixed with the nobles, all strolling with measured leisure, waiting their turn to be lined up and called into the grand ballroom at the bottom of the stairs.

The military wore decorative sabers. Chests, shoulders, arms marked with stripes, braid, ribbon, medals, ornamentations of gold and silver, bearing and entitlement, contrasting against the formality in black and white of the protected. The women wore gay-colored gowns, a rainbow of yellow, red, green, and blue with high coiffures festooned with ribbon, sparkling jewels, more gold and silver. They wore furs, white arm-length gloves, so much brightness on creamed skin that it was hard to see how the strained smiles fit. Older women flashed white teeth while their eyes revealed the dulling effects of patience, flattery, and self-absorption. They conducted themselves without deference, stood independent and strong. Free citizens propping up the system. They all bunched in brushed wool, silk, high collars, all manner of regalia and insignia, all held up by stiff backs, but tensed by simple pleasantries.

Rudd led Usell to the open side of the stairs that led down to the empty grand ballroom below.

To Usell's side a woman in a red gown and twirls of burnt brown hair dug her fingernails into the arm of her bristle-bearded companion, whose roguish eyes examined Usell.

A tremble of gooseflesh skittered across Usell's shoulders.

With a quick breath she looked him in the eyes and glared, something she would never do in Oylaif.

The man's smugness disappeared. He cleared his throat, turned back to the woman.

Rudd nodded at the balconies high over the ballroom. Perched above the dance floor at a height where rifles could cover every angle, soldiers stood their guard, guaranteed order.

"Relax," Rudd said.

"How can I? What if someone points me out as a Jew?"

"In these people's minds you are worse than a Jew. You're more perfect than them. You're a source of envy and resentment. They're jealous and fear you, want to be you or want you."

Glistening chandeliers threw shadows against the walls, stiff statues, locked-jawed men, flickering shades in black and white, floating, blurring into one another. The crowd created heat. Usell nudged nearer to Rudd. A line of couples formed against the right railing that led down to the ballroom floor, invitations in hand. Men, no matter whether they were braided with ribbons and metals or stuffed like penguins in black top hats, stared at Usell without regard for her modesty. They were barefaced and blatant in their examination, just like boys of Oylaif, who could see much less of her and could not keep the decorum of the shtetl.

"You're walking too stiffly," Rudd whispered.

"I know," she said. "I can't help it. I am an object."

"Yeah," he said. "I'm having a tough time keeping my eyes off you myself."

The smile creased into his rugged cheek.

"Nikolayevna decorated you," he said. "A creation for the men, a display."

The gathering slowed to a stop.

"What has happened?" Usell asked. "Why aren't we moving?"

"Patience," Rudd said.

"How can you be so calm?"

"If you weren't a child, you would know it's a little late to ask."

"Why do you continue to insult me?" she asked.

"Look where you are, Mademoiselle Bovary," Rudd whispered. "Can't you see? You're where every woman wants to be. At the center."

"I think these people are not themselves any more than I am," she said.

"These people have common commitments," he said. "They wish something from those in power."

"You do not understand, "Usell said. "I cannot do this. They will know I pretend to be someone I'm not."

"You don't look like a common village girl," he said.

The crowd pushed forward. A royal minister at the bottom of the stairs called out a name.

"The Grand Duke crown prince, Konstantin Andrea Ivanov Melikova, and his daughter, the Princess Ludivica Melikova, await the pleasure of your company."

Rudd slipped his fingers under her naked arm, broke through the crowd at the edge, and began to descend the curving white marble staircase while the line of guests holding themselves at attention on the railing waited to be received at the bottom of the stairs.

24 . . .

The ballroom sparkled. Colonnades buttressed the walls and supported a golden dome ceiling. Chains and anchors dropped crystal chandeliers from the heights and reflected blue gas flames onto the floor with its inlaid seal, the Grand Duke's, double heart - double sword. Faint orchestral tones from the hundred musicians at the far end of the ballroom lifted rising beats. Forte, pizzicato, poco a poco. To Usell's ear, far richer than Yehuda's violin or Madame Hoffman's fondness for screechy opera.

The violin players in the orchestra leaned against their instruments, and the quiver of strings trembled the air around the crowd on the mezzanine.

At the base the princess was dressed in white. She wore her hair up. Her diamond pendant dangled from its gold chain. She looked as though she'd been there a long time.

Next to her stood a bent old man with a balding head, white side hair, and a white sable robe dragging the floor. He paid no attention to the descending guests, but angled his sight toward the golden dome above the floor. His mouth was open and he tilted his head as if he watched something in the pinnacle of the dome.

The crowd on the mezzanine pressed toward the line as Rudd grabbed Usell's arm.

"Come on," he said.

Heading down in the center of the stairs, she trembled.

The crier's echoing voice called out, "Announcing, Count Martrusky, Prince of Serbia, with his concubine, Magdalena of Spain."

The Grand Duke continued to stare at empty space. He seemed to be watching something circling inside the dome. His head rather than his eyes rotated the transit. The count and his concubine bowed before him.

The princess shimmered in her silky white, but held herself stiff and tight as if she were confined. The count clicked his heels. The princess, who wore gloves, extended her hand to be kissed and nodded with a strained smile.

Behind the princess and the Grand Duke, Rotovak stood in a red jacket, black trousers, and brass buttons. His braid erupted from his crown and curled on one shoulder. His attention focused on each guest as if they were Nihilists ready with a knife or a bomb.

"Get hold of yourself," Rudd said.

"The captain knows I'm not who I say I am."

"Nikolayevna counted on it."

"Why should she care what happens to me?" Usell asked.

"I suspect she understands something you don't. Follow through. I don't need that long a time in this paradise and neither do you."

"I have to go," Usell said. "I have to get out of here."

She lurched back up to the mezzanine, but his grip restrained her.

"If you run now, they'll just chase you. Everyone will chase you."

"I can't do this," she said.

The Grand Duke screamed. "My brother is dead."

The princess waved her hand. The orchestra, as well as the undercurrent complaints, whispered to silence.

"The Jews have murdered my brother," the Grand Duke wailed.

Rudd loosened his grip on her arm.

His drama concluded the Grand Duke nodded at the count as if they shared a secret. With the quickness of a younger man, the Grand Duke spun around and pointed up the stairs. The eyes of his attentive gallery followed his crooked fingertip aimed right at Usell.

"That one," the Grand Duke said. "I want that one, the one in black. Bring her to me."

A young officer stepped out of the receiving line. He stood at attention in front of Usell. With a glance at the Grand Duke he said, "He is old. His mind wanders. He wishes company and selects for youth and beauty. I'll accompany you down to accept this honor and would be pleased to drive you home in the morning."

He extended a white-gloved hand.

Usell didn't move.

"You are summoned," he said. He turned his palm over.

She did not take his hand.

"You must come," he said. "Be grateful the uncle of the new regime favors you for the night."

"No," Usell said.

He grabbed the soft flesh of her underarm and Rudd stepped in front of her, between them.

The officer released Usell.

A smile twitched on Rudd's lips and then like an uncoiled spring, his fist twisted from the hip and crashed into the officer's jaw with the speed of a catapult.

The blow lifted the young officer out of one boot and arched him into the line of guests awaiting announcement. The queue collapsed down the stairs, tumbling like an avalanche to the feet of the Grand Duke.

All on the mezzanine gasped one audible breath. The Grand Duke stared at the moraine at his feet. He set his foot on the back of the count and his hands on his hips. He threw his head back and then he laughed.

The princess pasted a grin on her face and stiffened in place.

"Do it again. Do it again," the Grand Duke said. Then he grew serious. "I will find the assassins and introduce them to their graves."

When the French minister, lying next to the woman, lifted his arm, the Grand Duke kicked it aside. He smiled without showing his teeth and then he turned to Rotovak and pointed again.

"Get me the girl."

Rotovak emerged from behind the princess. Rudd stepped to Usell's side and put his arm around her shoulder.

Rotovak's long braid slipped from his shoulder. His shoulders trembled and then he leaped two stairs at a time, his stiff pylon arm and thrashing legs knocking aside anyone in his way.

Rudd slipped his hand beneath his long-tailed coat to a pistol behind his back.

"No," Usell said. She stepped away from him.

Rotovak raced up the stairs like a charging boar. Despite his press he came to a stop in front of her, his black eyes angry, his jaw forward, and breathing through his teeth.

With a tremble Usell smiled. A puzzle twisted the symmetry of his face. The scar flattened against his brow, color rose to his cheeks.

"Captain, aren't you glad to see me?" she asked.

"What are you doing here?"

"You are not happy to see me alive?"

Rotovak cleared his throat.

"You are intact?" he asked.

"I was rescued."

Rudd leaned forward, his shoulder brushing hers.

Rotovak adjusted his stance and rose to his full height, matching the American's.

Usell looked from one man's tight jaw to the other. The two men set their heels. For a moment she wished to let the two bulls have at each other, but with a sudden flush she stepped between them.

"Captain," she said. "Allow me to introduce the man who rescued me."

She turned to Rudd.

"He is arch Baron Cothman from America."

Rudd and Rotovak ignored her words, leaned toward each other.

"This man saved my life," she said.

Rotovak's squinting eyes twitched.

"Dmitri, Dmitri," the princess called from below. "Is that my Emma?"

Stiffening to attention, Rotovak's manner withdrew to professionalism.

"The princess has been worried about you," he said.

Glancing at the black ribbon about her neck, he followed the line of skin to her cleavage. With a low growl he withdrew behind his soldier's mask.

"You will both come with me," he said.

With a narrowed gaze at Rudd, Rotovak signaled his Cossacks. Four of the dozen men broke from their chain about the Grand Duke. As Rotovak led them down the staircase, the Spartan Cossacks filled the space behind.

The princess stretched on the tips of her toes, hopped in place, squealed, and ran towards Usell.

"Emma. Emma. You are alive."

Racing up the steps, arms extended, her high-pitched delight screeched from her pink mouth. The jewel swayed like a pendulum on its golden chain. The princess slammed into Usell, and hung there, a child missing her mother.

"I thought you were dead or worse," she said. "I imagined the most horrible things happening to you."

"I am safe," Usell said.

Releasing Usell, she stepped back. Standing with her back bent, her head rotated on its slight neck and she stared back at the guests watching with open mouths.

"What are you looking at?" she said. She stomped her foot. Every eye looked away, save Rotovak, who clenched his jaw.

The princess smiled at Usell with girlish happiness.

"Black is such a man's color," she said. She brushed the silk with her fingertips.

Rudd nudged Usell with his hip.

"Princess," Usell said. "This is the man who saved me from the rebels that attacked your train."

The princess's eyelids fluttered at him. A smile lightened the dullness of jade. She removed her glove and lifted her hand to Rudd.

He kissed her fingertips and stared at the jewel.

"How many did you kill?" she asked.

"Princess Ludivica Melikova," Rotovak interrupted. "Allow me to introduce you to Monsieur le Baron von Cothman from America."

His voice dripped sarcasm.

"Friends call me Rudd," he said. His boyish smile appeared.

The princess giggled. She grabbed Rudd's arm and closed hers around it, her skin flush against him.

"You must tell me all about America," the princess said. "How many wild Indians have you scalped?"

"Highness," Rotovak said. "Your receiving line."

"Oh, poof. Father can stand in the line himself. I want to talk to this brave young man."

"Your betrothal ball, your highness."

"Do you see him? Do you see the prince here, at HIS betrothal ball? Where is he?" She waved a hand at the captain, flourished it about his stoic face.

"His delay is temporary," Rotovak said.

"I will take this handsome Baron and we will waltz," the princess said. "And you . . . .." The princess wiggled her finger at Usell. "I think I would like to meet your seamstress. Send her to me."

She flashed a smile at Rudd and then spun him around heading to the dance floor.

"Just where do you have your lands? Will the American King sell me a territory I can rule? How many peasants would I have to take with me to America? Do you have the same trouble we do with them? We have such problems here. In America people like us can be free to rule. We are somehow magically linked, don't you think?"

The strings of the orchestra rose on cue and from beneath the pillars holding the golden dome, clots of young women approached the dance floor, as if they'd been readied for the occasion. In their coteries their eyes settled on the attractive young men who gathered to their cliques.

"Come, Dmitri," the princess said over her shoulder. "Bring my dear friend."

"Majesty, I must insist," Rotovak said.

"I'll do the insisting," she said. She did not look at him but smirked in that way that said she was a Princess and she would do what she liked.

Rotovak's firm grip tucked Usell's hand around the crook in his arm as the Grand Duke waved to him.

"You there with the fading braid on your head," he said. "And you . . ." He pointed at Usell. "You come to me."

"Don't be afraid," Rotovak whispered. "This is theatre."

With an easy stride and a swing of his arm, he escorted Usell to the Grand Duke.

Standing at attention, Rotovak said, "Konstantin Melikova Grand Duke and Uncle to Alexander Alexandravich Emperor of all Russia, allow me to introduce you to . . ."

"I don't need names," the Grand Duke said. "Come close, child."

Rotovak release her.

"Delicious," the Grand Duke said.

As she stood in front of the old man with his stooped posture, Usell tried to ignore the strong smell of an un-bathed man. With a smile, a pointy chin, and too much wrinkled and gray skin, the Grand Duke leaned close, his eyes searching hers, the distractedness gone.

"I saw what happened," the Grand Duke said. "It was about you. Men fight over breeding rights."

The Grand Duke put his hand on her breast. Usell froze.

"This is what they wanted," he said.

He retracted his hand and stared at the golden dome again.

"Why just yesterday at Sevastopol," he said. "I climbed the battlements where they had us rightly surrounded and I ordered the scuttling of the fleet. Better not to fall into their hands. But the Admiral refused. And yes, it was I who put the bullet in Admiral Andronikashvili's brain. For disobedience."

The Grand Duke covered his eyes and let out a pathetic sob. His thin frame curled like spoilt celery and he fell into Usell's arms, pulled her to him, his touch hard, locking, in control. His mouth nestled at her ear.

"Captain," she said with half a breath.

Rotovak closed his eyes.

The Grand Duke whispered.

"The captain is tired. He and his men are loyal, but they need rest. They need love."

The Grand Duke's hand crimped her shoulder.

"Take him to the balcony to view the sea," he said.

He nudged Usell's face toward a balcony behind ballroom windows and French doors.

"Lead him there," the old man said. "Alone with you he may yet find relief."

Her retreat caused the Grand Duke to grip tighter.

"The sooner the better," he whispered.

Straightening himself, the Grand Duke pushed away. He took his position in front of the receiving line as if Usell no longer existed. He spoke to an obsequious gentleman and a tall gray-haired woman accompanying him.

"Don't you love their smell?" the Grand Duke asked.

He lifted his arms to the guests coming down the staircase. He raised his voice.

"Curse them all. Crush the infidel to pulp. Put them to the torch. My daughter will be queen of Prussia, her heirs German. And then even if they pray to their God, the fires of hell will put them to ash."

The ballroom guests clapped energetic applause.

Rotovak took Usell's arm and like a man jerking a dog, he pulled her away.

"When the wolf howls, the sheep tremble," he growled under his breath.

25 . . .

With the choral of strings, a bridge of trumpets, and the twitter of a Pied Piper flute, the prelude to a light peasant waltz filled the great hall and a cold itch crawled up Usell's back as Rotovak's shoulder brushed her at the edge of the dance floor. Not daring to move or attract the eyes of anyone who might look at her she lowered her head to prevent anyone seeing through her disguise. She licked a taste of salt as the people around her chortled with gaiety.

Rotovak stood silent. He smelled of mint, a sprig sticking out of the pocket in his jacket. His jaw clenched and unclenched, his eyes shifting from the princess to Rudd as they stepped onto the dance floor.

The orchestra played its rhapsody, and when the princess lifted her hand to Rudd and smiled, he took her fingertips in his. Rudd, with his back straight, allowed the princess to close and then as if every movement was written in stone, he presented his arms for her to enter.

Over the double heart they leaped into the spun on the down beat. With rhythmic swirls and accomplished technique, the two held one another in this world's proper, spatial embrace, arms extended, the lightness of the dance creating a magical convention where joy embraced reality and the undercurrent of sensual throbs beat in their hearts.

The princess laughed as she whirled. They bounded and skipped with flourishes so free she appeared to fly off the empty floor. Rudd's permanent smile cocked to one side of his mouth, the wet glisten disguising his secret intent.

Rotovak rocked on his heels and along the edge of the dance floor a female server in silvery sashes slipped between the guests carrying a tray of gold-tinted champagne glasses.

The server shook her tail of slick black hair, rotated her hips, and with a familiar smile headed right at Usell, her dark gypsy eyes accepting the recognition.

Stopping in front of Usell, the gypsy girl lowered the tray to her waist. "Champagne?" she asked.

"Not now," Rotovak snapped.

With a shrug of her dark sculpted shoulders, the gypsy girl spun away, the tray of glasses on her shoulder, her hips swaying in diaphanous silk. She disappeared into the crowd like a summer haze.

On the second stanza of the music, couples joined the princess on the dance floor. Rotovak motioned with a nod to his troops. Cossacks formed their safety net.

"I'm troubled by this," he said. "I know of this man, Cothman. He is a common mercenary. There is an investigation about an incident involving Cossacks sent on a specific mission . . . The man is nothing but a *condottiere*. But he has diplomatic connections."

With a short breath and a straightening of her back, Usell said, "Captain, please. No business tonight. Please. Can't we just be?"

"We?"

"The two of us, together."

Rotovak's shoulders relaxed. He exhaled through his nose.

"I'm grateful to be reunited with you," he said.

"I am in your debt."

His brow crunched tight. His eyes squinted. "I thought you meant . . . You owe me no debt," he said. "The princess blamed me for your fate. Now she will stop her complaints."

He stopped rocking on his heels.

"She worried that when you were in Nihilist hands they . . ."

"I was not there long," she said.

"With information from you we might root them out," he said.

"Captain," she said. "This is not what I wanted to say."

"What you say is what you say."

A smiling dancer and her partner whipped by and stared.

"Captain, why are they looking at me?"

He paused for a moment and then said, "They see you are different."

She released his arm.

"How am I different?"

"You receive the princess's touch. They envy you. They cannot place you but they understand what influence you have. They are smothered by fears and they recall what happened to the deceased Grand Duchess."

"What happened?"

"Influence. A stranger became her confidant and changed the Duchess's vision of the order."

"Was this the woman the princess spoke of on the train?"

"The same."

"Where is she now?"

"She disappeared under suspicious circumstances when the Grand Duchess committed suicide. No one knows."

Rotovak's dark eyes met Usell's.

"Why so strong an interest in her?"

With a swallow and her head facing the dancers, Usell asked, "Have I done something to offend you?"

"I am Cossack. I have my duty."

"Duty, yes. Everyone has their duties."

The princess swirled around the dance floor. Rudd looked into her eyes with false admiration his intent to steal her jewel and give her up to Nikolayevna. The gypsy girl passed by again, eyes hot.

"Captain," she said. "Could you not put aside your duty, just for this evening? The music is beautiful. The lights are gay. Please. Let me spend these moments with you."

Rotovak lifted his chin, searched for answers in her eyes.

Usell did as Nikolayevna suggested and settled her gaze on him. Clearing his throat, he faced the dancers.

"You smell like cherry blossoms," he said.

Three young noblemen pressed across the dance floor and inserted themselves in an arc fronting Usell. They began presenting themselves to her with pointed-toed bows, names with long titles, laughter, chests thrust out, bends in their backs, a protocol to ease the tension of black-bowed, formal gowns, smooth combed hair, cloth smelling of musk and lilac, smiles maintaining eager eyes, and charming voices raining compliments on her.

"You outshine the princess."

"Perfection of hair."

"What exotic land holds beauties like you?"

"We are going to ski the mountains after the ball."

"Might one have a dance?"

Rotovak bristled. Several other young men joined them and tightened the circle about her, separating her from Rotovak, their cognac breaths filled with excited gossip.

"Did you know that Alexandra Breznevich and Katrina Prokhorov stayed, un-chaperoned, in Paris for a week?"

"With war brewing in the Balkans, there's sure to be opportunity to display one's bravery."

Usell shook her head either a yes or a no and did little to stop them. She caught her breath and blinked at those who pressed for recognition with self-indulgent wit, charm and a bearing that consuming her with attention.

They flattered her. They outdid each other with practiced technique. She flushed and flushed again at the things they said, charmed as much by their words as their confidence and eagerness. She accepted all as tokens of a desire she had only read about.

"Have you heard?" one dark-haired gentleman with brilliant white teeth said. "They arrested the head of the science academy at the university."

"We are well rid of that Jewish scum," another handsome young man said.

Usell set shoulders. Rotovak turned to the Cossacks behind him and for a moment she thought he might have them shoo the gentlemen away, but instead his shoulders slouched.

Pushing through the young men, she said, "Give way. Captain. Leave me be. I am only for the captain." Breaking through their orbit, she headed for Rotovak.

An angry retort followed her back as the young men filtered to another young woman. "Foreigners. The Jews infect them too."

Taking Rotovak's arm she said, "Why didn't you rescue me?"

"I did not think . . ." He glanced away. "I am the envy of every man in the ballroom."

"And I the envy of every woman," she said.

"You deserve more. You deserve royalty."

"I prefer quality to an accident of blood."

"You should choose a younger man," he said.

"I am wise enough to know what I feel in my heart," she said.

Rotovak cleared his throat.

"It would be an honor to dance with you."

"I am a novice," she said.

"Then it will be my pleasure to teach you."

With a bow he extended his arm.

In practice in her garret she danced without direction, but surrounded by bright light, and a thousand faces full of a seductive elegance, she took his naked hand and remembered her father's words. *Hardened yourself.*

Rotovak's demeanor softened. He clasped her hand with gentle pressure. She looked into his eyes and he back to her. With easy counting nods and his other hand on her hip, they leaped onto the ballroom floor and into the stream of swirling dancers.

Though she tried to hold onto his eyes, the spin required concentration. Rotovak swept through all the dancers and they made way for him, stepped aside to watch until there were only two couples commanding the floor. The princess and Rudd – Rotovak and Usell – circling in polar orbs.

She closed her eyes. Her head leaned back and she swung round and round in the arms of a man. He pushed harder against her pace, supported her step, and joined her swing about their gravity without fear of the bull or predator in the wings. Arching her back, she exposed her throat. He swung her like a stone straining at the end of a sling to a destination without a target, a perfect circle in an orbit around a double heart - double sword, the swirl so dizzying and perfect, her reserve slipped away.

Her mind swirled as she danced. Her heart raced. The princess's flirtatious laughter echoed across the floor. "Look at Emma," she said. "How beautiful she is."

Rotovak extended himself; his shoulders straight, and his sturdy arms carried her with the momentum of his balanced control.

Look him in the eyes, Nikolayevna had said. But she could not.

The climax rose, came and went, and she ached as they slowed, her breath uncontrolled and short.

As he stopped, she miss-stepped on Rotovak's foot and tripped. He caught her, set her upright.

"I'm not very good at this," Usell said.

"I have not danced since my cadet days," he said. "*They* insisted we learn to behave like gentlemen."

"You do not need training for that," Usell said.

"Flattery? For a man born on the steppe where the weather is raw and wind is wild, useless words get lost."

"There is nothing they can teach you," she said. She slid her hand down his arm as the princess dragged Rudd toward them.

"Emma, my dear. You stumble like a Jew."

"It was my mistake," Rotovak said.

Another waltz began.

Princess Ludivica spun around and stomped her foot. "I'm not ready to dance." The music dissolved to squeaks of strings, exhaling brass, and squawking winds.

"You are very beautiful," the princess said. "I am not used to someone else being the center of attention."

"You are wrong, majesty," Usell said. "There is only one princess of beauty here tonight."

The princess flushed.

"I'm going to continue my dancing with the Baron here." She clasped a hand to Rudd's wrist and placed his fingers on her shoulder next to the chain around her neck.

"We are going to dance the night away," she said. "And I hope my little Prussian boy hears all about it."

Rudd's hand slid along the nape of her neck near the clasp of the jewel.

Rotovak glowered as the princess set her arms in position to dance, pressed herself closer than was proper, nuzzled her cheek against his shoulder, and said, "Where do you confine your Jews in America?"

26 . . .

With the quick tap of the conductor's baton the music began again.

The Grand Duke flapped his hand in front of himself as if he were warding off an attack of bees. Attendants swarmed around him. Emerging from the fuss with a cane and a shuffling gait, he left the receiving line and headed for the antechamber beneath the curving stairs. His white sable robe dragged behind him and the bronze arm of the gypsy girl brushed his back.

They disappeared with a wide swing of her hips, and a portion of Cossack guards splitting off from the ballroom, following them. Usell gripped Rotovak's arm.

He watched Rudd take the princess round and round the floor. The princess laughed a throaty trill, and the dancers gave way to her flight. Behind the princess near every possible exit were the captain's guards. His Cossacks. They did not move, but watched the captain's eyes like hounds waiting for their master's signal. They were all young men, none past 25 years, their braids shoulder length or longer, their faces weathered, dark, impenetrable.

"Captain," Usell said. "There are so many young women and not enough men and you have so much youth at your command."

He squinted at her, the black in them fixed.

"You would have me leave us exposed?"

"With all this military around, nothing will happen." She pointed at the guards in their recesses above the dance floor. "Fill the young girls' hearts as you have mine. Save them with your gallant troops. Just for the night."

Rotovak snapped his fingers without taking his eyes off Usell.

Lieutenant Yazukov appeared at his side.

"Status, Lieutenant," Rotovak said.

"All is quiet. The Grand Duke has gone to his quarters. The princess is within sight."

"Give the men their leisure tonight," Rotovak said. "Let them revel in the event."

"But, Captain," the lieutenant objected.

"Quiet, Yevgeny," Rotovak said. "There are more ways to catch a rat than there are cats to do it."

At attention the lieutenant clicked his heels. "One thing more, Captain," Yazukov said. "We've cleared most of the north and west. Okhrana forces are working their way south and will be in Odessa soon, but there are many Jews to round up."

Lieutenant Yazukov inspected Usell's uncovered shoulders.

"Eyes front, Lieutenant."

Rotovak was the fuller man and more commanding. The lieutenant did not salute, but reversed and marched to the double line of guards. He muttered an order. The men hesitated. The lieutenant barked under his breath and the obedient soldiers spread from their positions toward the crowds of young women, who, with their fawning shyness and their clusters, added high-pitched voices to the new attention.

"Now," he said. "Have I satisfied your wish?"

"I wish to be alone in your company," Usell said. "I could use some air."

Thick muscles in Rotovak's jaw tightened. He glanced back at his lieutenant, but Yazukov leaned over a pale-haired girl fanning the air from her face. None of his men caught Rotovak's eyes as they occupied themselves with the smiles of the dozens of eager young women.

Usell clamped Rotovak's bent elbow and held on.

"A short stroll then," he said.

"In the night air." She glanced at the balcony.

Easing through the excited gaiety of the ballroom with Rotovak at her side, the expressions on the faces of the people had changed. They nodded. They smiled as if reassured.

Rotovak's brow smoothed as they wandered through the glass doors leading to the balcony and onto the veranda. Snowdrifts dropped from the palace roof three floors above. Icy wind stabbed at her naked skin and Usell covered herself with her arms.

Rotovak removed his red jacket, slipped it over her shoulders, and stepped behind her. He rubbed the material to her as if he were a tailor smoothing the garment to fit her smaller frame.

She clasped the collar closed as the wind whipped Rotovak's blouse against his chest and tore at his braid tucked into his belt.

The balcony was framed with milky-eyed statues of stone warriors with their pila and gladius. Rotovak's boots crushed the thin layer of ice. The raw weather hid the music's song and moonlight peeked from breaks in black clouds.

"The night hides many secrets," he said.

"Perhaps in the morning they'll be revealed."

"I do not like secrets."

"You do not say what you mean," she said.

Sculptured balusters supported the sandstone border at the edge of the balcony, and extended around the arms of the palace like a belt. Rotovak stopped at the stone railing. The frothing sea below crashed against the cliff.

With a sudden jerk of his head he stared hard at Usell as if he were having an argument with her. Turning back to the icy railing, he looked off at the funnel of hills tumbling toward the twinkling lights of the city.

"On the high reaches of the steppe," he said, "the Spartan wind dries the sweetness from every man it touches. It is where I was raised, who I am."

"Yes. I know," she said. "You are rooted to the earth."

"If you have a criticism of me, speak it."

"I don't know what you mean."

"This is not supposed to be," he said.

"Is there something wrong?"

He faced her, looked into her eyes.

"Captain, have I displeased you?" she asked.

"No. Call me Dmitri."

"Dmitri?"

"I feel the hungry spider," he said. "But I'm not a moth to be caught in its trap."

"I'm not a spider."

"Yes, you are." His tone scoffed. He turned away.

She touched his arm.

"You should not have come back," he said. And then he turned and hissed at her. "I am a soldier. I have my duty."

Against the railing she pulled the jacket closed, glanced at the ballroom.

"I'm sorry I don't please you, Captain."

"Don't do that," he said.

"What?"

"I am Dmitri."

"All right," she said. "Dmitri. I think I would like to go back."

"Now?"

"Yes. I've stretched my legs."

Lifting the gown, she took two strides toward the doors.

"Stop, Usell Binah," Rotovak said.

A web of clouds floated overhead and shielded the moon. Torches anchored to the walls blew tails of yellow. She turned around.

"You know who I am?"

"The Gods are angry," Rotovak said. "But you cannot flee them. They are everywhere."

He stared at a single distant light on the horizon.

"How long have you known?" she asked.

"Since the first moment I saw you. You are Samuel's daughter. I have seen you with him."

"My father," she said. "You know my father? He is dead."

"I suspected. So be it."

"How do you know him?"

"I was a boy when I first met him," Rotovak said. "We fought a common enemy in war. He was a spy with important papers and his blade was between a British officer's saber and my throat. When the war ended, I had a debt to repay, but he was still a Jew."

"And you still Cossack," Usell said.

He folded his arms across his chest. "Coming back here, you've endangered yourself," he said. "We will capture the rebels. The new Tsar demands it. You are in the way."

"I now have your warning, Captain." She backed toward the doors.

"Dmitri."

She squeezed the jacket tight against the whistling wind.

"I told your father," he said. "The Tsar wanted cooperation, token cooperation. Your people would serve the country and you could travel outside the Pale. You could own property. The peasant, the bourgeoisie, the proletariat, even the nobility bend to the Tsar's wishes."

"He wouldn't help you?" she asked.

"I couldn't convince him. He had his own desires and he said it was up to your people to decide their own fate."

"My father believed in reason," Usell said.

"Look at me when I talk to you," he said.

She straightened her spine.

"My father wanted citizenship," she said.

"Your father was a fool. He should have done more."

"So your men in silver and black had him killed."

"Alexander would not order it. Your father had value, connections. He was loyal in his acts. He paid his debts, but I've never paid mine to him."

He slammed the base of his palm on the concrete railing. Ice spray disappeared into the Black Sea below. Inside the lighted ballroom the orchestra, visible from where Usell stood, worked their instruments in their black formal wear, their hands manipulating and their chins tightening to the rising drama and force of their notes. Rudd and the princess no longer danced on the floor.

"Dmitri," she said. "What happened to the boy on the train?"

"What do you care about a fate you cannot control?"

"He is like me," she said. "From my village."

Rotovak faced the darkness. "He is lost. There is no hope for him, but you can flee. I won't stop you."

"You're letting me go?"

"Your attempts are futile. You have no chance. The rebels will fail. Go. Find what family you still have if you can."

"No chance?"

"You will be arrested like the rest."

She glanced at the sea below.

"Dmitri," she said. "Call your men back. Have them protect the princess."

"Why?"

"I was to lead you away," she said. "I was captured. I had no other choice."

"Why are you telling me this now?" he asked.

"I am throwing myself on your mercy. I do not know what else to do."

The Black Sea sparkled with moonlight that sliced through parting clouds.

Rotovak nodded. "I am glad you told me," he said. "We are not fools. We know who this *Baron* Rudd Cothman is. We know his connections."

"He is after the jewel."

"I am sorry about your father," Rotovak said. "If I'd known, I would have warned him."

His braid whipped off his shoulder and against his white blouse. Thick and folded, it hung like a towline. He shook his head as if talking to himself.

"I had not counted on this," he said.

"On what?" Usell asked.

"From the moment I saw you my fate was sealed. This does not happen to Cossacks."

"What has happened?"

"You overwhelm everything," he said. "And yet you don't see."

"I am alive, Dmitri. You've paid your debt to my father."

"You do not decide how I pay my debt."

His face took on weariness, a thing she'd seen on the faces of men with unhappy lives.

"Usell Binah," Rotovak said. "You have stolen my heart and I cannot bear what it is doing to me."

An icicle broke from the roof and smashed against the stone. The percussion instruments overwhelmed the music and beat in her chest. She stepped close, angled her face to his. He blinked at her with a frightened stare.

A rush of icy wind swirled around her as she lifted her mouth to his and pressed against him. Tightening his grip, he bent her back, wrapping his arms around her and nestling her in a gentle embrace.

The explosion that ripped from the ballroom and blew the windows and doors onto the balcony knocked both Rotovak and Usell against the stone railing as a ball of flame erupted over their heads.

27 . . .

Smoke and fire whirled from the darkened ballroom. Rotovak lifted Usell to her feet. Glass, marble, and stone lay scattered across the balcony along with a woman's shoe, a torn scrap of red cloth, and a twisted trumpet. A medal with a wind-whipped ribbon still attached flew over the railing into the night. Usell clung to Rotovak's right arm. A few guests stumbled through the smoke onto the balcony, coughing and carrying each other. The young officer that Rudd Cothman had knocked down the stairs staggered out of the ballroom and draped himself over the arm of a Centurion statue. He stared at Usell. She leaned behind Rotovak.

"You did it," the officer said. "I know you did it, you Jezebel."

Rotovak removed a pistol from under his blouse and shot the man in the forehead.

Cossacks, ruffled, dirtied, and bloodied, charged onto the balcony with their shashka swords drawn.

"Here is the saboteur," Rotovak said and pointed at the dead officer. "Investigate his confederates thoroughly."

As Rotovak ordered the business of placing blame, the high wind from the balcony blew through the ballroom and defused the smoke to gray and then white and then nothing but lingering smells and servants dousing fires.

Lieutenant Yazukov waved smoke from his path, marched to his captain, and saluted.

"Captain," he said. "The Grand Duke has been kidnapped."

With just a glance at Usell, Rotovak ordered a Cossack sergeant to his side.

"Watch her, and see that nothing happens to her."

He marched into the ballroom with his lieutenant.

With the sergeant three fresh Cossacks in burnished wool jackets escorted Usell through the wreckage.

Scattered about were the guests' bodies. Partial or whole, in mixed silk, wool, cotton, jewelry, and furs, they claimed attachment to the disparate arms and legs, refusing to let go.

Rotovak stood on the mezzanine. She caught him watching her, but when the Cossacks marched her up there, he was gone.

The wounded lay on the marble floor. A bloodied young woman with a torn tangerine dress glanced at Usell, at the Cossacks guarding her, and then set her frightened eyes straight ahead. Servants with buckets washed away blood and debris as the rich and powerful that were still standing contained their glazed stares and wobbled about like strays.

Usell tightened Rotovak's jacket. Wind howled through the shattered windows. The Cossack sergeant pointed to an iron chair. His square face showed nothing and when she sat he disappeared.

Infantry soldiers escorted what was left of the guests out of the ballroom and a blond-haired boy that Usell had seen attending to the princess's coach passed by. He wore soldier blue, not the caramel and white of palace guards as before. He carried the feet of a dead woman helping another soldier who carried her shoulders across the mezzanine.

The blond-haired soldier returned, his furtive eyes as secretive as the boys of Oylaif. In his eagerness not to be seen looking at her, he was not watching where he was going and stumbled into the Cossack sergeant as he came up the stairs. The young man bounced off the thick man's chest and scrambled to his feet.

"Attention," the sergeant ordered.

The blond-haired boy stiffened and saluted. He glanced at Usell.

The sergeant, his stern jaw set, slapped the boy's cheek and slapped him again.

"Back to your duties," the sergeant said.

Cowed, the blond soldier scurried down to the dance floor. Once there, he looked up at Usell again before bending to more dead.

Stopping in front of Usell, the sergeant said, "Stay here with her."

Reversing, he left Rudd standing in his wake. Wrinkling his nose at the sergeant, Rudd sucked on the scraped skin of his knuckles. A flop of hair hung in his eyes. A red bruise marked his temple. He sat down next to her.

Pinching Rotovak's jacket, he said, "Joining their army?"

She jerked free.

"I was this close," he said. He pinched his fingers together.

"They kidnapped the Grand Duke," she said.

"Probably their plan all along. A live royal is worth more than a dead princess."

"Why would they want to kill her?"

"Delays the alliance," he said. "I was moments away from snatching the jewel and getting clean away."

"What are they going to do with us?" she asked.

"Find a deep dark hole and drop us in it."

"Dmitri knows who I am."

"Dmitri?"

"He protected me."

Rudd laughed. Shaking his head side to side, he drew a deep breath and looked at her.

"Perfect."

"What?"

"You're a plant. Sent here to grow roots. Blackmail. Your Cossack's hanged himself."

"What do you mean?"

"He's not going to tell anyone who you are and neither can you. Perfect for the double agent."

"He wouldn't betray his duty."

"And yet he can't expose you without exposing himself, so what do you think Nikolayevna will do with that?"

"I don't care. I don't care about any of this. I just want to find my mother."

Rudd grabbed the collar of the captain's jacket.

"Concentrate on this," he said. "The rebels will do anything to topple the government. They will sacrifice anyone. They have the advantage now. The Tsarists will protect what they possess and they'll sacrifice anyone or anything to keep their power. The nobles feel the same. All this means is that the government will tighten their grip on the law and between them and the nobles and the rebels they'll crush everyone in the middle. That's us. We don't matter."

He wiped his mouth. "We have to get out of here. Squinting around he said, "I doubt any warm-blooded male could refuse you anything. I watched what happened with that blond soldier boy. If he comes up again, smile at him. Take advantage and if you can't get him, try the princess."

"What?"

"While we were dancing, she watched you, the way the men watched you."

"I don't know what you mean," Usell said.

Running his fingers through his hair he said, "These people make their own rules, live by their own appetites, and shape their own behaviors." He licked his lips. "Get what I mean?"

"That is not in my nature."

"Neither is dying, sweetheart. Neither is dying."

28 . . .

A half dozen Cossacks surrounded Usell and Rudd and marched them down the long, high-ceiling hall. All boots stomped to a stop at a room with a single guard dressed in a black and silver uniform. His hands were wrapped in gray cloth.

"American," the Cossack sergeant said.

Inside the room was a straight-backed chair with leather straps and large buckles on its arms and legs. Behind the chair was Lieutenant Yazukov in a different uniform, black and silver with two lightning bolts on his sleeve. He slapped a black glove in his palm and paced back and forth. When Rudd was shoved inside, Yazukov stared him in the eye and then struck Rudd across the face with the glove. Rudd jerked his knee into the lieutenant's groin and watched him fold before the soldier, who'd been at the door, slammed the butt of his rifle into Rudd's middle.

Wrestling Rudd to the chair, two men in silver and black buckled belts on Rudd's wrists and ankles.

Lieutenant Yazukov struggled to stand from his crouch. "Close the door," he said.

With a rifle stock pressing Usell forward, she followed the Cossack sergeant. The corridor changed direction. The Cossack privates turned left and the sergeant marched her right, down a hallway of bland blank walls on both sides.

Opening a door, the sergeant pushed Usell inside where the matron, Adrianna, stood with her arms across her chest.

Leaving them alone, he closed the door.

The room was long, brightly lighted, reflecting a gloss from a shiny wood floor. Except for an embroidered chair, the room was sparse.

"Please sit down," Adrianna said. Loose skin and vertical lines below bony cheeks marked her aging face.

At one end of the room was an altar with a large wooden cross on the wall.

On the other walls were dark oil portraits of royals, men in military garb, chests filled with colorful ribbons and medals, but on the wall Usell faced was a portrait of two women wearing dark heavy gowns and high tight necks. Their dresses were the same; perhaps they were sisters. The formal portrait of two women with pulled-back hair resisted ornamentation. Neither woman was bedecked with jewels or accessories. Plain. Severe.

Adrianna stood like a vertical green bean. The bun at the back of her head pulled her eyes tight. One hand covered the other over her middle. "Alexi's court has questions for you," she said.

Usell unclenched her hands. "What is it they wish to know?"

"*They* wish to know if you are acceptable."

"What is acceptable?" Usell asked.

"They must know if you are the right sort."

"What is the right sort?"

"Right is right," Adrianna said.

"Who decides what is right?"

Adrianna folded her other hand over the former top one.

"You must be cleansed before they can approve your travel with the princess."

"I'm to travel with the princess?"

"She has requested it."

"Is it all right if I have questions of you?" Usell asked.

Adrianna flinched.

"You may command."

"A request," Usell said.

Adrianna's forehead creased with a single horizontal wrinkle. A film cleared her retreating eyes. "What is it you wish to know?"

"Who are those women in the portrait?"

Usell pointed at the portrait. The two women held hands, half facing each other but half turned toward the artist without smiles.

When Adrianna looked up, she said, "You remind me of the other." She gestured at the portrait.

Both women were in their early twenties, both dark-haired, one with a hint of rust, the too portrait formal, their expressions stern.

"The Grand Duchess and a friend," Adrianna said. "It was before she took her own life."

"What happened to the other woman?"

"It's not talked about. They say it was unholy love."

"What was her name?" Usell asked.

Just then the door swung open and the princess, surrounded by her boy guards, stormed into the room.

"What are you doing to my friend?" she asked.

"We must discover if she is pure," Adrianna said.

The princess glared at Adrianna until she backed away. Hooking Usell's arm, the princess pulled Usell outside and marched down the hallway with her entourage of young palace guards.

"I've been looking all over for you," the princess said.

Her boy guards surrounded them and hop-stepped in their boots to match stride.

At their backs the Cossack sergeant waiting outside the door followed. "The captain has given orders," he said.

The princess ignored him.

"He will be angry," the sergeant said.

The princess spoke to a boy guard with pimpled skin. "Tell the fool that I will have him castrated if he says another word."

The Cossack sergeant said nothing more.

"The American?" Usell asked.

"I have my guards tending him," the princess said.

With Usell hooked by the arm, the party marched with the echoes of the footsteps into successive ceilings of Byzantine crowns and into the heart of the palace where the rooms were immense and the doorways gild on white.

"They will suffer for it," the princess muttered. "Taking my father. I will vivisect their women in so many pieces they will have to have burials all over the empire." She clamped Usell's arm. "Say something encouraging to me."

"I'm sure the captain will see to the Grand Duke's return."

"What does the captain know? He's a man. He is addled with love. Oh, yes. I saw him dance with you. I saw his face. And it wasn't enough you took the captain, but all those young nobles were mesmerized by you."

Usell's face flushed.

"You should not take them all from me," she said.

"I meant no . . ."

"That Deutsche boy sent word that I must cleanse myself for him, but he's not coming now. Not until the trouble is over. Trouble. It's all their fault."

She shook the curls off her brow.

"Don't you think the Baron is handsome?" the princess said. "He's so rugged, so . . . He smiles at me and I tremble inside."

Usell closed Rotovak's jacket, stared at her feet kicking from the gown as the hall echoed with the boy guards' footsteps.

"I was very impressed by you," the princess said. "You were perfect. You enticed them all, you held them without a smile, and you made them feel like men. I was jealous. I was told you bewitched them, made them blind to what was happening around them, so they did not see the plot. Some of them blame you. They are calling you a witch and a Jew. Do you see how foolish men are?"

The princess stopped at a gilded arch above white double doors.

"Where is the Baron?" Usell asked.

She pointed at double doors across the hall guarded by blue uniformed soldiers. Turning to the matching double doors in front of her, she said, "This is my boudoir."

Two boy guards with nervous eyes pulled open the boudoir doors. Two others raced inside. They came out with flushed faces, spear points averted. The princess walked by them, slapping the air away.

"The apologists are always making excuses," she said. "I don't want to talk about it, anyway. The kidnappers want the jewel. That nasty cousin of mine, this new Tsar, wants his alliance immediately. He won't give up the jewel even for his own uncle. I don't want to talk about it. Let's talk about you. I want your powers."

"Majesty?"

"Ludi-vica. Call me Ludivica."

The doors closed behind them. Usell took a breath. The space inside the room was immense. The outer wall of high French windows poured moonlight onto the shadowed furniture. The room separated into three parts: a dressing area with a vanity and armoire; a mammoth poster bed with canopy; and a sitting area with a sofa, side and long tables, all decorated in the purest white and finely stitched material.

The princess disappeared into the tortured shadows and in a moment the room brightened with blue gas flames.

Releasing the turnkey in the wall, the princess said, "This is it. This is where I spend my life in the southern palace. I hardly leave it while I'm here. All I see are my guards and the servants except when there's a ball or some important guest that wants my opinion about the Jews."

On her right and overlooking the boudoir from a high-ceilinged wall was a three-meter portrait of Alexander II done in the old style, romanticism, formality, Godly exaggeration. He stared down at Usell with an impassioned sneer, his uniformed poise demanding, hand on hip, sword under his arm, his five- or six-year-old son at his side.

The cherubic face of Alexi added to the impression with a superior curl in one nostril. His look said that with the lift of a white-gloved finger he could take life as easily as any supreme being.

Usell sat down on the sofa, folded her hands in her lap.

"I am angry with the captain," Ludivica said.

"You are always angry with him."

"He wants you for himself. I can tell."

Usell stared at her hands in her lap. "My father would not approve," she whispered.

29 . . .

With her bony arm, Ludivica reached behind her back and tugged at her bows of white ribbon.

Turning her back to Usell, she said, "Undo me."

She slipped the sleeves of her gown off her arms, letting them fall to the side, exposing the tight wrapping of her corset. "I can't stand this thing. Come on. Hurry up."

"Your highness. Your servants . . ."

"Do it," Ludivica said.

Standing at the princess's back, Usell's fingers fumbled with silk and metal eyelets.

"Faster," Ludivica said. "I only wore it for that stupid boy who didn't come because the Jews have rebelled."

"I thought they were Nihilists," Usell said. "Naradnaya Volya."

"You are not to argue with me. Loosen the ribbons all the way down. That boy didn't come. I'm glad he didn't come. I like the Baron."

At the bottom of the corset, the ribbons' knots were too thick to pull through the eyelets, but when Ludivica lurched away, the ribbons holding up the corset caught Usell's fingers and the entire construct opened and hit the floor with a clack of whalebone. Ludivica stepped out of it. She undid the laces that bound her bloomers, and then peeled off silk and emerged like a stick exiting a cocoon. Her body was as straight as a boy's. She swooped with exaggerated grace to the armoire and yanked it open. Her back was white; the spine was a ripple of bone held together by pliant flesh; the skin had to stretch to connect shoulders to neck.

Wiggling into a sheer golden petticoat, she stroked the front of herself.

"That's better," she said. "Help me with these shoes." Marching with floppy steps, she plopped to the sofa onto her back. She held up the laced ankle boots, and played with the jewel.

"If I give this to the rebels, they'll return my father. He would be grateful to me."

Usell bowed her head. "I'm sorry about your father," she said.

"You think it's pretty, don't you?" Ludivica asked.

She dangled the jewel.

"I will kill them," she said. "I will kill every last one of them and then I will destroy them. I will burn them up and when I get to my new home, they will pay for what they've done."

With a short coughing cry, she buried her face in her hands. "If they hurt one hair on my father's head . . ." Her tears ended as quickly as they began. She pointed at the right shoe, lifted the heel.

"Do that one first."

Usell undid the laces, tugged the heel, and the boot slipped from foot to floor. Her feet were large, long and thin.

Ludivica twirled the diamond around her finger.

"I bet you wish you had this," she said.

"What would I do with it, Princess?"

"Ludivica. Here. Feel it." Leaning forward, she let the jewel dangle from her neck.

Usell cupped it in her hand. The symmetrical facets were heavy on her smooth palm.

"It's hypnotic," Usell said.

Jerking it away Ludivica rose and limped to edge of the bed. "Unlace my other boot," she said.

Usell undid the laces on Ludivica's boot.

Ludivica kicked it off, got up, and paced back and forth before throwing herself back onto the immense bed as if she were exhausted.

"Have you ever met Alexi?" she asked.

"I have not met a Tsar, new or old."

"Do you know that bratty boy once tried to stick himself into me? Take off my stockings."

With a hesitant touch of Ludivica's calf, Usell rolled one stocking down.

"He was too fat," Ludivica said. "He couldn't catch me."

She laughed, a high-pitched trill rolling from her throat.

And then she slumped back down against her bed, a sullen twist to her mouth.

"Now he is Tsar and he does not have to chase."

With a wren-like skittishness, she bounced to the bedpost where she yanked a tasseled red ribbon.

"Would you like some French wine?" she asked.

In short, three young women entered. They wore two-toned dresses with aprons and lined up with folded hands. Bows on their foreheads masked their faces. White cotton flop hats perched on their crowns.

"Wine. Get us some red French wine."

They disappeared. In a few moments a carafe on a stand with two glass goblets was set in front of the sofa. Ludivica poured one goblet to the top and drank it down. She poured another and then one for Usell.

"Drink. Sometimes I wish God gave the birthright to someone else. It's so demanding to have descended from Him who gave his life for us. In our blood is the blood of kings and only those kings can truly understand the mystery of it all and oh, the heavy burden of decision."

The mirror on the vanity reflected windowpanes and starlight.

The princess clutched the jewel and downed her second glass of wine. With mischief in her jade eyes, she poured another and handed Usell hers.

"To us," she said. "We are more than sisters."

Ludivica tapped the crystal against Usell's goblet.

"Let's get that thing off you," she said.

Usell crossed her arms as Ludivica, with the wine goblet spilling, ripped the ribbon off Usell's neck. The button rolled across the room. The princess tugged at the ties on the gown. Releasing the knotted ribbons, she finished the goblet and refilled it again before gulping what remained. She wiped her mouth with the back of her hand and tugged at the ribbons sewn into the garment.

"What kind of stupid seamstress did this?" she said.

Ludivica marched to a knife on the vanity and back to Usell, where she attacked the ribbons of Usell's dress. With a tug, the dress dropped over Usell's hips to the floor.

Usell folded her arms over the undergarments.

Ludivica didn't seem to notice.

"I told the captain I'd refuse that ugly boy's touch," she said. "He said the Prince would be a lawful husband with the right to do what he wants. But I don't care. I will never allow that sour-faced boy into me, even if I have to leap from the palace balcony into the sea like my mother. I would do it, you know. My life is all that is truly mine."

Ludivica's chin lifted. Her eyes glistened, but a hint of frailty pinched her brow.

"I have nice things for you," she said. "Come look."

She opened the amour and pulled the drawer open. "Take yours off. Try this," she said and tossed Usell a silk petticoat.

Usell slipped it over her head, only then removing the undergarments beneath.

"Do you love me, Emma? Do you love your princess?"

"Yes," Usell said. "Of course."

With a giddy bounce the princess grabbed Usell and pulled her back onto the bed.

Pinning Usell's arms, she examined her chest.

"With what you have, you could have any of the best noblemen," she said. "Take your pick. I'll give one to you. Forget about Dmitri."

"I am cold," Usell said. "Can I wear one of your robes?"

Ludivica ignored her and looked down the neck of her own undergarment. "Cherries," she said. "I will never grow up."

She threw herself onto her pillows, rolled over, and stared up at the loops of laced linen overhead.

"They're going to hurt my father, aren't they?" She covered her eyes.

Usell slid off the bed.

"If they hurt him, I'll . . . I'll boil all their children in pig oil. Their God won't like that, will He?"

Ludivica grabbed Usell's goblet and downed the contents.

"What am I going to do?" she cried. "He's my father, he's all I have." With weepy eyes Ludivica reached out her hand. "Come hold me."

Ludivica wrapped her arms around Usell.

"Oh Emma, Emma," Ludivica said. "I'm so glad I have you as a friend. I won't let the Captain rip into you."

"He wouldn't do that."

"You don't know Cossacks," Ludivica said.

"If a man loves a woman . . ."

"I love you, Emma. Tell me you love me."

"I . . . I love you, Ludivica," Usell said.

The princess kicked her feet out and pulled Usell down with her. Crawling on top of her, Ludivica kissed Usell with hard stiff lips and then sat up. She undid the clasp of her necklace.

"You keep it for me," she said. "When the time comes, you will give it to them to get my father back."

She removed the necklace.

"Turn around," Ludivica said. Noosing the chain around Usell's neck, Ludivica snapped the clasp and let go.

"You will safeguard it for me," she said. "Because YOU love me."

Ludivica yawned.

"Later we will see what marriage can do for us," she said.

Crawling onto her pillows, the princess tangled in the covers. Watery jade eyes blinked and then all the tension left her body. Her head collapsed into her pillows.

"Ludivica," Usell said.

She didn't answer. Her eyes were closed, the body slack.

At the end of the chain around her neck Usell raised the diamond to the blue gaslight. Rolling the cold stone in her palm, she watched the light bounce off the facets. They reflected a dozen angles of blue.

Swiveling off the bed, Usell shook the princess. She did not wake.

Picking up the knife from the floor, she sat down. With the diamond in one hand, the knife in the other, she looked up at the portrait of the all-powerful Tsar, a God to decide the fate of men.

"I have to get out of here," she said.

30 . . .

Usell disguised herself in a robe of feathers that sprouted about her face. She pulled up her hair, imitating the princess's style, and then turned down the gaslights. The diamond hung from her neck. Closing her eyes, she thought of her father's teaching.

Think your way through each situation, analyze what you feel, and be clinical in your logic.

She shivered. She wondered if what she about to do were even possible. Alternatives. Discovery. Death. What did Dmitri want? Closing her eyes and taking a deep breath, she exited into the torch-lit hall. Yellow flares defined three forms.

Two sleepy infantry soldiers and the order-prone Cossack sergeant guarded the hall. The sergeant snapped to attention, his eyes blinking awake.

With her heart racing, Usell said, "Sergeant. Bring the American. Immediately."

She lifted the diamond to the light and reflections danced about the hall, disclosing only what was there, walls, floor, emptiness.

"Princess, I have orders," the sergeant said.

"If you do not do what I say, I will . . . turn you into a Jew."

With a disturbed pause the sergeant saluted. "At alert. At alert," he said. The two groggy privates roused themselves.

Usell closed the door and leaned against it. Holding her breath, she removed the robe, tucked the jewel beneath the princess's tight-fitting riding jacket and twirled her hair in a tailed knot. The too tight boots ran her leg to the calf, adding support to a wobbly height. Adjusting the light to shadows, she propped the princess up on pillows in the bed and slipped behind the curtains next to it.

With the short military raps on the door, Usell raised her voice. "Enter."

It opened. Rudd stumbled forward in manacles. Wearing his trousers and white tieless blouse he had no shoes on his feet. His wavy hair hung in his face. The sergeant pressed his hand on Rudd's shoulder, holding him in place.

"Remove his bindings," Usell said from behind the curtain.

"Princess," the sergeant said. "Princess. He is a criminal."

"Unbind him and leave if you know what's good for you."

"I cannot push the captain's orders beyond this."

"To hell with the Captain," Usell said. "And to hell with you if you don't do as I say."

When the sergeant didn't move right away, she said, "I will order you to hang yourself if you do not release him and leave this instant."

The sergeant keyed the cuff and ankle locks. Rudd bent down and handed the manacles back to the Sergeant.

"Go," Usell ordered.

With the close of the door a lopsided smile creased Rudd's cheek. "It's good to see you again, princess," he said.

Usell broke from the curtain. "It's just me," she said. She turned the key that lifted the blue flames. Rudd stared at her for a moment and then marched to the princess. He opened her robe at the neck.

"Where is the jewel?"

"A servant took it away in a box," Usell said. "She's passed out."

He glanced at the empty wine carafe.

"How do we get out of here?" Usell asked.

"I thought your Captain would take care of you."

"I no longer think that's enough."

"Not bad," Rudd said.

Usell fastened the last two buttons of Ludivica's jacket.

"Does she have any weapons in here?" he asked.

She handed him the knife.

He gripped the handle and lifted the last few drops of wine in the carafe to his mouth.

"I can order them away," Usell said.

"No, you can't," he said. "I'll handle this part."

Opening the door a crack, he winked at Usell before leaping into the hallway.

With two abrupt cries, a smack of fists, and a heavy grunt, followed by one long exhalation, the hall was quiet. The door opened and torchlight shadows flickered in the hall. A hand reached into the room, grabbed Usell's arm, and dragged her out.

Rudd tore the sergeant's jacket off and slipped it and the pants over his own clothes. Though the pants were short and the boots too large, the shoulders of the jacket fit, as did the pistol shoved in his belt.

"Let's go. They'll find them soon enough."

He grabbed the torch and hastened down the corridor. She ran as quietly as she could, but the tap of her heels echoed down the arcade. They ducked behind a statue as a patrol passed. The corridor led them to a portico at the ground level. An overhang shielded the moonlight to dark shadows at the edge of a garden.

Open to the sky, the garden was surrounded by three walls. An iron gate with a spear-point fence separated the garden from the grassy lawn outside. Frozen statues in the garden were covered in crystallized snow.

Usell headed for the gate before Rudd jerked her back. He pointed.

Two soldiers stood just outside. They smoked. Their muffled voices complained about the cold.

"Why is it we are always chosen for winter guard?"

"It is almost spring."

"They do not trust us."

"They do not trust conscripts."

"They think we will run away, but we cannot go home?"

"I tried once, but we see the world differently now."

The guard's stringy black hair peeked from wool karakuls.

"Wait here," Rudd said. He crept into the garden, slipped behind a statue of a maiden pouring a frozen icicle into the upturned mouth of a cupid. The icicle snapped.

"What was that?" one of the soldiers said.

"Norse Gods," the other said.

Rudd slipped back to the shadows.

"Too much exposure," he whispered. "We have other problems. I could see the concourse. Arragos is taking *Utto* away."

"Driving?"

"Hitched his horse to it. We have to get it."

"We're taking that noisemaker?"

"I need *Utto*."

"Why?"

"I'm not leaving my gun."

The two soldiers stood in the moonlight just outside the gate.

"No other way out," Rudd said. He drew the pistol.

"A shot will raise the alarm," Usell said.

"There's no cover," he said. "No way to sneak up on them,"

He drew the bloody knife from his belt and peeked around the column.

"I'll distract them," Usell said. "I'll leave the gate open."

"Too dangerous."

Removing the princess's jacket, she fluffed and ruffled the blouse. It squeezed tight against her. Rudd reached over and slipped the two top buttons open.

"That should do it," he said.

She ignored his smile.

"Take the pistol," he said.

"I won't kill."

"Take it. Threaten them with it."

He handed her the sergeant's pistol butt-forward and disappeared into the cloisters around the garden wall. She shoved the cold gun in her back waistband, set her shoulders, and headed across the garden.

The soldier's heads jerked to face her.

She waved.

A cigarette dropped from the mouth of the older of the two. The other snapped to attention as she walked to the gate, lifted the iron latch, swung it open, and passed through.

"Isn't it a wonderful night, gentleman," she said.

The older soldier fumbled with his rifle. "Huh, huh ... halt," he said. His cap fell off, revealing a shag of straw brown hair.

The second – a young man with a pointed chin and no facial hair – opened his mouth. She smiled at him. And then both jerked their bayoneted rifles at her chest.

The older man blinked twice before lowering his rifle and pressing the younger man's aim to the ground.

"Gallant soldiers," she said, "What's the matter?"

The younger man trembled.

"You are cold," she said. "She reached for his collar. He didn't move when she slipped the top buttoned into its eye.

Out of the corner of her eye she watched Rudd slip along the shadow of the icy wall.

"What are you doing here, Mademoiselle?" the older man said.

"I couldn't sleep and wanted to test the night air," Usell said. "Despite this . . ." She held out a naked hand to catch the crystals of falling snow. "Isn't it spring yet?"

"No one may be out this night. Mademoiselle, please," the older man said.

"But it's so beautiful."

When Rudd reached the moonlight shining on the open gate, she backed away from the guards toward the grass lawn.

"Mademoiselle. We must report this to the captain," the older man said. "We have specific orders. No one is to leave the grounds."

"Oh, Dmitri knows me," she said. "He knows my foibles."

"You are the most beautiful woman I've ever seen," the young man said.

The rifle hung limp in his hands.

The older man laughed and the young man, embarrassed, turned around. It took him a moment before he saw Rudd at the gate and like any good soldier, aimed his bayonet and charged.

Rudd's knife deflected the steel point and his fist hit the young man's jaw knocking him off balance. The force of his charge tangled Rudd in his fall, and the two spiraled to the ground. Rudd rolled on top, and struggled for control of the rifle.

The older man's weapon clicked, the hammer locked, the stock lifted it to his shoulder.

"Stop," Usell said. She pointed Rudd's pistol in his face. He looked at Usell with a puzzled tilt of his head.

Rudd twisted the rifle from the younger man's grip. The rifle fired. Blood exploded from the older soldier's chest and sprayed Usell's face. The soldier stood for a beat of his punctured heart and then fell forward like a chopped tree.

The two fighters rolled onto snowy ground and Rudd scrambled on top. He pressed the stock of the rifle against the young man's throat until the soldier's body lost strength and resistance and Rudd stood up.

"There'll be an alarm now," he said.

31 . . .

Pulling on Ludivica's riding jacket, Usell hurried behind Rudd through the south garden to the front of the palace where they'd left *Utto*. Arragos and the machine were not in the torchlight of the driveway.

Carriages and coaches lined up caravan style along the curb at the bottom of the broad stairs. Harnessed Lippizans, Friesians, Andalusians, and Lusitanians slept with flicking tails in front of their bent over drivers, who leaned forward in the cribs covered by dark wet capes and glinting headgear. They did not wake when the main entrance lights erupted on the lower floors or when the palace guards exited the doors with hurried, agitated voices.

"Stop shaking," Rudd said. He clasped Usell's arm.

"I can't." She wiped the blood from her cheek.

"Grip the weapon in your hand," Rudd said. "It will give you something to concentrate on."

He pointed to the road leading out of the concourse. A thin trail of smoke rose from the stack in the moonlight.

"*Utto*," Rudd said. The Azerbaijan with Arragos in the saddle had pulled *Utto* toward the sentry stand beside the road. There were two guards standing there, one with his hand raised to halt.

"Here's what we're going to do," Rudd said. You have to drive *Utto*."

"I don't know how."

"You saw what I did. You watched me. It's not hard. Button, switch, push the second and third lever forward, steer with the tiller between your legs, pull the last lever back to release the brake."

"I can't do it."

"Okay, you cut the horse loose and tangle with the Mongol."

Torchlight from the palace grew brighter as soldiers poured from the entrance. A line of nervous coursers fought their bits as the young palace guardsmen in their half-on uniforms clutched heavy rifles and stumbled into formation. Lieutenant Yazukov shrieked at them. He waved his sabre and the coursers shied and tugged away from the inexperienced horsemen.

Flying clouds uncovered the full moon.

Arragos dismounted and headed toward two sentries standing in front of a pitched roof shelter beside the road.

"It's now or never," Rudd said, and before she could draw a breath, he pushed her forward and they ran down the angled slope of crunchy snow onto the parking road and toward the sentry station. The two guards there pointed at the machine and laughed at Arragos.

Arragos laughed, too.

"It needs the horse," the first sentry said.

"I'm taking it away to be fed," Arragos said. His head tilted backward in good humor.

Usell reached *Utto* first and ducked in the moon shadow of the machine's lee.

Then one of the two sentries grew serious.

"No one leaves the palace tonight."

Arragos drew his curved blade and sliced across the man's throat. Before the second soldier could react, Arragos's forearm smashed his jaw and knocked him down. Straddling the second sentry Arragos stabbed him in the chest once, twice, three times, both hands slamming the knife to the hilt.

Rudd grabbed the Azerbaijan's reins attached to *Utto*.

Usell jumped on the running board, opened the door. Setting the pistol on the bench seat she bounded inside.

Planting her feet on both sides of the driving tiller, she pressed the first button on the panel and the furnace belched with heat. With the flick of the switch, a chain engaged. Hesitating over which lever to push first, she shoved two forward. The chains grabbed gears and clanked into place, jerking into Rudd as he stretched across the snout cutting leather and sawing with the princess's food knife.

Arragos's head snapped up with the compression of steam.

Rudd waved. Usell yanked the third lever back and *Utto* leaped forward, the tiller twisting back and forth between her knees as she tried to grab it. *Utto* wobbled and lurched, one way and then another, the wheels twisting on the road. Rudd cut the last rein and the Azerbaijan darted into the dark.

Arragos leaped at Rudd and *Utto's* front wheel smashed into them, knocking both aside and off the road.

Utto hiccupped a burst of steam and the machine rolled into the grasses, the wheels wobbling, the tiller whipping back and forth.

Arragos jumped on the running board and yanked Usell's door open. He grabbed her arm, pulling her hand from the twisting tiller. *Utto* swerved, unbalancing Arragos. By the time he righted, Usell had grabbed the pistol, cocked the hammer, and shoved it in his face.

The drooping mustache enclosed glistening yellow teeth, but instead of stabbing her with the bloody knife in his hand, he kicked backward, surprise on his face as Rudd, running alongside, yanked his dangling mustache.

Arragos fell off the running board and under the weight of the rear wheel. The crunch of his skull sounded like a gourd split on a rock.

Rudd tumbled into a cushion of snow.

Utto swerved. She grabbed at the tiller with both hands and was jerked around the cabin by its twists. Picking up speed, *Utto* wobbled down a slope, spraying snow as she headed right at a bare-leafed oak.

"Whoa," she cried. "Whoa."

The machine slammed into the trunk. Four wheels lifted off the ground and the metal ached as it stopped. She pitched forward, hitting her head on the panel.

The machine settled in a wheeze of steam. Moonlight on the white snow dimmed behind passing clouds. Flashing stars dropped from the sky.

A blast of cold air was followed by Rudd bumping her over with his hip. He pressed buttons and jerked all three levers at once. *Utto* backed off the tree as her head cleared. Twisting the tiller, Rudd altered *Utto's* direction and headed across a clearing.

"Nice stop," he said.

She pressed her hand on her forehead and wiped her wet palm on Ludivica's riding clothes. "Blood," she said.

Rudd's sleeve was cut and soaked red.

"It's just a nick," Rudd said.

Pings on metal hit the carriage and shattered the glass on her side of the cab. Sparks of rifle fire winked from the darkness.

"Shoot at them," Rudd said. He slammed the levers forward to their limit.

Usell leaned the pistol out the broken glass, pointed at the sky, closed her eyes and pulled the trigger until the hammer clicked on empty chambers. The young riders veered away. Rudd pressed a plunger. The machine compressed faster and in a short time the galloping horses following them faded from view.

Bouncing, rattling, and hissing through a field and a cherry orchard, they turned onto a smooth road.

"It's not safe for us out in the open," he said. "We have to stop."

"Where?" she asked.

"Away from here," he said. He wiped his mouth and leaned over the tiller.

"I have to get to the city," she said.

"Don't be stupid. The secret police are everywhere. They're vicious people who torture women and children and enjoy it. What do you think they'd do to you?"

"I have to find my mother," she said.

"This is what I warned you about," he said. "This is a war. You, me, we're standing in the middle of a fire. Nobody matters. Nobody can do anything about it. Dancing with your captain does nothing more than race your heart."

"He's not my captain. Why do you keep saying that?"

Utto chuffed and rattled. Usell leaned against the open window as a light snow began to fall. Icy wind whistled into the cab and even the pulsing heat from the brass chimney behind them could not subdue the cold.

32 . . .

Taking the long way around Odessa, they veered onto a snow-covered path and through a flat empty expanse. With *Utto* compressing steam and bumping over rock and ruts, a burned-out husk of a farmhouse appeared in the shadowed moonlight.

A single wall stood next to a brick chimney that was mounded in snow. 30 meters away a second structure, a barn, off plumb, tilted like a man leaning on a walking cane, but supported a roof.

Rudd jerked two levers back and one forward and *Utto* squeaked to a stop in front of the barn. One panel door lay crooked and broken. The other blocked the entrance. Usell leaped out and tugged the hinged panel open enough for Rudd to drive *Utto* inside. In silence the two of them shouldered both doors closed.

The chug of *Utto*'s compressors stopped in a corner of the dilapidated structure. Trudging out of the shadows, Rudd's tall frame hardly swayed. He dug his heel in packed ground and built a fire of broken wood and wet straw. When the fire blazed, both Usell and Rudd rubbed their hands before it.

"We'll rest the night," Rudd said. "In the morning we'll head into the city on foot. It's not far."

In the firelight his face was taut; bones were sharp along jaw and cheek, the skin glistening like a polished saddle.

"You did a good job getting us out of there," he said.

He snapped a board across his knee and threw it on the fire.

"I may have underestimated your skills," he said.

"I took advantage of a child," Usell said.

"The princess is no child. She's a monster with the power of God behind her."

"I hate your perceptions," Usell said. "They are cynical and cruel and uncaring. She is just a child who cannot see."

"And your reality is an illusion of flying in the arms of your Cossack lover," he said.

"Stop saying that."

"What little fantasy was going on in your mind when you danced with him?"

When she didn't answer, he sprang to his feet and marched to *Utto*. He returned with a brown wool blanket in one arm and a gray tin can in his hand.

While she cleaned her face with her own spittle, Rudd jabbed two holes into the can with the princess' knife. Working it open, he set the can on the fire.

A light snow began to fall through the holes in the barn's roof.

Hardly satisfied with her swabbing, she gave up and squatted by the fire.

"When we get to Odessa, we have to part ways," he said.

"You're leaving me again?"

He scratched the side of his head. "I'm getting out of this place before I get killed," he said. "There's no chance to get the jewel and you should consider coming with me."

"Go ahead," she said. "Go. Leave now. I cannot go with you."

He shook his head. "I'll get you to Odessa," he said. "In the meantime . . ."

When the stewed meat inside the can bubbled, Rudd removed it from the fire. With the knife and holding the can between the sergeant's unlaced boots, he dug out a chunk of meat covered with thick brown sauce and handed it to her.

The meat was salty and over-cooked.

"Is that jewel so important?" she asked. "Getting rich?"

"The princess will send troops after you."

"I'm hoping she thinks you kidnapped me."

"Well, I might," he said.

"I'm not worth a ransom."

"Who said I wanted to ransom you? I might just keep you."

"You wouldn't like me," she said.

"Oh, I might."

"I am too damaged. I wouldn't make a good wife."

"Who said anything about marriage?" he said.

"You're not chivalrous."

"Never claimed to be."

"I am not a person who lends my heart," she said.

"How do you know if you haven't tried?"

"You are without honor."

"Listen, sister," he said. "We're on the run. Honor, duty, compassion, all that crap is mixed up with getting dead."

Grabbing the knife back, he stabbed it into the meat and stuffed the lumpy contents on the point into his mouth.

The wet wood sizzled in the fire. Metal nails burned to a red glow.

"I appreciate your helping me," she said.

"Yeah, I keep making the same mistake," he said.

Cold hard ground cracked of brittle straw. The brown wool blanket bound Usell to the ground. Breath clouded about her nostrils. A hard muscled arm confined her movement. Rudd's body nestled against her in a fetal curve. His eyes were closed and the spray of morning sun sliced through the cracked and weathered boards of the barn roof.

The dawn chased the night sky white. It was silent. A light snow fell in floating flakes. Crystal piles sparkled on mud and straw, making mountains and valleys for elves and fairies. In Oylaif, when she was a child, the first snow brought smiles to people's faces as they went about their day, minded their own business, worked, and enjoyed their children. It was only when the snow stayed day after day, month after month that their expressions turned sour.

But with the first snow Yehuda would play his violin and Madame Hoffman would screech her arias. As a child, Usell would stand on her stool and look out the window, watch Yehuda stroke his instrument as if nurturing an infant; when he finished testing his violin, he'd look up at Usell and nod a hello. When she was older, she danced with an imaginary man, a man without a face, a man who held her with such gentleness that she needed only to respond to his imaginary touch and fly about her attic floor. Happiness. At the ball she'd closed her eyes. It was somehow the same, somehow different with Dmitri's arms holding her.

A drip of snow melted on Rudd's eyelid and he flinched. His hollow breaths warmed her ear. She lifted his arm by the wrist and put it on his hip before easing out from under the blanket and standing over his limp body. His hat had rolled off his head. Snow clung to his hair.

"Rudd Cothman," she said. "Boy catching butterflies. Hey."

Rudd squinted at the bright light and then blocked the rays with his hand.

"Up so soon," he said.

He pressed to his elbow – assessed the morning.

Rolling to the dead fire, he blew on gray ashes until the un-burnt wood reddened and ignited. He added more and warmed his hands to the small flames.

"Sleep well?" he asked.

"You should not take liberties with me."

"Your cheeks are flushed. Sleeping with a man becomes you."

"I'm not frightened by you," she said.

"Maybe you should be."

"You wouldn't hurt me."

"I wasn't thinking of hurting you," he said.

"You wouldn't do that to me, either."

"Don't be so sure."

"Let me remind you, I'm betrothed," she said.

He shook his head and his hair dripped melted snow.

"Who is this person you're going to marry?"

"A boy I thought did not like me but then he saved my life."

"Where is he?"

"I don't know. In their hands, maybe dead."

Rudd broke a long board with the heel of his boot.

"I need to get into the city," she said. She buttoned the princess's jacket at the collar.

"Hold on," Rudd said. "Give me a hand up." He stretched out his arm.

When she took his palm, he grabbed her wrist and jerked her on top of him. She did not fight him. She said nothing as their close faces warmed each other with meaty breath and their eyes looked into each other. And then she kissed him. A long full-mouthed kiss yielded to her search.

Breaking away and standing up, she closed the last two buttons of her jacket.

"No good will come of this," she said.

"That isn't what you just said."

"I said nothing."

"You don't have to talk to speak to me," he said.

"You understand our people. We have laws. You would not do this without my consent."

"One plus one, huh?"

"Yes."

Rudd's shoulders relaxed. "Okay," he said. "But . . ." He winked at her. "You'll let me know if you change your mind."

Her shoulders relaxed. "I need a friend," she said. "My father said our people need friends."

With a shrug, Rudd returned to *Utto* and came back wearing his broad-brimmed hat, and long coat. Stopping in front of her, he strapped his holstered pistol to his thigh.

"Time to go," he said.

33 . . .

Odessa appeared in a white gleam against the flat black of the harbor. The seaport bustled. Ships loaded and unloaded. Fluttering sails banked against belching black smokestacks.

The city was the color of ecru sand. Dozens of onion domes, mosque minarets, and spires reflecting Tartar, Turk, and Russian preoccupations with their Gods. Usell's feet in the princess's shoes ached from stumbling over rocky ground.

The sky, troubled by distant turbulence, hesitated to blue. Rudd's set chin made his face appear blocked and cornered. Preoccupied, he tucked chin to chest and caught Usell's jacket, slowing her down. He put his arm around her shoulder.

"Slow down. We need to act like we're together," he said.

"You are too familiar," she said.

"If you're talking about the kiss – you did it."

"I should not have."

"You wanted more," he said.

"You cannot know my feelings. You cannot. I did not say." She hastened her pace. "You are too brash."

"Yeah," he said. "You're not all that different from other women."

"There is only one me. I am most certainly different."

"You're more naive."

"I'm not a child," she said.

Rudd shook his head. She removed his arm and marched away from him. Pressing her stride for a half dozen steps, she slowed. Waiting for Rudd to catch up, she brushed the mud from the cuff on her sleeve.

"Might I travel with you, miss?" Rudd asked. He bowed, the smile warm, honest, and humorous.

"All right," she said. "I did feel a want, but I cannot think of it and I will not act on it again. I need your help. I need to trust you."

"I wouldn't put all my eggs in that basket."

In a clutter of buildings, dating back centuries, traffic swarmed. The people of Odessa scurried about their morning, a tangle of carriages, wagons, and coaches. Police manned every corner. Street signs read: Eupatoria Street. Theodosia Street. Gadzhibei. Deribasovskaya. Pushkin Street. Greek. Tartar. Turk. Lithuanian. Russian.

Two soldiers pointed at a young girl rushing through the market.

Usell covered her nose at the strong smell of fish. Sellers, hawkers, and buyers competed for products and profits lined up on sober display.

Above the tables fringing both sides of the street were white-tented roofs of cloth strung to stakes in the dirt, poles at angles, squared to buildings, all shading the goods from an intense sun. The ropes connected one merchant to the next and white cloth flapped in a steady breeze. Dry fruit dangled next to brown meat, split fish, turnips, nets of chocolate, mounds of cabbage, snails, seaweed, the smell of brine, all hovering above the clogged river of searchers.

In the bustle Usell and Rudd became part, but not participant, not susceptible to the call of merchants who raised their heads, lifted their wares, and shouted prices as if there was a duty to purchase because they were there, the goods were there and they expected those who looked, smelled, and heard had a duty to buy.

Despite the commerce the people of Odessa were as diverse as their clothing. No single fashion. Some women wore farm skirts to their ankles, different colors, muted patterns, stripes, solids, puffed hats. Still others wore fitted dresses with tight necks and European bustles. Those men engaged in sales and merchandise wore tunics to the thigh, wadded ties at the neck, and scarf-belts, not unlike the orthodox *gartel* that divided upper and lower body parts in Oylaif. Other consumers fashioned their clothes after European styles and held themselves at a distance, but examined the wears with eager eyes.

In the street's gutter the beggars sat in their lumpy leather shoes. The skin on their dirty ankles was as bruised and purpled as the worn looks on their faces.

Rudd stopped. He rubbed his hands in front of himself. "Would you like an orange?" he asked.

In the nearby carts there was no fruit, only those items that could be stored over the winter.

Rudd had moved ahead without her.

"Coniheutzski, you dirty thief," he said. "I will cut your throat."

In front of him six black Tartars pivoted from a circle made around a single occupant. The six – with black mustaches cupping their mouths to short beards – reversed and formed a phalanx that pushed through the crowd in blousy black trousers and leathery vests over swarthy, barrel chests. A stride from Rudd, they stiffened to attention and stopped. Green sash belts cradled curved golden daggers.

Breaking through the Tartars, pushing them aside, a woman, her body heavy, wrapped in black and yellow silk sashes from head to toe, stared at Usell above a veil shielding her face. The crimp about her eyes was padded and short-lashed. With a tense shake of her head, two fleshy hands reached out and grabbed Rudd.

"You womanizing, smuggling traitor," her husky voice growled.

She wrapped him in tentacles of silk and lifted him off the ground.

"Coniheutzski," Rudd said, "You still think you can cheat the devil and live?"

"Never more readily than in the presence of their couriers," she said.

The woman opened her arms and did a small circular dance, scarfs twirling about her pear-shape. Catching Usell's stare, she stopped, and looked Usell up and down. Wrapping one thick arm around Rudd's neck she said, "What brings you to Odessa?"

"Oranges," Rudd said.

Light angled below the brim of his hat, exposing his cocky smile.

"I was just about to tell my friend here," he said, "that you are never without them."

Slipping a hand behind folds in her middle, Madame Coniheutzski exposed an orange. She pinched the soldier's jacket peeking from beneath Rudd's long coat.

"Have you enlisted?" she asked.

"Disguised."

"And who is the dirty noble you travel with?" Coniheutzski's gray eyes measured the princess's jacket, stared at the crest of double heart/double sword on the lapel.

"She is . . ." Rudd cleared his throat.

"An apostate," Madame Coniheutzski said. "Yes. We have seen warrants. You disappeared from the palace where the Grand Duke was kidnapped and there were murders on the grounds. The drawings don't do you justice."

For a moment the orange retracted, but then Madame Coniheutzski's veil – hiding all but her dark inquisitive eyes – blew outward. She laughed and turned the fruit into Usell's palm.

"There is a large reward for you," she said.

"And how are your courtesans, Coniheutzski?" Rudd asked.

"Touché," she said. "As ever, I avoid the authorities."

Across the street a bent shrimp of a man scribbled in a small leather book and glanced up at the commotion around Usell. Pressing his thin brows together beneath a dangling cloth cap, he spun away, pushing through the moving congestion in a hurry.

Rudd eyed the man's movement. "Coniheutzski," he said.

He put his arm around her.

"You can see we have a problem."

"We?" Coniheutzski said.

The shrimp man appeared at the far corner, followed by two policemen.

Madame Coniheutzski glanced at them.

"Come this way," she said. "And . . . bring your beautiful champagne."

34 . . .

Usell stayed next to Rudd as Madame Coniheutzski's six protectors sawed through the crowd and away from the thin man's pointing arm. She led them through back streets. Rudd looked over his shoulder, the parade attracting more attention than when they were alone. Moving in a hurry, they wound through empty streets and stopped at a high-walled building that looked like a prison.

At a barred gate one of the Tartars yanked a bell and a bear-sized black man wearing white muslin robes and pursing rubbery lips appeared. With suspicious beady eyes and a grimacing jaw, he unlocked the gate, stepped aside, and, once the entourage entered, locked the bolt with a key.

The Tartars fanned away and Madame Coniheutzski led Rudd and Usell past an open courtyard strewn with broken stone statues.

"What happened here?" Rudd asked.

Sculpted chunks of rock lay about the patio. Half naked male figures still posed but had their faces and genitalia demolished, broken to shards. Usell ran her fingers across the Greek letters on a bust with the head missing. A name. Hylas. Another nearby, Daphnis. And another, Hermaphroditus. Greek youths seduced by the Naiads.

"My garden," Madame Coniheutzski sighed. She swayed into the center of the rubble and covered her eyes with puffy white hands. "Some nasty boys paid me a visit. Ignorant boys, who obey the hatreds of their confreres. Look how they savaged my poor darlings."

"Why?" Usell asked.

"I hope they suffer before and after they die," Madame Coniheutzski said. "You see how art is treated when truth and beauty are not in harmony."

Usell was about to ask more questions when Rudd set his hand on her shoulder.

With a flourish of her wrist, Madame Coniheutzski shuffled inside a large square house. In a spacious room with un-curtained windows, she threw herself on a backless Roman couch decorated with square, tasseled cushions. She opened her palm to Usell and Rudd, suggesting they squat at the low table on the Persian rug.

Usell examined an ancient carpet on a wall, the weave a portrait of a curly bearded man with a crown. Babylonian. He held a hooked cane scepter around the neck of a whip-tailed dragon.

Rudd sat on a floor pillow.

"With one God there are so many disappointments," Madame Coniheutzski said. "That is Marduk, the last of the noble polytheists. You would like him. He charmed the other Gods to get his way."

"Marduk's dragon ate infants and children," Usell said. "Until Abraham dethroned him."

"Ha," Coniheutzski said. "You know the myth?"

"It is a foolish myth," she said.

"Myth is reality," Coniheutzski replied. "It is how the people follow their leaders. It is culture. It is why we behave as we do."

Usell squatted to a pillow at the low table. Setting her hands in her lap, she pasted her lips into a smile as Madame Coniheutzski continued.

"I have always wondered," she said. 'I have never been so fortunate as to engage the words of the aristocracy. Tell me. What do you think?" Her eyes twinkled above the veil.

"I think," Usell said, "that when myth is more important than reality, the people are in trouble."

"Not all the people," Madame Coniheutzski said. "The educated and the uneducated have different values, but they all spring from similar myths."

She laughed and continued it in a long giddy string and then she flopped back in a heap of sash and pillows as if she'd been shot. She lay there with arms out. The breeze from the open window lifted the hems of sashes and billowed them above her waist. Layers of veils swirled over her.

Usell sat up.

Beneath the circulating silk were two thick hairy legs, a paunch of belly, and a pale fat shrunken caterpillar twisting in her crotch.

"You are a man," Usell said.

Rudd gripped Usell's hand.

163

She twisted free.

"Things are not always what they seem," Rudd said. "Grow up."

Coniheutzski smiled. "On the inside I'm just like you."

"Like me?"

"Ahhhh," Coniheutzski sighed. "I lack beauty and youth; the things every woman wants, but the feelings . . ." He turned a fat palms up. "Are we not similar in some ways?"

"Maybe," Usell said. "I also wish to choose my own way."

"You are a Nihilist," Coniheutzski said.

"I am not a rebel," Usell said.

"If you do not conform, you are a rebel. Women cannot choose."

Rudd sat forward. "Coniheutzski. Do you have something to eat? A change of clothes? Hospitality to connect us to the people we need to see?"

Coniheutzski tapped his lip. "A smuggler wishes help and a noble thing has wants she cannot provide herself."

"I'm looking for my mother."

"I know many people in the city. Perhaps I can help."

"Her name is Vera Figner."

Coniheutzski sat upright.

"The Grand Duchess's consort?"

Usell shrugged. "Do you know where she is?"

Coniheutzski folded his arms, his fat brow constricted. "Perhaps," he said. "Where are my manners?" He lifted his head and called, "Cleomachus."

The huge black man slipped between a curtained entryway. He wore his blousing white muslin Roman fashion. He picked up a pillow and laid it behind Coniheutzski for support. Coniheutzski grabbed him around the back of the neck and kissed him hard on the mouth. Then he pushed the servant away, saying, "You need a shave. We are hungry. Serve us."

The muscular black man left the room, his flat-footed walk duck-like, exaggerated.

"Now tell me, my friend," Coniheutzski said, nodding at Rudd. "The warrants all over the city, but no explanations. They want you. They want her." He smiled at Usell. "Alive. What did you do to the princess to deserve this?"

"I need to get to my ship," Rudd said. "I'll need you to give me an escort to the harbor and her, to . . ."

"Pushkin Street," Coniheutzski said. "I know people at the market. Dangerous. Okhrana. Cossacks. Police. But information."

The strapping black man reappeared carrying bowls and bread in his muscular arms. His set mouth showed no emotion, but his eyes inspected Usell as if her touch might infect the grapes overflowing his bowls. He set one bowl on the couch next to Coniheutzski and handed him the largest loaf of bread. After positioning the rest on the low table between Rudd and Usell, his quick short steps scurried away.

Coniheutzski waited until he left before saying, "Cleomachus dislikes royal blood as much as the Jew."

"Be careful, Coniheutzski." Rudd leaned forward. "This is a perilous time. If you pick the wrong foe, you make many enemies."

Coniheutzski shrugged. He bit a green grape in half. "They have closed commerce in many places. Spies are everywhere. They hunt the Jew."

"What are they doing to the Jews?" Usell asked.

"Why worry about them?" Coniheutzski asked.

Usell straightened her back. "People who sneak in the shadows should worry about those in the light."

Tilting his head, Coniheutzski lifted both his chins. "They gather the Jew in pens."

"Pens?"

"Cattle pens. At the docks. No one is allowed there."

Beneath the table Rudd gripped Usell's wrist.

"Why? What have they done?"

Coniheutzski's fat fingers thrummed his lips. He shrugged. "It is ordered. They pay extra for traitors who masquerade."

"You would be wise, my friend," Rudd said, "not to cross this young woman."

"Then perhaps she should not call attention to her opinions," Coniheutzski said.

Usell locked her fingers together.

And then Coniheutzski sat forward and righted himself with the grace of a fitter man. He brushed the front of his clothes.

"I will secret you to the market," he said. "I have contacts. I will ask about this Vera Figner. No one will see you. For now,

Cleomachus will take you to rooms after you eat. You can freshen yourself while I make the arrangements and . . . I have costumes for you both."

Flopping his hand at the wrist, he looked around at his furnishings, sighed, and with rotating hips slipped between curtains and was gone.

"I don't trust him," Usell said. "He keeps talking about rewards."

"He likes his comforts. He'll do what we ask," Rudd said.

After eating, Cleomachus led Usell and Rudd to side-by-side rooms.

"Call out if you need help getting out of your outfit," Rudd said.

In her small chamber, light poured through a single un-open pane of glass.

A bare wooden stand held a basin, a pitcher of water, a fragrant soap, a hand mirror, a comb, a scissors, and a folded cream-colored towel. Clean clothing draped over the high-backed chair, cloth slippers at the foot. Shapeless peasants wear. In the corner a wooden bed with a quilted comforter on top supported square pillows fringed with gold braid.

Usell sagged onto the edge of the bed. She removed Ludivica's jacket. Once again she was to change form, slink from one kind of shadow to another, disappear like a brown wren into the flock.

Holding the mirror, she examined the girl without the snood hiding her hair. She was filthy. Her face was smudged with blood and something else looked back at her, a disturbing steady gaze that sought nothing. The eyes were tired, tired of running, tired of hiding, tired of the senseless stupidity and hate. Clutching the jewel around her neck, she slumped with her arms between her knees. When she looked up, she squinted at the girl in the mirror, grabbed the scissors, and with a clump of hair in hand, she cut.

35 . . .

Rudd—dressed in the costume of the Turk—opened the door to Usell's room. Kaftan and embroidered robe with a floor-length knitted vest hung like curtains over the burnoose.

Behind him Coniheutzski laughed.

"From noble to peasant, a great fall."

"Not so much as you think," Rudd said.

"Did you find out about my mother?" Usell asked.

"What I found was that you need to ask the rebels, people I do not communicate with. That is all I know."

Leaving the stronghold, Usell followed Cleomachus, Coniheutzski, and Rudd. Keeping her head down she watched her steps as they engaged the people of Odessa going about their visible tasks of buying and selling.

Without his guards Coniheutzski pressed his bulk through the streets, his orange silks riding the ribs of his pumpkin frame, the glances of pedestrians simple, perfunctory, and without comment.

If there were suspicious eyes, they followed the black and Rudd, but no one noted Usell except an evacuating donkey attached to a wagon. The police, the shoppers, and the merchants, rats and cats, dogs and mules, all drained down the cobbled streets with common inclinations.

Rudd nudged Usell forward as they strode past a pillar of stone engraved with the words *Pushkin Street*. Rudd jerked Usell's tunic and pulled her close.

"If anything goes wrong," he whispered, "the rebels have a sanctum. There."

With a nod he aimed past a bakery, a jeweler, and a winemaker's shop at a sign on a green building with yellow trim, *The Inn on Pushkin Street*. Flaking plaster, dilapidated, an ordinary place to mark the poet who championed the people.

Coniheutzski stopped a dozen strides ahead at a warehouse and hammered on the black door.

With a reply from within, Coniheutzski entered and tromped three steps down from the short landing to a packed mud floor. Rudd and Usell followed. Cleomachus stationed himself on the landing with his arms folded across his muscled chest.

A single kerosene lantern hung from a rafter shedding sallow light in a warehouse. Coffin-like crates piled four high divided the room into military rows. One crate was open and tilted against the others. In it were a half dozen percussion cap rifles lined up like soldiers. Against a windowless wall a man in a hooded tunic sat on a sack of wheat and worked a fat-bladed kukri on an abrasive stone.

"Wait here," Coniheutzski said. "Cleomachus let no one enter."

The man sharpening his kukri stood up tall.

Coniheutzski waddled to him and they whispered to each other.

"Something's not right," Rudd said. "That's government weaponry."

Rudd slipped the dead sergeant's pistol from beneath his garment. "Stay behind me," he said.

Coniheutzski headed back to the steps, the hooded man right behind. Smiling at Rudd, Coniheutzski said, "I'm afraid doing business with you is no longer possible."

The man with the kukri removed his hood and Lieutenant Yazukov's golden hair reflected the light.

Rudd kicked Coniheutzski in the gut, sending him sprawling into Yazukov, knocking both to the floor.

Behind them Cleomachus raised his long dagger and leaped down the steps. Rudd's pistol exploded, the bullet ripping through Cleomachus's open mouth. The falling body hit Rudd in the chest and knocked him to the floor. Cleomachus didn't move.

From the shadows sabers flashed and grim faces raced down the aisles. Lieutenant Yazukov struggled beneath Coniheutzski.

"Get out of here," Rudd said.

Soldiers launched themselves at Rudd. He fired three times as Usell scrambled out the door, twice more as she raced from the darkness to the blinding light of day.

36 . . .

Diving into the busy market of barkers and buyers, pig, poultry, and swarming flies, Usell scrambled into turbulence of hagglers.

Behind her, pushing into the thick crowd, soldiers erupted from the warehouse in a blue swarm.

Usell sliced through the people and found space between backs and shoulders and chests of the men and women, who stood like posts buried deep in a stream.

A sergeant at the head of soldiers called to his fellows and pointed a finger.

Usell twisted behind a fishmonger with his back turned. Jerking the underside of the table, she dumped flounder, mackerel, and goby into a stream of slimy scales in her wake.

The sergeant – close on her heels – slipped and landed on his backside, tried to stand, but he could neither rise nor ignore the angry fishmonger swearing at him and brandishing a knife.

Usell ducked through a chicken hawker's stall as a bird with its neck stretched on a block screeched. The hawker severed the chicken's head. With the thunk of the butcher knife on the block dickering voices bid and blotted out the soldier's alerts. Usell stooped and then crawled on her knees to a wall as the headless bird ran in circles.

The pursuers charged into the buyers, who locked in their demands, produced a stubborn grid and repelled the soldiers like a rocky cliff does the shore.

Usell stood up along the wall, slipped from one connected building to the next until she reached the lime green and yellow structure with a curtained door and the sign above it reading *The Inn on Pushkin Street.* She plunged into the dim candlelight and stumbled to a stop. A layer of smoke hovered above her head.

The darkness reshaped from black to gray. Deep growls lowered to a hush. Below the layer of tobacco smoke shadows moved. Chairs scraped on wood floors.

In the middle of a dozen tables, sweaty faces with tough scowls stared at her. A brawny man in a sheepskin vest lifted his bearded face and lowered his glass mug. Next to him a second man with one eye sewn shut glared up at her.

"Peasant," the vested man said. "Are you one of us?" He didn't wait for an answer, but stood, and lifted his glass. "To the revolution."

"To the revolution." Bodies stood up from the tables and raised their mugs.

The man with one glaring eye hunched forward, and stayed in his seat. On his jacket was a silver lightning bolt. Okhrana. On the table was an open sack of gold coins.

Usell stepped back. At an adjacent table someone slammed a mug down. A chair squeaked wood on wood. The gypsy girl from the rebel camp pressed to her feet.

"Soldiers of the Tsar," Usell said. She pointed at the door. "In the street. Following me."

The gypsy girl's chair kicked over backward and in three rocking strides she grabbed Usell's arm and drew a short pointed dagger from her belt. She brandished it at the seated one-eyed man.

"You and your money are no longer welcome," the gypsy girl said.

Clasping the bag, the one-eyed man rose from his chair and moved around the table toward the door. The vested man grabbed the bag from One-Eye's hand.

"For our time," the vested man said.

One-Eye scowled, but then disappeared into the bright street.

The gypsy girl jerked Usell through the tavern, pulling her behind a serving counter. There she set the point of her knife in the wall and a panel slid open.

"Get in," she said.

A hole in the earth behind the wall was large enough to fit a body. Pressing her hand on Usell's neck, the gypsy girl bent Usell into the space. Dross rained on Usell's head as she scraped the sides and ceiling of the enclosure. Granulated rock chafed her knees. Grains of sand blinded her eyes and when she turned on her back, her head hit the roof and showered her with earth.

"Be quiet," the gypsy girl said. "Or this will be your grave."

She smoothed the dirt into the mix of straw outside the panel and closed it.

In the darkness Usell wiped her eyes, banged her head twice before holding still.

Pounding boots on the wood floor trampled into the tavern. Usell held her breath.

"Where is the girl who came in here?" someone barked.

"You can shove your questions up your ass for all I care," an annoyed voice answered.

"Arrest him."

Shouts erupted.

A whistle blasted.

Sounds jumbled. Scraping of wood. Screeching chairs. Swearing of angry men.

"For the revolution," someone yelled.

"For revolution."

"Revolution."

The pop pop pop of a pistol produced a momentary silence.

"Arrest them all."

"To the death, comrades."

Glass shattered. Wood broke and the smack of meat and bone resisted what Usell could distinguish. Amid obscenities, screams, and cries of pain, gunfire exploded.

With the peal of police whistles and barking orders, boots trampled wood floors and the rage of men became the anguish of collisions.

Usell closed her eyes. She covered her head.

Someone slammed against the wall outside her panel, showering her head with debris.

And then the noise subsided. Someone hollered, "Okhrana," and she heard the click of many metal bolts locking into place. The barrage of explosions ended with the smell of cordite seeping into her cave.

Groans followed gasping breaths.

"Take them all away," someone ordered.

Boots outside the panel stomped the floor.

"Is she among them?"

Usell recognized the voice. Yazukov. She held her breath. Pebbles and dust trickled down her back.

"She must have gotten away," a second voice said.

"She's hiding among the Jews. Round them up."

"I will inform the captain," the subordinate voice said.

"No. You will not," Lieutenant Yazukov said.

Her head bumped the earth above and a chunk fell between her legs.

In a short time the sounds of movement, moans, and grumbling led to complete silence.

In her hollow she could hear her own breath. Nothing more. Time, like a Leviton preparing to consume her, usurped the confined space.

Usell clenched her fists and tightened her grip on its inevitable passage, holding her fear back, keeping the prescience of the next moment from the demands of her thoughts.

There was once a time when her mother held her, rocked her in the bond of birth and nature, the carry of one body in another, but the connection once close never grew beyond that moment of entering the world on her own. How could that be? She had seen mothers love their young. Why was she unloved? What was wrong with her? What was so important that the love of her daughter could be denied?

Something moved outside the panel. Usell leaned between her knees and scratched at the panel's edge. She could not budge it from the thick grooves.

There was a tap on the panel.

"Are you there?"

A block of earth fell behind Usell, filled the gap at her back.

"Help me. Help me," she cried. "I'm being buried."

"Be quiet."

Usell kicked against the panel. "Get me out. Get me out."

A heavy rock pressed on Usell's head. The panel slid away. Brown light outlined the opening.

She tried to straighten her legs and when she couldn't, a hand reached in and pulled her ankle, twisted her out onto the floor behind the counter as the hole collapsed in a gush of dust.

Wiping grit from her face and eyes, she squinted at the dark tavern. A spray of light from the entrance sharpened the shadows. The serving counter was pocked with bullet holes, as was the wall around her cave.

Leaning against the counter in a pool of blood was the gypsy girl, her head tilted at a broken angle.

"Get up," the woman's voice whispered. The shadow moved away, cloaked in black, a hood about her head.

Usell rolled to her knees.

"Who are you?"

"Come on," the hooded woman whispered.

Dirt falling off Usell sprinkled the wood floor as she stood. The woman yanked Usell by her blouse. She stumbled after, through the scattered wreckage of the empty tavern, through a back door into an alley where Usell covered her eyes in the bright sunlight.

"Stay up," the hooded woman said. She yanked Usell to the end of the alley, and then crouched next to the wall looking onto the street. The air filled with burning wood and angry voices.

A man on a wagon roused a crowd around him.

"The Jewish boys wait for our girls, wanting to seduce, contaminate their blood. They hate the whites. There is no filth or crime without a Jew being involved. We must cut the sore, the maggot from their rotting bodies."

Cheers from the crowd echoed on the walls.

"Tear them from their covens."

"Strip them of all they've stolen."

"Burn their idols."

Usell lurched back, but the hooded woman jerked her close.

"Let's go around," the woman said and led Usell up one block then across another before they scrambled down a wide alley flanked by sand-faced stone buildings.

Halfway through the alley the woman stopped at a handle on a slanted cellar door. The warped wood leaned at a low angle against the foundation of a building. She unlocked the bolt and yanked the poorly made doors open.

Shoving Usell down the first step of a vertical ladder, the hooded woman climbed in after. On the fifth step down Usell slipped and slammed onto her back against a mud-packed floor. She grabbed her shoulder and winced.

"Quiet," the hooded woman said. She stepped halfway down the ladder backwards, crouched against it as she pulled the doors closed. Using a length of wire through the cracks, the woman slid the large scraping bolt into its iron anchor until the lock clicked.

"They went this way," someone outside said.

In the alley, boots echoed against the stone walls until the sound faded. A shadow froze above the cellar doors. Hard yanks failed to budge the lock or the rusted iron bar. A drizzle of dust fell through the sunlit slits.

The shadow above the cellar doors disappeared into the slap of boots.

"Who are you?" Usell asked.

With a pale palm toward Usell, the woman said, "Shh."

The noise from the alley faded and Usell struggled to her feet. She wiped dirt from her hair. She licked her fingers, cleared her eyes, and swallowed.

The woman backed down the ladder and pulled her hood off. She brushed her fingers through her short black hair.

"What are you doing here?" Nikolayevna Fillipova asked.

Bars of light crossed her tight face.

"Nikolayevna?"

"I asked you a question," Nikolayevna snapped. "Why aren't you in the palace with your Captain?"

"I . . . escaped," Usell said.

"Why would you do a stupid thing like that?"

"What?"

"Now we're blind," Nikolayevna said.

"The captain put me under arrest."

"Did you damage your relationship with the Cossack?"

"I did nothing," Usell said. "He knew who I was. He knew I was a Jew. He said he loved me and then you kidnapped the Grand Duke."

"As I suspected." Nikolayevna said. "But escape was stupid."

Usell dug her nails into her palms. She started to shake. Dust trembled from her clothes.

"You have to go back," Nikolayevna said.

"I what?"

Nikolayevna stepped in front of Usell and slapped her face.

Usell touched the cheek. The sting cooled against her hand and she leaped at Nikolayevna both fists swinging. Nikolayevna dodged the swipes, grabbed Usell's wrists, and folded them behind her back.

"Submit," she said. "Submit."

37 . . .

Usell dropped her shoulders and lowered her head. Nikolayevna Fillipova released her grip and stepped away.

"Come with me," she said.

Striding into the cellar shadows, she climbed a ladder straight up between two posts supporting the beams of the floor above and disappeared into a trap door.

Usell wiped her arms across her chest. Dirt fell from her peasant clothes. Faint light seeped through the cracks. The basement was empty. No shelves full of winter canning. No stored quilts. No potatoes left over from the November harvest.

Rubbing her hands before shaking the chill from her shoulders, she took a deep breath, held it in, closed her eyes, and then let it out. After rolling her head on her neck, she followed Nikolayevna up the splintered cross planks of the ladder, and balanced on the edges of the opening. Nikolayevna shoved two slim doors open and stepped into bright light.

Leaning out of a cupboard, Usell stood in a kitchen. An iron stove with lion's claw feet throbbed with heat. Vapors of hickory rose from the hot metal. A blaze of yellow light showered through a pane glass window above a table with two chairs.

On the table a brown bottle with no cork sat next to an empty glass. The adjacent wall was interrupted by an open hallway and trailed into darkness. Cabinets lined a third wall above a gray sandstone worktable where a basin, pitcher, and red iron pump interrupted its rectangular lines.

"This is where I live," Nikolayevna said.

Usell rubbed her wrists. "Sparse," she said.

"It's clean and it's safe."

She removed her cloak. Beneath it she wore a plain wool dress that showed the curves of a firm body and slim waist.

"Who are you?" Usell asked.

"You know who I am and you need to learn to control your anger."

"Are you a Jew?"

The glare from Nikolayevna's black eyes glinted with sunlight.

"Your insults will get you nowhere," Nikolayevna said. "I need you in the service of the revolution."

"I'm not joining anything."

"Do you know where the American's gun is?" Nikolayevna asked.

"Why would I tell you?"

"Is it hidden in his machine?"

"I will not answer your questions," Usell said.

Nikolayevna smiled.

"You are upset," she said. "I understand, but time is short. I'll get right to the point. We need your help."

Usell slumped into the chair. Looking at the woman with the slim nose, Usell ran her finger down her own. The woman's eyes spread too far apart, the hair was thick and coarse and tinted by the sun. The skin was lighter in color, the brows thicker. Nothing connected.

"How badly have you damaged your relationship with the Cossack?" Nikolayevna asked.

"I betrayed him," Usell said. "I escaped. His men were killed."

"The warrants in the city say otherwise. They want you alive, not arrested. Someone wants you back. I say it is your captain."

Usell pressed her palm over the jewel beneath the jacket.

"I doubt it," she said.

The muscles below Nikolayevna's cheeks tensed. She lifted her chin. "He has touched you, hasn't he?" She patted her heart. "Did you look in his eyes when you danced with him?"

Usell didn't answer.

"Were you a foolish romantic taken in by moonlight and a strong, powerful man?"

Usell looked away.

"Well?" Nikolayevna said.

Usell shrugged.

"No matter," Nikolayevna said.

At the counter Nikolayevna levered the handle of the red pump until water gushed from the spigot into the pan. She transferred the pan to the stove.

"The war continues," Nikolayevna said. "We are gathering our men. We will take the American's gun and we will send the new Tsar a message about his ultimate destruction."

"Rudd may be dead."

"He's not dead. Your captain has him."

"Is he safe?"

Nikolayevna shook her head. "Only a fool allows her heart to govern her mind." She grabbed the bottle and poured a frothing brown liquid into the glass.

"Drink," she said. "It will clear your head."

Swallowing nothing but dryness and grit, Usell clasped the glass and glanced out the window, seeing only bright sunlight. With a gulp of beer she coughed.

"Russian beer," Nikolayevna said. "You must learn to drink with the common man. When you go back, you will mingle with the royals, taste the best, but never forget you are part of the proletariat."

"You ask a lot and offer nothing."

"I offer you a chance to do something, be someone important, to be more than yourself. Help build a nation of powerful citizens."

"My people?" Usell said.

"All people," Nikolayevna said.

"Why should I believe you? You're nothing but a . . . a politician."

"And she's very good at it," a crackling voice said from the dark hallway. "She is an artist at convincing people of her sincerity. That's why they follow her."

Framed in black shadow was the Grand Duke. He was still in his white sable ball garments. He strode toward Usell, hooking his cane on his arm, energy in his step.

Nikolayevna removed cloth towels from a cabinet and set them on the counter next to a tin of liquid soap.

"You got him on the balcony," the Grand Duke said. "He is a good soldier. He maintains order. He follows orders. We need him."

Nikolayevna folded her arms.

"You're part of this?" Usell asked.

177

"None of this would be without him," Nikolayevna said. "We're wasting time."

She retrieved a map from a cabinet and spread the parchment on the table. Leaning over it she said, "I need two things from you."

"Wait a minute." Usell pointed at the Grand Duke. "The Tsar was your brother. Ludivica is your daughter. Ministers, nobles, military, all the people at the ball. YOU blew them up?"

"They were carefully selected," the Grand Duke said. "Accidents happen and if there is to be blame, we need only to choose who and call for justice."

"And there are fewer left who oppose our politics," Nikolayevna said.

"Every once in a while," the Grand Duke said, "the stock needs to be thinned so the strongest can emerge."

"But your own blood," Usell said.

"I concluded it was necessary. Alexander was a frightened vole. He was making agreements with everyone, solidifying his power. He was giving everything away."

The Grand Duke seated himself at the table and rested his hands on his cane. "The Prussians, the Poles, the Hungarians, the Romanians, the Lithuanians, the Finns. He gave to them what had always been given to his most trusted supporters. He chose the wrong allies."

"But Alexander made a mistake," Nikolayevna said. "He gave Jews citizenship. A bargain to obtain their support."

"Soon they will be scattered like the four winds," the Grand Duke said. "We are doing what the people demand."

Usell lowered her head. "To satisfy the mob," she said.

"It is a balancing act," the Grand Duke said.

"What are you going to do with my people?" Usell asked.

"Some we will send away," the Grand Duke said. "We will use some for labor, library, wealth. Some, well, some are useless."

"You're going to kill us, aren't you? Like you did my father."

One of the old man's eyes closed. A corner of his thin lips lifted.

"Whoever is in the way," Nikolayevna said. "Now. Listen. The docks need to be cleared so we can get delivery of our weapons."

"The docks?" Usell said.

"Trains carry prisoners there day and night from all over the Pale," the Grand Duke said.

"I remember you, now," Usell said. "You were there in Havens. With her. Plotting to kill your own daughter. I heard you."

"Ah. I'm discovered," he said. He lifted his bony hands in surrender. "Political expediency. The people would be sympathetic. They would demand I take my brother's throne."

"But they haven't," Usell said.

"Alexi grabbed the reins," Nikolayevna said. "He appealed to the people by pointing at the leopard endangering their children."

"He is a weak minded fool," the Grand Duke said. "We must strike again. Once I'm back in the safety of his court, we can proceed to dislodge him."

"You have no conscience," Usell said.

"We're wasting time," Nikolayevna said.

The Grand Duke laughed. "You do not need to worry. As long as you work with us, no one will know who you are. You are safe."

"Can we get back to business?" Nikolayevna asked. She bent over the map.

"This is where we are." She pointed to a dot in the center of the city. "The dock is down the Richelieu Stairs past the industrial district to the harbor where the American's ship lies. There are problems. Orders not to unload the ship. Your captain thinks ahead, but the American has connections to the government that will use whoever it can to stay in power. Alexi is interested in the weapons. If the American intends to betray us, we need to have your captain eliminate him. That they contend for you makes it an easy choice."

"Dmitri is a man of duty," Usell said. "He will not break faith with the Tsar."

Nikolayevna lifted one eyebrow. "You underestimate your influence."

The pump's spigot dripped to the counter and from the counter to a pool on the floor.

"If you expect me to help, you have to stop what you're doing to my people."

The Grand Duke smiled. He nodded.

"You see," Nikolayevna said to the Grand Duke. "It is only a matter of reasoning with her."

"A temporary amnesty," the Grand Duke said. "But I cannot control all the forces against them."

Usell rose from the table and walked over to the pan of hot water. She dipped her hands into it. The water muddied with dirt; the liquid soap soothed her fingers.

"I'll do what's necessary," Usell said.

"Good," Nikolayevna said.

Drying her hands in the towel, Usell opened her palm to Nikolayevna.

"Give me back my mezuzah," she said.

"What?" Nikolayevna asked.

"I need it."

With curiosity in the lift of her brow, Nikolayevna walked to a kitchen drawer and removed the silver tube with the embossed *Shim* on its shiny surface.

"Here," she said and slapped it flat on the table. "I see you are still one of them. I thought you were smarter."

38 . . .

"We must gather our forces," Nikolayevna said. "They are in the city and the Tsar has agreed to the exchange for the Grand Duke. You must wait here."

"An exchange?" Usell asked.

"For the diamond."

"Once I'm in their hands again," the Grand Duke said, "I'll simply tell them where to find you. I trust our Captain will then do as we assign."

"Your Cossack will exchange the diamond for the Grand Duke in the plaza in front of the Library of Odessa. It will be crowded this time of day, and our forces will be on hand to avoid trouble."

Usell pressed her palm on the jewel beneath her blouse. She squinted in the sunlight streaming through the windows.

"I think you are stepping into a trap," she said.

"When you understand the way the empire thinks," Nikolayevna said, "your opinion will carry more weight."

After they left, Usell traced a line on the map down the Richelieu Stairs to the port and fixed both position and destination in her mind. Whatever suspicions Usell had about Nikolayevna's identity and her mother's whereabouts would have to wait. She looked like the woman in the portrait, but Nikolayevna was not a mother Usell cared to encourage. What good would it do to give her the jewel? These people didn't care about the people of Oylaif or anyone else as far as she could see.

When the lie is so evident, her father once said, *it is time to consider a different action. Trust rests on truth. Lies make co-operation impossible.*

While the government and the rebels were at each other's throats, scheming and plotting, Usell considered going to the docks to see if she could find anyone from Oylaif.

Take him to the docks, Dmitri had said about Moshe Gimmel on the train. If he was there or if he wasn't, her people were being rounded up and she had to find out if it was true. If it was, maybe with the jewel she could do something about it, bribe someone or trade it for their lives.

Washing herself from the basin of hot water, she selected clothing in Nikolayevna's wardrobe. Though slightly smaller and mannish in style, the clothes fit. She strapped her chest tight and pulled on loose trousers. Buttoning a blouse with a stiff collar, she presented herself to a mirror. When she shoved her arms into a camel's hair long coat and combed through her short hair, she perched a gray Homburg on top. If no one looked too close . . ..

"See if you can find me now," she said.

In Nikolayevna's stiff black boots Usell peeked out the door onto the street.

Multi-gabled buildings were set side by side in hues of cream and dry wheat. Above the peaked roofs, glazes of black chimney smoke rose to a blue sky. No broken furniture in the street, no burning pyres in the rain, and whatever anger gathered for trouble, it was not yet chaos.

Stepping from Nikolayevna's house, Usell adjusted her hat and set her direction for the harbor just as a column of soldiers turned the corner. At each door they banged their rifle butts. "Come out," they said.

One door opened and a family of five, three children – one stepping higher than the next. They huddled to their parents, who clenched them close as the soldiers poked their bayonets at the clothing, lifting jackets at point with stone faces and sober intent.

Usell slipped behind a passing wagon as two soldiers appeared in front of her. Taking a quick breath, she tipped her hat.

"What is happening?" Usell asked.

"We are searching for Jews," one soldier said. "Move on, sir."

Walking between them, she thrust her hips forward without a sway. The two soldiers watched her for a moment, but when Usell turned the corner, they banged their rifle butts on another door.

Following the map she'd memorized, Usell pressed through the streets and apartments, shops and warehouses that were squeezed together like the sedimentary rock. Whatever planning the city once had in mind, it was lost in the hurry to capitalize upon the growing population of the industrial age.

When she reached the stark gray ministry buildings on both sides of the Richelieu Stairs, she stopped. From the top of the broad and wide steps to the avenue below looked like four or five falling stairs, but something was wrong with the perspective.

The "200 Steps," they called it. The plaza where Nikolayevna was to meet with Rotovak was at the bottom, but it was submerged in a light mist. The harbor and sea beyond was lost in it too. But the scale was all wrong, an optical illusion, the distance dropped too far. The fabled steps and the park on both sides of it were empty.

In the street at the top she stopped between gray ministries built with classical Greek fronts. Entablature and pediments, columns and triangular roofs framed the appearance of the buildings with forced grandeur, a notion of stability, an announcement of faux importance.

Built onto the center of the street at the top of the steps was a monument, a statue in greening copper, done in the Romanesque style. The figure was that of a man of middle age in a toga with a laurel wreath about a full head of hair, a scroll tucked to his side and an arm stretched-out offering an explanatory gesture of pride in the city.

The plaque at its base said *Armand-Emmanuel du Plessis, Duc de Richelieu, Frenchman. For his service to Catherine the Great in founding Odessa.*

The sun beat on her skin, but the wind off the sea whipped cold at her ears.

"Don't go down there."

Usell spun around.

A girl, perhaps ten, in a baggy wool sack that covered her torso from neck to sandals, stood with a sour face and worried eyes in front of the statue.

"Why shouldn't I go where I wish?" Usell asked.

"Specters," she said. "They're all around."

"Ghosts?"

Another girl, older, a teen, stepped out from behind the statue and put her arm around the younger girl. She, too, dressed in ragged garments made of shabby wool, and spotted with stains.

"They are killing people," she said. "Blood is everywhere."

"What happened?" Usell asked.

"Cossacks ordered for everyone to go to their homes."

"But you are here."

"We have no home. Jews have eaten our parents."

Usell squatted next to the younger child. She curled her chin to her chest. Usell brushed the hair out of her eyes.

"Tell me what happened here," Usell asked.

The older girl looked over her shoulder, first in one direction and then another.

"Ghosts came out of the mist, down there." She pointed to the plaza at the bottom. "They swallowed everyone. And then there was a black carriage with human passengers, a woman in a man's suit and an old man in white fur. There was a growling of voices and then from the top of the steps hundreds of screaming Jews raced down toward them. But from the park on both sides of the steps ghosts attacked. There was a battle, and when it was over, the spirits swirled into a mist, covered the plaza down there. None survived."

"What happened to the woman?"

"The protector Cossack had her taken away in chains."

"And the old man?" Usell asked.

"The Cossack went away with him in the carriage. You must not go down there. The people are frightened. They hide. They fear the ghosts of Jews."

Usell stood. The girl clasped Usell's hand. "Don't go," she said.

"Don't worry," Usell said. "I have a way with ghosts."

39 . . .

Five long and broad patios divided the 200 steps. The Library, the place where a minister, her father's friend, might nominate those worthy to a post, flanked it at the bottom.

If things had stayed as they were and there was order and reason and tolerance, perhaps she might have persuaded her father to let her go to university, find answers by study and learning, but there was no wisdom there now.

Usell came to a halt on the third section of the 200 steps. The mist covered the vague outlines of the harbor beyond the plaza below. In following her father's words she had not thought about him. Find your mother, a mother who had other causes. A mother not wanting to nurture a child. What kind of mother is that? Why would her father want her to find that kind of mother?

With the lifting of the mist, citizens emerged from their hiding places and filtered onto the broad patios both above and below Usell.

As she reached the plaza, she stopped near two library lions resting sphinxlike in gray granite with half-opened eyelids. Guardians of the imposing library, reflecting an idea: a lion of intellect.

A rider on a white gelding stopped on the other side of the nearest lion. Lieutenant Yazukov. He pointed at a man in a black cloak.

Usell crouched in the shadowed side of the lion. The riderless man pulled his hood back.

"Did you find the girl?" Yazukov asked.

"She was not where the Grand Duke said she was."

"Search the streets," Yazukov said. He sat tall in his saddle and stretched his neck as he looked around the plaza.

Usell adjusted her hat, turned away, showing only the back of her head.

"What about the Grand Duke?" the man in the hood asked.

"Alexi sees plots everywhere. He protects himself. He has secreted the family to the palace outside Saint Petersburg. He will not be a Tsar that is as easy a target."

"Do they know the Grand Duke's complicity?"

"Alexi is no fool," Yazukov said. "Stay hidden. Your disguise lets you mingle amongst the rebels. Report to us. The girl will turn up."

"If I find her?"

"Rotovak still controls his men. If you find her, make sure she never gets away again."

Usell's muscles constricted.

Yazukov's gelding took its own head and rotated in a circle. Yazukov jerked it to obedience.

"Make sure the citizens understand the danger of the spirit world," he said. "Keep spreading the word that they haunt the harbor. It will keep them away."

The standing man pulled his hood back over his head.

Yazukov waved his arm in the air and kicked his gelding in the flank and it galloped up the 200 steps. The hooded man disappeared among the crowding citizens, who gawked at the blood pools marking the plaza and said prayers to the sky.

Usell closed her eyes and exhaled a long breath.

"Sir," a voice said from behind her said. A policeman on a gray mare approached. "Why are you crouched there?"

"I was headed to the library when the ghosts attacked."

"Jews have infected the library. It is closed."

Behind him, four hooded soldiers in black and silver uniforms descended the library steps. The soldiers dragged a struggling woman between them. Coniheutzski. He twisted to free himself, his sashes tangling in the soldiers' arms. One side of his face was flushed. His veils were gone and his hair frayed into an exploded ball of bristling twine.

"You cannot do this," he protested. "You know who I am? I have helped you. I have turned them over to you. I am a trusted agent."

Scuffling with the soldiers on the steps, he gained traction with his heels, making his bulk difficult to control. He twisted one arm free, jerked loose of their grips, and ran toward the Richelieu Stairs.

The soldiers grabbed him and yanked him back. As he struggled his eyes met Usell's.

"There." He pointed. His stumpy arm thrust at her.

The soldiers tried to twist him away.

"She's one of them," Coniheutzski said.

"This gentleman?" the policeman asked.

Usell leaned into the statue's shadow.

"He doesn't look like an unbeliever," the policeman said.

"I'm not," Usell said.

The soldiers struggled with Coniheutzski. "She is one of them, I tell you. Can't you tell? Just look at her."

The policeman's eyes blinked with disapproval. "I'm sorry, sir," he said to Usell. "Criminals always try to deflect attention from themselves."

"She is a girl," Coniheutzski squawked. "She is wanted. She is one of them. Let me go. There is a price on her head."

With a muscular jerk Coniheutzski broke free again. Just before reaching her, the soldiers grabbed him, but he yanked the Homburg from Usell's head, exposing her hair, revealing the whole of her face.

The soldiers dragged him onto the center of the plaza.

"You see," Coniheutzski said. "Look at her. Who has hair like that? Who has a face like that? She is one of them. Not me."

The policeman opened his pistol holster and drew his weapon.

"Why do you disguise yourself in this awful fashion?" he said.

"I am a citizen," Usell said. "I dress as I please."

"You'd better come with me," the policeman said.

Once again Coniheutzski freed himself from his captives and ran at Usell, yelling, "It's their fault. Blame them. Don't blame me. I'm a businessman."

The soldiers drew their weapons and fired. Bullets slammed into Coniheutzski, and with a surprised look on his face he pitched forward onto the stone plaza. A gruff-looking soldier with a square-set jaw pulled his hood back and marched to the corpse. He fired three more shots into Coniheutzski's back. The body jumped with each explosion. He holstered his pistol.

People in the plaza looked the other way.

"I have heard there are more of them in the Jewish section," a burgher with a red sash tie said.

186

"Out of the way," the policeman said. "Prisoner here. Out of the way."

A well-dressed woman wearing white broadcloth stepped forward and spat on Usell. "Curse you, you foul bitch."

A woman with a head of straw hair threw a rotten piece of fruit that smashed against Usell's forehead.

"It was she who witched my son. He has no voice. He cannot speak."

An old man raised a gnarled stick and brought it down on Usell's back. "Heathen liar."

Usell ducked her chin and pitched forward, her shoulder crashing into the man's chest. He stumbled back, and cried, "The Jew is trying to kill me."

Fists from the crowd pummeled Usell.

A merchant in a bloody apron said, "Set the devil to fire."

A group of middle-aged women, who followed along the edge of the crowd, closed around Usell like ants funneling into their nest.

"She is a whore," one said.

"Go back where you came from," another said.

A woman with a round pretty face and wide innocent eyes said, "You are the reason I have no money."

And then they all converged around Usell and pounded her about the head and shoulders until the policeman grew tired of their interference and pushed them off, shoved Usell through them, and beyond their reach.

40 . . .

The police officer kicked at Usell's back as he pushed her toward the harbor. The mist thickened. Despite visibility being only an arm's length, the clear-sensing horse pressed ahead until a breeze near the water swirled the vapors and lowered them closer to the ground. The policeman came to a halt on a wide avenue across from the docks. Ships of all sizes sunk deep in the water. Some oozed black smoke; others rocked against wavelets with folded sails. All waited for the midnight tide.

"Cross," the policeman said.

Usell dragged her feet across the avenue where a camp of blue uniformed soldiers gathered about a large open fire. Behind them, horizontal panels of cattle pens stretched the length of the avenue.

Faint voices strained against the crash of waves hitting the stone barriers separating land from sea. Faces on the other side of the pen glinted campfire light.

A soldier approached, a young man, his uniform soiled, the collar unclipped. A shock of blond hair fell across his forehead. It was the boy who had stared at Usell when she was held on the mezzanine in the palace. The azure longing in his eyes had been replaced with a dull hardened stare.

"Another one?" he asked.

The policeman shrugged. "What are you going to do with them all?"

"I don't know," the blond soldier said. He looked right through Usell.

"Give this one to your dandies," the policeman said. He reined his mare around, re-crossed the avenue, and did not look back.

The blond soldier grabbed Usell by the wrist and bound her hands behind her back.

"Please," she said. "There's been a mistake. Don't you remember me from the palace? Don't you know who I am?"

With his rifle gripped in both hands, the blond soldier shoved the stock of his weapon against her.

"Move," he said.

"I saw you look at me at the palace," Usell said. "You looked at me. We exchanged a fascination. We saw into each other. We traded looks . . . you remember?"

"Move along," he said.

"This is a mistake," Usell said. "You must help me. Didn't you see me dance with Captain Rotovak?"

A ghost of his innocence flashed in his eyes, but as quick as it appeared, it vanished to a film. "Keep moving," he said.

Stopping at the side of the pen, shadows of the captives took form in the mist. The faces looked gaunt. Sunken eyes stared at her.

Blank expressions without focus. Packed tight, they strained for space.

An older soldier approached the blond.

"There's no room," he said. "The gate is broken. We can't open it against the press of these parasites."

"How will we get her inside?" the young soldier said.

"I don't care. Throw her over the railing."

"Wait please," Usell pleaded. "Captain Rotovak. Dmitri Rotovak. He knows me."

The name caused the older man to step back. "How do you know the Cossack?" he asked.

"Remember me," she said to the young man. "We looked into each other's eyes and you worried for me. I saw it."

"You are mistaken," the blond man said.

"It's all a mistake," Usell said. "None of this should be happening."

"What would he know of a Jew," the older man said.

"You must tell Captain Rotovak that Emma is here," she said. "He'll reward you."

The young man's glazed eyes hardened to slits.

He ignored Usell's request and together he and the older soldier lifted Usell over the railing and threw her into the pen. In a twisting fall, her head smacked against a post and she remembered nothing after that.

Usell regained consciousness with her hands unbound. Her back leaned against the long boards of the horizontal fencing. It was dark. Cloudy. The mist lifted off the water and waves splattered against the seawall. Trying to stand, she slipped, splashed down in muck.

She pressed her hand on the back of her head and winced. Ghostly shapes moved in a low mist. She hardened against the fence when a slumped skeletal man spoke to someone on the other side.

"Why are you doing this to us? I have three children."

"We're looking for a woman," the invisible voice said.

"What do you want of us?"

"She's a woman who charms men, infects them. She is young."

"We have done nothing to harm you."

A spark exploded from the other side, the pistol shot echoing into the crash of waves. The skeletal man crumpled. Other shapes behind the downed man backed away and dissipated into the gray.

An athletic man in silhouette climbed over the fence and was followed by a thicker shadow with a grunting voice.

"Stinks in here," he said.

The two shades stomped in the muck to the bunched people standing waist deep in the mist. The heavyset man grabbed a prisoner by the throat, another by the hair, kicked a third in the groin, and asked questions.

"Do you see a woman?"

"Please, I have nothing to do with Jews."

The pistol fired again and a twisting body disengaged.

"This will get us nowhere," the fitter man said.

"The fog will lift in the morning. It'll be soon enough to find her."

"She may have been taken away with the women."

"Where?"

"Where soldiers find their comforts."

"Then we may yet find her alive."

"Let's get out of here. I don't want to be around when the ministry comes to clean up this mess. They ask too many questions."

The two clambered back over the fence.

Usell stood. She covered her nose. The soldiers' bonfire licked at the night.

"What do I do now, Father?" she asked. "What questions make sense to ask?"

A shadow on the ground moved toward her. "Usell. Usell, is that you? Do you hear me?"

"Father?"

The shadow, on his knees, crawled toward her.

She scrambled forward, stretched to a hand that grabbed for her. As soon as she clasped it the hand pulled her down.

He was wet. He was muddy. There was no Kippah on his matted hair. His cheeks strained to smile, but his lips and face were so bruised and swollen she choked back a cry.

"Moshe Gimmel. Moshe Gimmel."

She flung herself on him, wrapped him tight and held him close. His fragile voice croaked sounds she could not understand. He was cold, his skin sticky. She shrugged out of her camel hair long coat and pulled his arms into it one at a time.

Rolling him on his back, she set his head in her lap.

A briny wind whipped her face as she buttoned the coat around him.

"There, Moshe Gimmel," she said. "You are now a proper gentleman."

His eyes blinked. His body was without tension, and then she wrapped his head in her arms and rocked him back and forth.

41 . . .

Waves crashed against the rush of the Black Sea. Mist chilled her face and she cleansed Moshe Gimmel with torn scraps of Nikolayevna's blouse and her own spittle. If he was aware of what she was doing, he did nothing to stop her; he did not say it is not permitted. He did nothing but breathe.

The faint sound of galloping hooves clapped louder on pavement and then slowed, quieted to iron wheels on crunching gravel outside the pen near the soldiers' fire. A squeak of wood against wood mixed with the strains of leather bridles, and horses protesting the pull against their bits. Usell leaned Moshe Gimmel against the fence and stood to see.

Friesians tossed their wet stringy manes as their raiments rattled. Soldiers standing near the flame became statues as they stared at two columns of Cossacks dismounting around a white coach. A Princess's velvet curtains with golden tassels wavered in the carriage windows.

Cossacks – with tall braids erupting like coxcombs – formed a barrier around the coach. They pushed away the curious soldiers as if *they* were somehow intruders. A young palace guard wearing a cream-colored uniform jumped down from the driver's bench, opened the door, and backed away.

Rotovak's head and shoulders rose out of the carriage door. He wore his black uniform, grim-faced, no hat or helmet, his braid draped down his back. He surveyed the soldiers, the fire, the line of cattle pens, and then dropped from the vehicle into the mud.

"Where is the private?" his deep voice said.

The young blond soldier approached Rotovak and saluted.

"Where?" he barked.

The young man pointed to the pen.

"Give the boy a commission," Rotovak said.

"Sir." Lieutenant Yazukov dismounted his white gelding. "The boy is a conscript from the Pale."

"Lieutenant. I am still captain of this guard."

Six Cossacks carrying torches pulled open the broken gate and tromped into the pen, pushed through the thinned remains of shadows who formed the border shading Rotovak's marching path.

Usell set her shoulders, faced the captain, caught his gaze as it focused across the torchlights, and locked onto her.

He marched past the captives, through his Cossacks, his black leather boots splashing, his shashka sword slapping against his thigh. Reaching her, his hard stare weakened as her eyes defied him.

"You have offended the princess," Rotovak said. "You fled the palace."

"You confine me."

"For your own protection."

"A strange way to show concern," she said.

"My way."

"I do not like it," Usell said.

Moshe Gimmel moaned and she knelt to him.

"What are you doing?"

"It's the boy from the train," she said.

She set Moshe Gimmel upright against the fence.

"What is this leech to you?" Rotovak asked.

"He is who I am."

Rotovak put his hand to his shashka.

"Dmitri. No. Don't hurt him," she said.

"You love him?"

"Dmitri," she said. "He is like me. We are the same. Harming him harms me."

Rotovak glanced back at the carriage. "This is obscene," he said. "The Okhrana are amongst us."

"What do they want?"

"They obey orders."

"Whose?"

"Now is not the time. Come." He took her arm.

She shook loose.

"I will not leave him."

Rotovak's shoulders slumped. "You must leave here." He turned back toward the carriage. "None here will survive."

"Then I die with them," she said.

Rotovak drew a long breath.

"Bring the new lieutenant here," Rotovak said to a private.

A Cossack with a thick black mustache and brows to match broke formation and raced through the gate.

"This conscript will have to do," Rotovak said. "He was probably taken from a village like yours when he was young."

On the run, holding a serviceable saber against his leg, the young blond in a lieutenant's jacket approached. Stopping short with a salute, he glanced at Usell and then back to Rotovak.

"Sir," he said.

"You see this man lying here," Rotovak said.

The blond lieutenant's nostrils twitched. "The Jew."

Usell stepped between his look and Moshe Gimmel.

"Your first act as an officer," Rotovak said, "must be with complete obedience. Do you understand?"

"I will honor my appointment as I honor our Lord Jesus," the blond boy said.

"What shtetl are you from?" Usell asked.

The young man's eyes shifted from Rotovak to Usell.

With a glare from Rotovak, the young man straightened his back and saluted.

"What are your orders, sir?" he said.

"Guard this boy with your life. Let nothing happen to him. Further instructions will follow."

The blond lieutenant's eyes worried. "I will stand my post, sir."

Usell knelt to Moshe Gimmel. Rotovak gripped her arm. She brushed his fingers and he released her. She bent to Moshe Gimmel's ear.

"Listen to me, Moshe Gimmel," she whispered. "I know you hear me. Do not move. I'll find a way. Have faith in me. Do not die."

His closed eyes squeezed tight and she stood back up.

With Rotovak at her side, she marched through his Cossacks, passed the prisoners, out the gate, through the barrier of bunching soldiers, right toward Ludivica, who stood outside the carriage and held a handkerchief over her nose.

"Someone clean this place up," she said.

The wind whipped Usell's blouse. Her short hair slapped wet muck against her neck. Ludivica, seeing Usell, jumped in the air, dropped her handkerchief, and ran with open arms. The collision with Usell bumped them both into Rotovak's chest.

"I am lonely. You must never leave me again," Ludivica said.

Then she pushed away from Usell.

"My God, you're cold and . . . filthy. You stink. Where did you get these clothes? You're hurt. Bruises. What happened to your hair? What did these criminals do to you? Why were you put in there?"

"It was . . .."

"Look what they've done to you," Ludivica said. "I will fix them. They will not escape the wrath of the empire."

She whirled around. "Captain," she said. "Dispatch these bloodsucking Liliths."

Rotovak spoke in a whisper. "If we start now, they will panic and bolt. Some will escape. We have not yet finished rounding up all of them. The army will arrive tomorrow and we will finish it."

"You haven't got them all?" Ludivica asked.

"They are like weeds, they've spread everywhere," Rotovak said.

"What incompetent fool did you put in charge?" she said. She stamped her white boot in the sticky mud. "I will speak to him."

"Speak with the Okhrana officer in charge." He nodded direction.

Lieutenant Yazukov turned as Ludivica, holding up the hem of her gown, charged toward him. "Lieutenant," she said. "Lieutenant. I'm going to have your head."

A squint, appearing like a quick smile, twitched in Rotovak's cheek.

Usell took Rotovak's arm.

"Dmitri. Where is Rudd Cothman?" she asked.

His scar knotted. "Be careful, Usell Binah. I gave you a life. Let that be enough."

"What do you want, Dmitri?" Usell asked.

194

"You know what I want."

"Give me the American."

"He has connections to the foreign ministry. He is under my guard. Here." He jerked his head behind the carriage. "We are releasing him. He is to leave the country, never to return."

"Release him now. I must say good-bye," she said.

Rotovak lifted his chin.

"Please," she said. "Do not frown so, Dmitri. I have said I am for you."

"Bring the American," Rotovak ordered without taking his eyes from her.

As Ludivica screeched and Lieutenant Yazukov backed away, a Cossack corporal – senior in years to the captain – shoved Rudd Cothman toward them. He was manacled again, wrists to ankles, hair in his face, bruised and dirty.

With a nod from Rotovak, the corporal keyed the irons loose and dragged them off.

"Thugs," Rudd said. He rubbed his wrist against his jaw and then met Rotovak's gaze.

"Dmitri," Usell said. "I need a moment."

Rotovak filled his chest and then reverse to his Cossacks.

Rudd pinched Usell's chin, turned her face to the side.

"He do that to you?"

"Listen to me, Rudd Cothman," she said. "You must help me."

"Your Cossack ordered me out of the country."

"Can you get word to your ship?"

"What do you want?" he asked.

"I want to free these people."

"Okay, Queen Moses," he said. "How are you going to do that?"

"I can barter for them."

"No one can release them. Not even your Cossack."

"The princess can," Usell said.

"You're going to get yourself killed."

She leaned close to his neck.

"You said I'm too pretty to kill."

"You're crazy." He shook his head.

"Will you help me?" she asked.

"These people are already in God's hands."

"I'm putting them in mine," she said.

Rudd filled his cheeks. His exhale clouded her face with hot breath in the chilled air. He glanced over his shoulder at the prisoners and took her hands in his. "You need bigger hands than these."

"Will you help me?"

"I'll come back with *Utto,*" he said.

"And your gun?"

His mouth twitched.

"I'll meet you here around midnight," she said. "I'll wait for you, but if I don't show up, have your ship take them." She nodded at the pen. "Use your gun for something good."

"And what do I get for that?" he asked.

"I have what you want."

"Don't tempt me." He leaned close to her.

She blinked and then blinked again.

"No," she said. "I meant I have something else."

"Nothing as valuable, I assume."

With her face still flushed, Rotovak strode back, leading a Spanish Dorado. Usell stepped away. Rotovak's glare focused on Rudd.

"You are an enemy of the Tsar," Rotovak said. "You should be hanged."

"But your superiors are more practical," Rudd said.

"Let him leave, Dmitri," Usell said.

"Go," Rotovak said. "I don't wish to see you again."

Mounting the Dorado, Rudd said, "Captain."

Rotovak lifted his chin.

"Take care of her."

And then Rudd kicked the stallion in the flanks and the Dorado's iron shoes beat an echo into the city night.

42 . . .

Rotovak leaned into the cabin as Usell seated herself next to Ludivica.

"Beat these horses to my doctor," Ludivica said. "My sister is hurt."

"We will hurry, Princess," Rotovak said. He closed the door.

She drew the curtains and hunched to a ball.

"I am in trouble," she said.

"What has happened?" Usell took her hands.

"I have lost my diamond. If the Tsar finds out, he will send me to his brothels."

Usell rubbed her chin against the jewel's chain. Outside the carriage Rotovak ordered the driver to go and the coach lurched. Friesians strained to a gallop and hooves echoed through the streets.

"I've looked everywhere. I don't know where I put it," she said.

"Delay the wedding. Give us time to find it."

"I'll be hanged for treason."

"You could say you are ill," Usell said.

"Yes. I can have Adrianna attest to it. I can say the Jews put a spell on me."

Swaying lantern shadows brushed Ludivica's cheek. Her jawline gathered an edge, the lower lip pooched with gloom.

"I will string their entrails from border to border for stealing my jewel," Ludivica said.

Usell withdrew her hands to her lap.

Upon arriving at the doctor's office, Ludivica said, "I can't bear to see your wounds. I will stay in the carriage."

Rotovak opened the door and marched with Usell inside a one-story building with a flat roof. The pedestrian office held a desk, a chair, medical books on shelves, and a long bench of dark-toned oak that shined in the pale gaslight. A certificate in a frame from the Heidelberg Institute hung on a wall.

The doctor in shirtsleeves stood up from behind his desk. A stethoscope dangled around his thick neck. With a snarl on his lips, the speckle-skinned man with gray bushy hair washed his hands in a pan of water.

When he approached, Usell curled away from him and clenched her blouse to hide the jewel.

Rotovak folded his arms and watched every movement the doctor made as he examined Usell's cuts and bruises without touching her.

"There's nothing seriously wrong with her," the doctor said. "Except her birthright."

"You will shut your mouth and do your business," Rotovak said.

"I'll not be party to this. Bringing Jews to my office. Do you know who I am? Do you think I don't know what is going on? You do as you wish. I don't care. I even approve. Just do it and say no more. Don't bring them here for care. They are not my problem."

The doctor puffed his chest and set his shoulders.

Rotovak slapped the doctor across the cheek, grabbed the collar at the back of his neck, spun him around, and with a fist full of the man's britches, he half carried the doctor to the door and heaved him into the street like a sack of grain.

"You will say nothing of this," Rotovak said.

From his hands and knees the Doctor said, "You'll pay for that, Cossack. You don't frighten me. I have friends in high places who have the ear of your masters."

Rotovak slammed the door.

"He knew I was a Jew?" Usell said.

"The herd panics. They run in any direction. It's impossible to control."

"Whose fault is that?"

"There must be order," Rotovak said.

The room smelled of alcohol and a hint of fresh varnish.

"Why are you involved in this?"

"I'm a product of order," Rotovak said.

"Is that who you are?"

"It is my duty to control."

"Yes, I see," she said. "I saw you there in Oylaif too. Don't deny it. You were part of it. You led the charge. My father's village."

His chin firmed and his stance withdrew.

"So this is pretense," he said.

"What about my father? Your debt?"

"You do not know what you saw in Oylaif."

"What did I see?" she asked.

"You saw a man preserving his position, nothing more. I knew it was your father's village and I wished to find him, warn him, save him, but I was too late."

"You allowed it to happen. You have men at your command."

"If I did as you ask, they would no longer be under my command."

Usell leaned away from him. "I don't believe you."

"The princess must marry the Prussian. After that Yevgeny will be in charge. Her need is all that keeps me present."

"You could do something to save my people," she said.

"I am Cossack. I am what I am. The Okhrana decides their fate."

"While you stand by."

"I can protect you," Rotovak said. "You are no real threat to them and I can get you out with the princess. You need only continue being Emma."

"But I'm not Emma," she said. "I'm tired of denying who I am. It betrays my heritage."

"To hell with your heritage. Say nothing and the princess will protect you after you're gone."

Medical books were stacked and bound in lizard-like leather, each with gold inlay along the spine, looking the same on the outside, distinguished only by their different gold markings.

Her eyes watered.

Rotovak folded his arms across his chest. "You cannot expect me to commit treason."

"Pay your debt to my father," she said.

"I told you. I decide how I repay my debts."

"Then we have nothing further to say to each other," she said. "I will find a way to persuade the princess to help me."

"She will not help you. She cannot overcome her ignorance or her hatreds and I cannot help you beyond what I've said. When the Tsar was killed, I was in charge. All those involved in any way are being purged. I have heard that I am to be court-martialed. I'll be sent to Saint Petersburg after the princess gets on the train to the German."

Usell sat up. "Then help me. I'm the only one loyal to you."

Rotovak folded his arms across his chest. "You want that boy or the American."

"I will stand by you, Dmitri, no matter what happens. I honor my word."

"Honor, but not for love," he said.

"I am here, Dmitri. I am yours. What more do you want?"

"To be done with sacrifices," he snapped.

Whatever strength she had left gave way. First a single tear rolled down her cheek. Her eyes filled at the corners. They dripped, and then unleashed a flood that became splatters on the floor.

Rotovak huffed, but when it continued, he touched her back.

Her sobs shook her shoulders.

He knelt, leaned against her, and held her hair to his chest.

"Stop," he said. "Please stop. I cannot bear it."

He kissed her hands and when Ludivica opened the door she stormed into the room right to them. Kneeling next to the Cossack, Ludivica shouted at him.

"What have you done? What have you done to make her cry?"

43 . . .

Back at the palace Rotovak gave orders and Cossacks hovered about Usell like a swarm of bees protecting their queen.

"If you are taken again," Rotovak said, "it will cost many lives."

"Where is the Grand Duke?" Usell asked him. "He knows who I am."

"He is no longer important. Alexi is not stupid. Anyone he suspects is handled. In the Grand Duke's case he will be sent to the winter palace surrounded by especially selected men who will bury him when he dies on that land."

The Cossacks marched Usell and Ludivica through the deserted corridors of the palace in a wordless parade of echoing boots. A faint smell of smoke hugged the air. All traces of ball gaiety were gone and in its place were shadowed walls, sycophantic servants, and sentries posted at every turn.

At her bedroom door Ludivica clasped Usell's arm, and dragged her away from Rotovak.

Ludivica ordered her servants to bring liquor and then drank vodka and chattered as if everything was as it should be.

"After the wedding my prince is to study the martial arts," she said. "You will come with me. We will travel, you and I. There will be opportunity for us both to find lovers. It's what they do in Europe." She gulped down the contents of the glass.

"What will your Prince say to that?" Usell asked.

"Why should he care? He is a child. How would he know?"

"He is a man, and jealous of possessions like other men."

Ludivica's thin shoulders shrugged; the gesture loosened a curl of rusty hair from ribboned coils. She crossed her glossy jade eyes to observe the strands tickling down the bridge of her nose. Shaking her head she closed her eyes and said, "Do you love me?"

"Of course, Ludivica." Usell said.

Ludivica leaped off the sofa and wrapped her arms around Usell.

"I love you, too. I grant you a wish."

"A wish?"

"Yes. Anything you want. Diamonds, furs, I can give you servants."

"Release those people penned at the docks," Usell said.

Ludivica stepped back. Shadows hardened her jawline. Her manner, so distracted moments before, sobered and grew rigid. Trained to speak as a Romanov and divined by birth to decide life and death, she said, "You are tired. Being held with the Jew has addled your brain. If you are unwell, you cannot come with me to my Uncle's funeral where my prince will meet with me and take us to our new home."

She yanked a purple ribbon by the bed.

"You must get some rest," she said. "You must think the thoughts that all of us think. The right thoughts."

~*~~*~

Two budding female servants escorted Usell to another bedroom. Six Cossacks followed. They sentried the door.

The room was freshened with a white lily in an Italian renaissance vase. A brooding portrait of a young vibrant Grand Duke, a man afraid of nothing, stared down from the wall. His stance exuded poise, a vision of strength coupled with the right to make demands. She wondered how his hatreds would manage locked up in a palace with guards around him.

Usell turned down the gas flames. She sat down at the three-mirrored vanity. In front of the center mirror was a brush, depilatories, white powder, beeswax, and a lip salve in a tin labeled Spermaceti. On the corner of the vanity was a framed dry plate photograph of two young women in riding gear. Brown-toned, their gloved hands reached across to one another. They stared at the camera without smiles. They were same women in the portrait on the wall that Adrianna said were the Duchess and her consort. One of the women's eyes strained as though uncomfortable. Either could have been Nikolayevna more than a decade and a half younger.

Usell lifted the frame.

"Which of you is my mother?" she asked. "Is this the fiction my mind creates? Is this what my father wants me to understand?"

Her thumb brushed the photograph. Shadows danced against the windows. Yellow moonlight caught glass and reflected the precise order of the bedroom.

Usell removed her clothing, removed the diamond, and set it on the table. With a basin of fresh water, soap, and towels she washed herself. Opening the large wardrobe, she selected a white silk robe from the cabinet, concealed the diamond, and yanked the purple ribbon beside the poster bed.

When the young servants appeared, Usell said, "Please have the princess's matron, Adrianna, come to me."

With glances at each other the young servants disappeared and in a short time Adrianna knocked at her door and entered.

"Do you wish to pray?" she asked.

"What happened to the Grand Duchess on the parapet?"

"I was not there."

Usell held up the framed dry plate. "Which is she?"

"It has been a long time," Adrianna said. "They looked like sisters."

"Who?"

"The duchess and usurper. Neither liked me. One's influence dominated the other."

"This one?" Usell pointed at the woman with the part down the center of her scalp.

"I don't remember."

"Whose bedroom was this?"

"The usurpers."

"Vera Figner?" Usell asked.

Adrianna shrugged.

"When you leave," Usell said, "would you have the servants tell Captain Rotovak to attend these chambers on the hour?"

With lifted eyebrows that said *it is not permitted*, Adrianna left.

44 . . .

As the sixth hour chimed, there were two raps on the door.

"Enter," Usell said.

Rotovak stepped inside the unlocked door. Dressed all in black—blouse to boot—his hand rested on the hilt of his shashka. A curl troubled his brow when he stepped into the soft candlelight.

Usell faced a mirror behind a black screen in the corner. She met his eyes in the reflection and lifted a red silk robe over her nakedness.

"I will come back," he said.

"No, Dmitri. Stay."

He glanced at the broad sprawling bed. The sheets and covers were turned down.

"The servant said you wished to see me," he said.

Closing the robe, she walked to him with a sway in her hips.

"I wanted to be alone with you," she said.

His braid slipped off his shoulder.

"The jewel," he said.

It hung around her neck and between the high seams of the robe.

"The princess was drinking," Usell said. "She does not remember where she put it."

"Alexi will crucify you both."

"Is that what you wish to happen to me?"

Rotovak frowned.

"Keep the jewel," he said.

"What about the princess's dowry, the alliance?"

"It no longer matters to me."

"Do I matter?" she asked.

"Think what you want."

He glanced out the windows to the balcony and moonlight.

"Was your kiss a lie?" she asked.

"It was just a kiss."

"And your words. Were they also lies?"

"What is it you want now?" he asked.

She turned away. "Never mind."

"You called me here. What do you want?"

She faced him. "I want to be back in my garret with my father watching over me."

"I've dismissed the guards," he said. "You can go whenever you want. I left my stallion at the south gate. Behind the opera house at the docks there is a small boat tethered to the end of the longest peer. Take it and go. With the tide there'll be many ships. Someone will pick you up."

"I can't abandon my people," she said. "Help me."

"I can do nothing. You would need an army."

"I need only you." She stepped close to him.

"Don't trifle with me," he said. "I've thought of nothing else for the past three days."

She slipped the nightgown off her shoulders.

"Then help me."

"You play with me like cat's yarn," he said.

"Prove you have a heart I can count on."

Rotovak held himself in his soldier's stance, rigid, tall.

"You are a child," he said. "Your games will not succeed and you will lose your innocence in the offing."

"You have no feelings for me?"

"I do not trust feelings."

"Trust this, then," she said.

She grabbed his entwined braid and tugged his head to her mouth and kissed him. His neck muscles corded and a growl rumbled in his throat. Gripping her waist, he lifted her without effort and threw her onto the bed.

Stripping off his sword and his clothes, he kicked out of his boots and reared over her.

The white canopy above the four sturdy posts of the bed fluttered in a draft. A terrible cold swirled around the room.

"No," she said. "I can't."

She lurched up.

His hand clamped her neck, pressed her back to the mattress. On his knees between her legs, he spread her. She twisted her neck.

"Let me go."

His grip hardened.

"If you do this against my will . . ."

"You must fight me," he said.

Positioning himself, he pressed forward.

She slapped at his face and pushed her palms against his chest. Her arms bent at the elbow as he lowered himself. She pounded his shoulders, hit at his head. He did not even flinch. Grabbing her ankles he pushed her knees to her shoulders, pressed down.

"No," she cried.

Holding her in position, he elevated himself and plunged into her.

Usell's half-stifled cry rolled into a guttural swallow.

The assaults began; each ram produced a sound from her she could not control, each withdrawal caught in a breath. She closed her eyes, clenched her teeth, girded herself against the next onslaught. His body was hard and heavy and each thrust slammed into her with the force of a blow. No escape. No escape. She opened her eyes and focused on the canopy above.

White muslin waved and shuttered with the shaking of the bedposts. The insect veils about the sides of the bed fell to the floor and goose feathers crackled with the compression of her body weighing on them.

And then Rotovak's shoulders trembled. The celerity of withdrawals and plunges diminished. On his knees he tilted his head back. He released his grip on her and strained every muscle in his body.

Usell turned her head aside and closed her eyes. A gush of warmth flushed her abdomen.

When his weight collapsed on top of her, she held her breath. The white canopy billowed in the hidden breeze and then it waved like fleeing ghosts. The bowl of linen took back its shape above the bed.

Rotovak did not move.

She squirmed to free herself. His hand gripped her shoulder.

"You are weak," he said. "The hunter knows to take the weakest."

"Get off of me," she said.

His head lifted. His eyes seemed to recoil. She twisted from beneath the hand at her shoulder.

"I am not a thing you have power over," she said.

"It is the Cossack way," he said. "The heart, mind, and body at war."

"Mine are not," she said.

"You don't understand," he said. He backed off the bed.

Usell pressed to her elbows.

He turned away.

"Cleanse yourself," he said.

Jelly worms of blood marked the sheet. Marked her thighs.

Usell rolled over. With a gasp, she clenched her teeth, bit the coverlet, and then rose. Dragging it behind the screen she washed her wound and robed herself.

"This is what comes of folly," Rotovak said.

"Is that what it is?" she said. "Folly?"

"Now you have no worth except to me," he said. "I have possessed you. I own you."

She turned around and stared at him.

"It is the way," he said. "You are no longer new."

"I am the same as I ever was," she said. "An action against me has been done, but I am still who I am."

"No. You're not. To others you are not."

"Then let me tell you this," she said. "I am enough myself that the next time you treat me like this either I will be dead or you will."

He stepped back.

"It is the Cossack way."

"Not my way," she said.

His shoulders shook. His thick unraveling braid spread across his front to his thighs. Looking at his feet, he said, "I have been taught to feel nothing. I had a wife. She was with child and I brought her to my major as proof my request was true: a delay of my orders so I might witness the birth of a Cossack. He did not like my Cossacks or me. He said *Duty waits for nothing.* And then he drew his saber and thrust. I turned to my wife's cry. The major's blade cut straight through her bulging abdomen and split her spine. *There,* the Major said. *Now there is nothing for you to witness.* I have felt nothing until I saw you."

Rotovak's head sagged. He hung like a black shadow in the silent candlelight fumes.

Usell clenched the jewel, felt each facet in her hand.

"We will find peace together," she said.

45 . . .

Within moments of Rotovak's leaving, Usell collapsed on the bed. She compressed her body into a knot. Something convulsed in her chest. It took her into herself and welled up in her eyes. Memories flooded back in waves of cold and timeless winter. She could hear the shofar calling the men of Oylaif to Sabbath prayer. They left their homes in their black rekels and shtreimel hats and she remembered how she hurried about her duties, preparing a meal for her father's return and yearning to get back to her reading while the women of the community tended their children.

Canopy linen fluttered. Wind and tide would come and go.

"I'm sorry, Father," she said. "I'm sorry I am disobedient."

Pressing up, the half hour chimed through the palace. The portrait of the Grand Duke on the wall stood frozen in the artist's invention of power and glory. The chime echoed through the halls. The walls vibrated.

She hopped off the bed and rubbed her palms together.

"I will get you out, Moshe Gimmel," she said. "I will come for you and get you out. And I will read again."

At the wardrobe she selected tight-stitched, musty clothing: loose-fitting pants, a black blouse, a woolen seal-oiled jacket. Inspecting herself in the mirror, she noted that every line fit. Her feet filled the sturdy boots. She brushed the hair from her face.

"Whoever you were," she said, "I replace you."

Retrieving the mezuzah, she slipped it in her pants pocket and tucked the diamond beneath her blouse before wrapping a long gray cape around her shoulders.

Rotovak knocked twice and when she opened the door, the Captain stood erect and splendid in his black uniform, the single red stripe on his shoulder. He inspected her like she was one of his privates and then entered without her acceptance.

Removing a revolver from his belt, he said, "This is a British weapon, an Adams double action revolver. Hold it like this." He put her hand on the grip. "All you have to do is pull the trigger and it will fire. Aim for the largest part of the target. Don't think of consequences. If you do not slay the predator, it will eat you alive."

She stared at the offered gun.

"We have to get you to safety. You will ride my black. He will break through the mobs of the street. They attack anyone not with them. Okhrana are stirring the pot. They round up those without proper papers. They have orders, but we will make the pier before the tide. I will stay behind and protect your retreat."

"No," she said. "I have a different plan."

His shoulders tightened. "You cannot . . ."

"We will get Nikolayevna Fillipova from captivity and she will fight the empire with her rebels. Create a distraction."

"For what?"

She touched his collar. "We will have more time together."

"You would make me a traitor," he said.

"Would you like to witness the birth of your child?"

Rotovak bunched his brow. His eyes watched hers lock on him. Coming to attention, he bowed. "Your servant, Mademoiselle," he said.

She slipped the British gun into her waistband.

They exited onto the balcony and she walked by Rotovak's side around the stone railing.

The black harbor tossed whitecaps from a stormy sea. Rotovak's shashka slapped his thigh. A cocked pistol stuck out of his open-flapped holster. At each post soldiers in brown uniforms saluted. Rotovak returned the salutes with a snap and the soldiers' obedient eyes stared straight ahead.

Entering the burnt-out ballroom, they marched up the curving staircase to the mezzanine and then toward the front doors.

Coming from beneath the stairs, Ludivica and her palace guards marched to the base of the stairs. Six boys in their cream colors and heavy gold braid formed a wishbone around her. She dressed in court nightwear, a tight-fitting jacket over a pants-skirt to the floor.

"Let me do the talking," Rotovak whispered.

"No," Usell said. "You wait here."

Before he could say another word, Usell ran down the stairs to Ludivica and threw her arms around the accepting princess.

"I am so sorry," Usell said. "My mind has been affected, but now I know what my heart feels."

"Yes. Yes," Ludivica said. "We must care for each other. I have come looking for you. I did not mean to be angry. You have suffered."

Rotovak signaled the six boy guards to hold where they stood and ushered the women to a nook in the wall. The sculpted head of a horned fury leaned over them.

"Princess Melikova," Rotovak said. "You should not be out."

"I'll do as I please," she said. "What are you doing with my Emma?"

Usell leaned in front of Rotovak.

"I have learned that the rebel leader who mistreated me is in your prison," she said. "I am going to confront her."

"You must ask my permission for that," Ludivica said.

"I did not want to trouble you. I asked the captain to take me."

"Yes. You would ask *him*," Ludivica said.

"I must purify my soul," Usell said.

"Yes. Yes. Purify their poison. We are so much alike."

Ludivica hooked Usell's arm and with lightness in her step pulled Usell away from Rotovak. He hurried after them.

"You should dress like this more often," Ludivica said. "We could appear as a couple."

Rotovak caught them.

"Princess," he said. "The hour is late. You must be ready to travel in the morning."

"I will go with you to the prisoner," Ludivica said.

"It is too dangerous for you," Rotovak said. "The rebels are still a threat. What if an attempt is made to rescue their leader?"

"Dmitri," Usell said. "The princess can do as she pleases. She represents the Tsar. No one questions her authority."

"I'm going and that's that," Ludivica said.

She lifted the hem of her split gown, bent over to a high-topped boot, and patted a black-handled pistol tucked neatly into a sheath of the leather. "I can protect myself. I will go."

"We must leave now," Rotovak said. "You are not dressed for the weather."

The princess snatched Usell's cape and swirled it about her.

"Now I am ready," she said. "Won't this be fun, Emma? You and me on an adventure."

She squinted at Rotovak. "Draw my carriage."

"I have horses waiting," Rotovak said.

"I wish to travel in my carriage."

"Ludivica, my friend," Usell said. "You must depend upon your Captain's knowledge and experience."

"Oh, all right, Dmitri," Ludivica said. "We'll do it your way. Perhaps after the Jew recants, we can ride to the port and drown the rest of them in the high tide."

In front of the palace they mounted three black Arabian stallions that pawed the wet pavement and snorted steam.

"You already have three horses here," Ludivica said.

"Your Captain anticipates your every thought," Usell said.

After helping Ludivica onto her mount, Rotovak led Usell to his black.

"My stallion is trained by me," Rotovak said. He patted the shiny snout. "He is obedient, but do not wave your hands in front of him or he will rear and bolt."

"Yes," she said. "He did that at the trough in Oylaif."

"That was you? I wondered what caused his rebellion."

In one motion he hefted Usell into the stallion's saddle. Once mounted, Rotovak pointed toward the city and they galloped into the darkness, the princess and Usell catching up with him before he left the grounds.

46 . . .

They rode hard from the palace down the sloping road into the city. The clatter of hooves ricocheted off the city buildings. Dull lantern light inside the homes passed in shadow glimmers. The Arabian beneath Usell raced on moonlit cobbles as she concentrated on controlling its muscled strides.

Once at the outskirts of Odessa Rotovak reined close to Usell and slowed. "Keep your eye on the princess and keep that pistol handy."

"I'm not going to shoot the princess," Usell said.

Rotovak looked at her as if she were a disobedient private, but then instead of a withering challenge he urged his stallion between the two of them.

Following the eastern edge of the city, the black harbor melted into the flashing starlight as the three galloped across a wide basalt plateau covered with camel grasses. Rotovak raised his hand to slow and then angled his stallion down a winding path leading over the moat of a walled castle.

"The prison at Sverdlovo," he said. "Most of the soldiers guarding the prison were sent to stop the massing rebels I reported."

At the entrance they stopped before an iron honeycomb gate.

"Who goes there?" a guard behind it said.

"Princess Ludivica Melikova," Rotovak said. "Here to interrogate a prisoner. Open immediately."

Two men leaned on the gate; one lifted a torch, the other keeper hid under an overlapping hood. The torchbearer stuck his head through the iron crossbars to get a better look. Half of his front teeth were broken or missing. Rotovak approached with his hand resting on the grip of his shashka.

"How do we know it's her?" Broken-Tooth whispered.

"She has a Cossack with her," the hooded man said.

"Where is her escort? She would not come without an escort."

Ludivica pressed her stallion forward. "Open the gate before I have the gallows readied for each of you."

"We must be sure there are no Jews with you," Broken-Tooth said.

"Do we look like Jews?" Ludivica said. She lifted Rotovak's braid and pushed Usell forward into the torchlight.

With just a brief look at each other, the two gatekeepers scurried into the shadows and turned a wooden sprocket, the counterbalance rattling and raising the gate.

The stallions stomping hooves echoed through the thick Romanesque archway to an open stone courtyard. The broken-toothed gatekeeper with his hooded companion ran into the yard behind them.

"It is a great honor, princess," Broken-Tooth said. Both gatekeepers bowed before Usell. Ludivica kicked her boot at Broken-Tooth's head, hitting his shoulder, knocking him down. He scrambled up and hid behind the other.

Ludivica dismounted. With a short whip in her hand, she swung at Broken-Tooth before she was even close. He ducked away, the blows landing on the hooded man, who closed his eyes and allowed the blows, one and another.

"We don't have time for this," Rotovak said. "You." He pointed at the broken-toothed gatekeeper. "Take us to the rebel leader's cell."

With a nod Broken-Tooth scrambled toward an arched entryway. Usell brought up the rear, with Ludivica behind Rotovak.

"Peasants," Ludivica said. "I hate peasants. They have no education."

Down stone stairways they followed the screw of wet steps. It smelled of algae and age. Crawling things skittered from the torchlight. At the landing of each floor withered skeletons hung like decayed fruit from iron arms and disintegrating hemp.

They descended five flights. On a broad basin floor of cut stone, concentric rings ended at a circular wall bordering the open space. Doors with square openings separated the cells every few meters. Drilled into the walls between the doors were iron shackles with open cuffs. A bellowed furnace smoked with white-hot coals, its heat pulsing off the walls.

Ludivica clasped the cape over her nose.

A man stepped from the shadows. "Who are you?"

"Are you the guardian of this sty?" Rotovak snapped.

"I am the chief jailer," he said.

The man wore no shirt over his rotund gut. He had a bald pointed head and collected the bullwhip in swollen red hands. His bony forehead dripped sweat. Without warning he snapped a whip in the air in front of the gatekeeper.

"Who are they?" he repeated.

"They're here to see the rebel prisoner," Broken-Tooth said.

"On whose authority?"

"It is the Princess . . ." He held out his hand toward Usell.

"No one sees the prisoner without written orders," the jailer said.

"Ready," Rotovak whispered. His hand reached for his pistol.

"This is ridiculous," Ludivica said. "Dmitri, give the man gold and be done with him."

She pulled a bowed sack from her pocket. Rotovak took it and threw it at the jailer's feet.

The jailer closed one eye, bent over, picked up the sack, and hefted it in his palm.

"I have business in the upper cells," he said. "Return my keys to the hook. She is in number five."

He disappeared into the rising staircase.

The gatekeeper lifted a key ring off a peg and pointed at the cell halfway around the circle.

Ludivica marched to the furnace and removed a hot iron poker from its embers. "We will make her squeal," she said.

"Alexi has ordered her intact," Rotovak said.

Ludivica shrugged. She dropped the poker into a puff of white-hot ash. The gatekeeper slipped the key into an iron lock, turned it and with the screech of the bolt he yanked the scraping door open.

Usell was first inside.

"Nikolayevna," she whispered.

Rotovak entered with a torch and the bloom of light sprayed the darkness of a windowless stone cell. Nikolayevna crouched against the wall, her mannish garments soiled and her feet naked. Her scowl was as threatening as a cornered animal.

"Get up," Rotovak said. "Hurry."

Ludivica's tentative step into the cell was followed by complaint. "Dmitri, it's horrible in here. It smells."

"Gatekeeper," Rotovak called.

The broken-toothed man shuffled to the center of the cell with his head bowed. He glanced about, a worried twitch in one eye.

"What have you done with my jewel, Jew?" Ludivica asked.

Nikolayevna glanced at Usell.

Rotovak drew his shashka from its scabbard and slammed the pommel against the gatekeeper's head. He crumpled to the floor.

Nikolayevna stood up next to Usell, eyed the pistol in her waistband.

"Go," Rotovak said.

"Dmitri, what's the meaning of this?" Ludivica asked.

Rotovak's sword crossed in front of her.

"Do not interfere, Princess," Rotovak said.

She stared at the double-edged blade blocking her movement.

"You threaten me? You dare to threaten me?"

Rotovak nodded Nikolayevna toward the door.

"The Tsar's army will arrive by sea in the morning," Rotovak said. "Mass your rebels near the port if you wish to trap them there."

Ludivica bent to her boot and removed her pistol.

"No," Usell said and pushed her arm. The pistol fired. Rotovak twisted to the wall and slid down it. The torch tumbled to the cell floor and ignited matchsticks of damp straw. Flames fizzled and died.

Nikolayevna grabbed the revolver from Usell's waist and slapped it on the back of Ludivica's skull. The princess collapsed on top of the broken-toothed guard.

Bending over her, Nikolayevna tore open the tie of her cape and searched her neck.

"Where is the jewel?" Nikolayevna said.

Usell knelt over Rotovak. He opened his eyes. She pressed her hand over his bleeding forehead. He opened his eyes. "Go," he said. "Just go."

"No," she said. "Let me help you."

His head lolled to the side. His eyes closed.

Nikolayevna removed the princess's cape, wrapped it around her shoulders, and pulled the hood over her head. She sniffed it and then she grabbed Usell by her collar.

"Come on," she said. "There's nothing you can do."

Dragging her out of the cell, Nikolayevna led them up the winding stone stairwell and to the landing inside an arched entry to the courtyard where she stopped and hid in the shadows.

47 . . .

In open moonlight surrounded by flaring torches the paunchy jailer cursed and shouted at the hooded gatekeeper and another bulky man in a long peasant robe and a club in his hand.

"Did you see written orders?" the paunchy jailer said.

"The princess was with them."

"How do you know it was the princess?"

"The Cossack said so."

"Cossacks are liars and traitors. No one trusts them anymore."

Nikolayevna peeked around the archway. "Is this the only weapon you have?" she asked.

The paunchy jailer led the two others toward the dungeon stairwell.

"Stay back" Usell said. "I'll talk to them."

"Wait," Nikolayevna said, but Usell stepped out from the shadows.

The jailer stopped. He uncoiled his black whip.

"The princess has finished her business here," Usell said. "We are leaving."

The jailer stopped, tilted his head at Usell.

Pointing with his whip in his hand, he said, "You there in the shadows. I see you. Come out."

With the hood flipped over her face Nikolayevna stepped out of the arch. The muzzle of the revolver peeked from her cape.

"Put that away," Usell whispered. "I will reason with them."

Nikolayevna's thin brow pinched. The pistol disappeared.

"What are you two talking about?" the jailer said. "Come out here so we can see you."

"Go ahead," Nikolayevna said. "Let's see if your beauty works better than bullets."

The three men braced themselves as Usell stepped within the whip's length. With a bowed head and her hands folded in front of her, she said, "Gentlemen. I honor your duty, but the princess has urgent business elsewhere."

"I piss on your urgencies," the jailer said.

"She is a Princess of the empire, a descendant from God."

"Where are your orders?"

"The bag of gold we gave you wasn't enough?" Usell asked.

"Gold?" the hooded gatekeeper said.

"You have gold?" the other asked.

With just a glance at the two men, the jailer took a waddling step toward Usell.

"I must see orders," the jailer said. "The Tsar himself sent word."

"The princess gives the orders in the Pale," Usell said.

"She has no authority here," the jailer barked. "Where is the Cossack?"

"I am here," Rotovak said.

Usell spun around. Standing beneath the archway, Rotovak leaned on the stone. Despite blood dripping at his temple, he walked with an imposing stride.

At Usell's side, his hand on his shashka hilt, he whispered, "Get to the horses."

"Are you all right?"

"No thanks to my ward."

"I need to see your orders, Captain, or I will have to hold you," the jailer said.

"You threaten the Tsar's emissary."

The jailer unraveled his whip.

Rotovak nodded at the three stallions reined to a nearby post.

The jailer mumbled something to the others before setting himself with his fists on his hips.

"You are bleeding, captain," he said.

"We are leaving," Rotovak said.

"Don't take that tone with me," the jailer said. "I don't like Cossacks. You are barking dogs, nothing more. You have no orders.

216

That does not look like the Grand Duke's daughter. Where's Ivan? How did you get that wound?"

The jailer leaned to the side to get a better look at Nikolayevna. She dipped her hood lower, but he was not looking at her face. He was staring at her dirty bare feet.

"The prisoner," the jailer said. "Get her."

The two men ran toward Nikolayevna. With the dexterity of a professional the paunchy jailer snapped the whip at Usell.

Rotovak pushed her out of its path and caught a meter of the whip wrapping around his arm. Jerking it, Rotovak pulled the jailer forward and sliced across the man's gut. His insides unraveled from and pale twisting intestines tumbling onto the stone plaza. The jailer dropped the whip, fell to his knees, and looked with astonishment at the coil of gray snakes falling from his abdomen. With a child's innocence he chirped, "Mother." And then his eyes rolled back in his head and he folded to the ground.

Before Nikolayevna could fire her weapon, Rotovak swung his blade across the swath of the scrambling others. Trembling the hooded gatekeeper dropped his short club, tripped over his own foot and fell. Rotovak hacked him in half from shoulder blade to the hip.

The third man fled into the tunnel in the rock wall. Nikolayevna lowered the pistol and grabbed Usell's arm. Usell shook loose.

"Get out of here before it's too late," he said.

Nikolayevna turned toward the horses against the wall.

"Come on, Dmitri," Usell said.

He tightened his grip on his shashka and pressed her behind him, looking in the direction of the open gate. A half dozen armed Cossacks rode onto the plaza.

At the head of the squad, Lieutenant Yazukov dismounted, and pulled out his pistol.

"Traitor." He pointed it at Rotovak. "Traitor."

The Cossacks dismounted, their shashkas drawn. They spread around Rotovak and Usell.

"Arrest him," the lieutenant said.

Nikolayevna tugged the back of Usell's jacket.

"So, my loyal comrades," Rotovak said. "How do you plan to take your captain?"

He wiped his bloody blade across his chest and held it up to them.

Lieutenant Yazukov dismounted and twisted through the short Cossacks' shoulders to face Rotovak.

"Put down your weapon," Yazukov said, "unless you wish to die."

"Would you kill a man of the sword with a pistol?" Rotovak asked. The Cossacks stared at Yazukov as if expecting an answer.

The lieutenant's left hand clutched his saber's hand guard, but his eyes jerked to the hooded woman taking a side step toward the three black stallions.

"Stand where you are," Lieutenant Yazukov said. He raised his pistol and pointed it at her. "Captain Dmitri Rotovak, you are under arrest."

Two of the six Cossacks half-lifted their shashkas.

"I deny your accusations," Rotovak said. "There has never been a Cossack traitor and there never will be. Cossacks are the empire's shield."

He lifted his braid and held it in front of the men of his order. Each of the men gripped his own.

The lieutenant aimed his pistol at Rotovak. "A man who consorts with Jews cannot be trusted."

"Yevgeny," Rotovak said. "I am Cossack. You are wrong."

"The Jew has witched you," Yazukov said. "You can no longer be trusted."

"I have fought along side these men," Rotovak said. He nodded at them. "Men of the sword are comrades. Yevgeny, you could be one of us."

"I don't trudge in shit without high boots," Yazukov said.

Six Cossacks glanced at each other and sheathed their swords.

"What are you doing?" Yazukov snapped at them.

"It seems, Yevgeny," Rotovak said. "That they would like to see the old bull fight the young one, or is that thing at your side just for decoration?"

The gun in the lieutenant's hand trembled. The plaza torches whipped like flags. Nikolayevna's hood blew off her head.

"The prisoner," Lieutenant Yazukov said. He cocked the hammer of his revolver. "Arrest them all."

But it was too late. Rotovak had closed the distance between them and his fist crossed into Lieutenant Yazukov's clean-shaven jaw.

Nikolayevna leaped onto the nearest stallion. In the saddle she drew Usell's pistol and fired twice. Two of the Cossacks crumpled. Rotovak slashed across the neck of the nearest, kicked the second in the groin, and skewered the third. The last slashed at him, but caught the sickle and hammer markings of Rotovak's shashka hilt. The ring of steel clanged across the courtyard as the smaller man parried Rotovak's blows. With a series of crosscutting charges the lone Cossack retreated.

"Go," Rotovak said.

A second group of men with cudgels erupted onto the courtyard.

Nikolayevna grabbed Usell by the collar and twisted her onto Rotovak's black stallion.

Rotovak engaged the lone Cossack, kicking him in the knee and then charging the prison guards.

With both sets of reins in Nikolayevna's hands, the stallions galloped off the plaza, through the stone archway, out of the prison, and across the moat.

Usell twisted in the saddle as Captain Dmitri Rotovak attacked the greater forces and forced them back.

48 . . .

Nikolayevna took the lead and once away from the prison she threw Usell her reins. With Usell keeping pace, Nikolayevna leaned forward without lowering her chin and seemed unbent for the hours spent in government hands. Like all sufficient riders of the day, she pressed her stallion hard. On a rise overlooking a lower patch of meadow on the outskirts of Odessa, she drew her reins to her chest and her stallion stomped to a stop. Moonlight glistened off patches of snow. Campfires burned with shadows moving across their yellow and red flares.

"Nikolayevna, wait," Usell said. "I have to get back into the city."

"Too dangerous," Nikolayevna said.

"There's a boy from my village in the pens at the harbor."

"You are a known enemy now. We have to plan, organize, gather our army."

Nikolayevna pressed her stallion forward.

"My people are being exterminated. You say you're for freedom. Doesn't it mean anything to you?"

"Listen to me," Nikolayevna said. "I don't know what that boy means to you, but he is probably already dead. You must fight with me, for yourself, for a better life. The boy means nothing."

"Because he's a Jew?"

"Because the cause is all that's important."

Standing in her stirrups, she pointed at the encampment. "My men are there. The American is there. We will have his gun and you'll help me rid this land of the Tsars."

Away from fireglows, *Utto's* chimney-stack puffed a film of gray into the moonlit night.

Nikolayevna urged her stallion forward and Usell followed in her wake down the gradual slope and into the open meadow. With the men standing up at the fires, Nikolayevna slowed, giving them time to recognize her, prancing the stallion toward them and coming to a halt.

"Comrades." She raised her voice. "We must stop the alliance with Prussians. We must find the jewel and bring the empire to its knees."

The men cheered. They shouted. They surrounded Nikolayevna and dragged her into their arms.

Usell dismounted and walked Rotovak's black toward *Utto* and Rudd's side. He hunched atop his bicycle seat. The Maxim gun, bolted on a tripod at the back of the wagon's bed, hung its long barrel at the ground. Rudd compressed bullets into a long spring-loaded casing.

"Things working out like you planned?" he asked.

"What are you doing here?"

"Her boys caught me as I headed back to the city. They want the gun, but they can't make it work. I have the firing pin in my boot."

With the novelty of her escape wearing off, Nikolayevna's men barraged her with complaints.

"Where are our provisions?"

"When will our army arrive?"

220

"The gun will not fire. He says he will not make it work unless we give him the jewel."

"Follow me," she said and marched to the steam carriage.

"Are you still going to help me?" Usell asked Rudd.

"First things first. We have to get out of here alive."

With her hands on her hips, Nikolayevna stood in front of Rudd. "Where is your ship?"

"It will be gone before too long," Rudd said.

"We will take your gun. Make it work."

Rudd slipped the firing pin from his boot, shoved it into the chamber, locked the casing in place, and pointed the barrel at her.

"Where's my jewel?" he asked.

"You will turn over the weapon to us," she said. "We'll give you rubles."

"You mean the Tsarist currency you're trying to destroy?"

"You give us the gun or we'll take it." Nikolayevna put her hand on the pistol in her waistband.

Rudd snapped a lever. A dozen men nearby reached for their weapons. Rudd lifted the sight at them and they froze.

"You cannot escape," Nikolayevna said.

"If you're all dead I can."

The rebels, like well-trained troops, spread out, firelight no longer defining them.

Rudd followed their arc with the muzzle of the Maxim gun and fired a burst at their feet.

"Give us the weapon," Nikolayevna said.

"Give me the jewel," Rudd said.

New arrivals coming out of the forest and in the shadows locked their rifle bolts.

"Stop this," Usell said. She placed herself between them.

"Get out of the way," Nikolayevna said.

"Move," Rudd said.

"No," Usell said.

"Don't be a child," Nikolayevna said. She reached out to grab Usell.

"No one move," Rudd said.

"Don't shoot her," Usell said.

"Aim sharply, comrades," Nikolayevna said.

More bolts locked in place in the darkness beyond the fires.

"I'll get you the jewel," Usell said. " I know where it is."

Both Nikolayevna and Rudd looked at her.

"Where is it?" Nikolayevna asked.

"Where the princess put it," Usell said. "I can get it within the hour."

Both Rudd and Nikolayevna relaxed.

"What is it you want?" Nikolayevna asked.

"To fight the Tsar," Usell said. "Isn't that what you want?"

"How do I know you can deliver?" Nikolayevna said.

"I was with her when she stowed it. I will get it before midnight."

Rudd wiped the back of his hand over his mouth. "The gun for the jewel?"

Nikolayevna nodded.

"Meet us before high tide," Rudd said.

"I'll get the jewel," Usell said. "We can meet at the piers."

"Can I trust you?" Nikolayevna asked.

"I got you out of prison."

"Go," Nikolayevna said.

"You drive," Rudd said, keeping the barrel aimed at the rebels.

Usell hopped into the carriage. Pressing a plunger, flipping a switch, and adjusting three levers, she grabbed the tiller as Rudd unhooked the Maxim and slipped inside the cab with it.

49 . . .

Once out of the meadow, Usell stopped *Utto* and Rudd took over driving. He aimed the machine into the moonlight and drove toward Odessa. On the outskirts of the city he came to a stop.

"What now, brown eyes?" he asked.

"What do you mean?"

"I don't believe one word of what you said. What do you have going on in that wishful head of yours?"

"I have a duty," she said. "You will get what you want."

"What about this fanatasy of yours, to find your mother?"

"I'd rather not be disappointed," Usell said. "The dream is flawed, but it is better than the reality."

"So you've moved on to saving the world?"

"Just a small part of it, with your help."

"What about the jewel? Can you really get it?"

"I'll talk to you about it when we're done," Usell said.

The city had come alive. In the shadows of a clouded moon the rook had awakened and taken flight. It had burst into flame. Its offspring swirled above the ecru walls, minarets, and onion domes, and set its nest ablaze.

The streets clogged with citizens. They rampaged through its grid. Mobs led by their magnates of industry rode in open carriages, shook their fists, and ordered their private armies to brandish their swords against the crowds of serfs who wielded hammers and sickles. Their clashes boiled with cries of rage and pain. Everywhere there was conflict.

Clattering horses raced on hardpack and the echo of iron hooves followed the riders. Nobility in their tight collars and brass buttons swirled their long knives and chased shadows of lone stragglers, anyone who could not escape the sweep of the pendulum.

"How will we be able to get to the water?" Usell asked.

"Is that where we're going?"

"I must get to the pens."

"Is that where the jewel is?"

"Yes," she said.

With a skeptical glance Rudd pressed the forward lever.

Lost in the cacophony of violence and burning buildings, *Utto's* hiss and rattle attracted little attention. Turning away from clashes, Rudd avoided kept to side streets, moving corner to corner, creeping shadow to shadow.

Close to the pens she smelled the brine of the sea.

When Rudd shut *Utto* down, the silence of the boiler tick, tick, ticking with cooling metal. The splash of waves against the seawall hid the distant sound of conflagration.

Down the block a gray mist lingered above the pens. Usell reached for the handle on the door. Rudd touched her hand, put his finger to his lips.

Across the avenue two soldiers marched with stiff precision in front of the pens. They stopped, reset their rifles to the other shoulder, turned, and marched back the way they came.

"Sentries," he said. "Be careful. Wait for my signal."

Salt spray rose in the moonlight and smashed over the pens.

"Give me a pistol," she said.

"A pistol isn't going to help you if you won't use it."

"Just give it to me," she said.

Removing his revolver from his holster, he handed it to her.

"It's heavy."

"Makes a big hole," he said. "Just hit what you shoot at. Cock, squeeze the trigger."

"I have something to say," she said.

"What a surprise," he said.

"I have not always been honest with you," she said.

"Somehow, I'm not surprised by that, either."

She brushed the hair from his forehead.

"I do as my father instructed. I do not think of right and wrong anymore, but I want you to know . . ."

"Don't say anything else," he said. "I'm going to help you."

"I just wanted to . . ."

"You just want to get me killed so you don't have to face how you feel about me."

"I have to do this," she said. "You know I have to. I don't know who my mother is. I may never find her. I don't know who I am. The only thing I know is that someone who cared about me needs my help."

He leaned over, cupped her chin and kissed her, a brief, sucking peck on her lips.

"I told you. I'll create a distraction. It'll draw the soldiers. You'll only have to deal with the sentries and maybe I can draw them away, too."

"How do I get to the piers?"

"Why?"

"I was told that there are boats on the piers."

"What are you going to do, row to the Bosporus?"

"If I have to," she said.

"Two city blocks down the avenue is Catherine Street. The opera house is at the end of it. The piers are behind it." He pointed west. "I'll support your retreat. My ship will be outside the harbor. Look for it."

A commotion erupted behind them. Many voices. Many feet. Running away from them.

Usell gripped the heavy gun, opened the door, and stepped onto the running board.

"Wait for my distraction," he said. He put on his broad-brimmed hat.

Launching herself at him, she knocked his hat off his head and kissed him - a hard, clumsy kiss - but when she tried to break away, he wrapped his arms around her, locked her to him, their embrace swelling with warmth.

She broke his grasp and pushed him away.

Leaping down, she closed the door, lifted the pistol, and headed for the avenue.

Utto hissed and backed away. Above the seawall a mist spread a gray blanket. White clouds puffed beneath a haloed moon.

The two sentries moved into the low mist. Across the avenue there were no soldiers guarding the pens. The fire was out. No shadows appeared above the top of the fence.

With one last look up and down the avenue, Usell raced across and climbed over the fence into the pen. As soon as she stood on the other side, the two sentries emerged from their path. They stopped. One leaned against a post. The other lit a cigarette.

She used the fence to walk the muck, but could not see forms.

"Moshe Gimmel," she whispered. But only a hard crash of wave responded.

Her boots sucked with each step. Crouching, she found the post where she left Moshe Gimmel. There was no sign of the blond lieutenant who was to guard him.

"Moshe Gimmel. Moshe Gimmel," she whispered.

No answer.

Tripping over something, she caught her breath. Kneeling beneath the height of the mist, she turned the body over. A man's black beard condensed droplets, and flies sat on the whites of his eyes. His pupils were dilated, terrified, even in death. Not Moshe Gimmel. Controlling a gag, she stood up.

Smoke from the sentry's cigarette across the avenue rose in twists of lamp light.

"Moshe Gimmel," she whispered louder. "Moshe Gimmel. Do not be dead."

A moaning sound nearby sent her to it.

"Moshe Gimmel."

"Here," his voice was weak.

She clutched his arm and did not let go. She lifted him to her. "You are alive. Where is the soldier left to guard you?"

"He thought I died," Moshe Gimmel said.

She hugged him. "I'm glad you didn't."

"I always wait for you," he said as if he were standing on the corner under the Gerber Brothers sign and looking up the street at her garret window.

"Come on," she said. "We've got to get out of here."

His legs wobbled as he strained to stand. She slipped her shoulder underneath his arm, clutched his gartel rope, and used it to help him walk. When his stare met her, she said, "I know. It's not permitted."

He blinked and with surprising ease they made the fence close to the open gate. She rested him against it.

The two soldiers across the avenue jerked to attention when Rudd's Maxim gun began to rattle. The sparks from its muzzle ignited in the mist. The sentries dropped their smokes, unwrapped their rifles, crouched to shooting stance, and pointed in the direction of the gunfire.

The machine gun's concussions were blocks away. The men looked at each other and then without words they got to their feet and ran in the opposite direction.

The Maxim gun fired and fired and then was silent. The bombarding that followed was a mix of rifle fire and cannon explosion more violent than the action attacking the princess's train.

Explosions erupted inside the mist where the Maxim gun had been. Moshe Gimmel slumped.

"Come on," she said.

Helping Moshe Gimmel up, she clasped his arm. Though he was not strong, he lifted his weight every other step. Nikolayevna's coat was gone. His black rekel was wet and torn, and both of them wore the muck of cattle. Before heading in the direction Rudd had pointed out, Usell tucked Moshe Gimmel's pais behind his ear and caught his glance as she hoisted him to her hip. Using it as a fulcrum, she rotated his body with her stride.

Down the two blocks to the waterfront, Usell checked every shadow, half-carrying Moshe Gimmel all the way to Catherine Street. The Maxim gun fired again, closer this time. The response was more violent than the last.

Moshe Gimmel took fewer steps. Flames erupted behind them. Smoke rose in its glow. She stopped at the corner of Catherine Street.

A broad public square faced the sea. Angry waves splashed on the wet stone. On the parvis in front of a three-story building with gray Greek columns, Usell leaned Moshe Gimmel against a pillar and caught her breath.

At the far end of the block the glass-domed opera house shimmered with light and pulsed with the faint orchestral sounds of violin springtime.

The plaza was a patchwork of crushed rock, brick and cobbles with streetcar rails snaking around the curve next to the opera house.

Moshe Gimmel lost all his strength and sagged against her.

There was no one around. Moonlight brushed the wet pools of the parvis in front of the ministry. Massive Greek columns held up a high portico, and their numbers, buried in shadow, staggered like a chessboard from sidewalk to the front of the building. Above the cornice a cross defined the words *Ministry of Religion.*

"Moshe Gimmel, you must get up, you must help me carry you."

He did not respond.

A clash of steel rang from the plaza behind a tall black monolith in its center. Emerging from behind it, a single man fought with a half dozen others. They beat the single man back, but he defended himself with a blade in each hand, a broad man with two shashkas and no braid fighting against shorter Cossacks.

Despite their numbers, the broad man halted each assault with an aggressive counterattack. Usell pulled her revolver from her waist and dragged Moshe Gimmel through the pillars to an alcove fronting the dark building. Laying him down, she said, "Moshe Gimmel. Don't move."

She made her way out of the parvis and watched the man with his back to the sea.

The opera house at the end of the block blazed yellow light. The smell of brine filled with orchestral song. Faust. Marguerite, a girl in her garret, sang her jewel, *Ah! je ris de me voir si belle dans ce miroir.*

The attackers closed around the broad man and when the sea wall reached his back, he lunged into them and the fight disappeared into the splashing mist.

The sea absorbed them and they all disappeared.

50 . . .

Moshe Gimmel cried out.

"Usell. Where are you?"

Rushing back into the alcove, she lifted his head and whispered, "You must be quiet, Moshe Gimmel. I am here."

She tried to rouse him, but his head lolled. She slipped her arm under his and pulled him up. "Moshe Gimmel you must help me."

Out of the shadows of the pillars, Rotovak, dripping seawater and grim, pointed his shashka at them. His braid was gone, the hair chopped up, scrapes and cuts on his scalp.

"Dmitri," she said.

"The boy again," he said.

"Yes, give me a hand with him."

"He is almost dead. Leave him."

"He is not dead," she said.

Rotovak glared at her.

"Dmitri," she said. "I will not leave him."

"Enough of this. Come with me." He grabbed her arm.

"Take your hands off me. I am not your property." She drew the pistol from her waist and pointed it at him.

Rotovak's eyes weakened, but the soldier in him straightened, and when she could not hold him up any longer he collapsed against her.

"What am I to you?" Rotovak asked.

"I don't know. Just help me."

"I come from the steppe," he said. "Even though the wind is harsh, I face it."

"I don't know what you want," she said.

"I thought not."

She lost her grip on Moshe Gimmel and he crumpled to the patio. Usell bent with him. When she looked up, Rotovak was gone.

Faust and Marguerite sang their love song, *Oui, c'est toi que j'aime,* their duet rising into the night sky. Moshe Gimmel's eyes opened and studied her.

"What is it, Moshe Gimmel?" she asked.

His eyes closed and she pulled him against her. The crash of waves against the sea wall splashed harder and a wind howled through the pillars.

Footsteps marched onto the parvis. Usell leaned Moshe Gimmel against the wall and slipped to a vantage point behind the pillars.

"Did you see the Cossack?" a voice said.

Men in black and silver uniforms – gray hoods hid their hair and faces. Their fists were wrapped in cloth. They formed a line in front of the ministry. The soldier at the head of the men tossed his hood from his head and a shock of blond hair rose like a crown. The young blond lieutenant puffed his chest and saluted. The four others in black and silver shook their hoods loose and snapped to attention, their bayoneted rifles pressed stock to ground. Behind the blond lieutenant, Yazukov with a captain's red kuntush accepted their salutes.

Usell lifted the pistol.

"Well?" Yazukov asked.

"He escaped his Cossacks," the young blond lieutenant said.

"What about the princess?" Yazukov asked.

"We don't know. She may be among the dead. He was with her."

"Her little prince wants her, anyway," Yazukov said. "He wants the jewel. The alliance must be made."

Usell cocked the stiff hammer of the heavy pistol, but it slipped from her fingers, clattered on the pavement, and exploded. The shot chipped stone from a pillar.

The men of the Okhrana lifted their weapons at alert.

Yazukov drew his saber. "Search the ministry," he ordered.

Four men in silver and black spread into the pillars with bayonets forward. The blond Lieutenant drew his pistol and advanced down the aisle to the doors.

Picking up her weapon, Usell cocked the action with both thumbs and slid sideways into the shadows of the pillars. She circled behind the advance. The lieutenant moved down the aisle where he stopped at the wall. Moshe Gimmel lay unconscious.

"I know this Jew." he said. "I left him for dead."

"Dispatch him," Captain Yazukov said from the parvis.

The lieutenant aimed his pistol.

Usell fired. The bullet splattered the lieutenant's brain on the wall. His body lurched forward and flattened. Two Okhrana soldiers emerged from the pillars. She cocked and fired, cocked and fired again as they aimed their rifles at her. Her bullets slammed into their chests, kicking them back.

Rifle hammers detonated as Usell leaped across the aisle to the nearest cover. The muzzle flashes swelled from the shadows and bullets heated the air, one whizzing through her hair and the other tearing a hole in the cloth of the blouse beneath her arm.

Setting her stance, she faced their bayonet charge. She fired at the closest. Her bullet stuck an eye and kicked the man from his feet. She cocked the hammer and squeezed the trigger at the charging man. Two strides away, her bullet bent him at the gut. He stumbled, dropped the rifle, and fell forward.

Captain Yazukov emerged from a pillar with his saber pointing at her. Usell cocked the pistol and aimed it at his forehead.

Yazukov flinched when she squeezed the trigger and the percussion slammed on a discharged cylinder. She squeezed the trigger again with the same hollow result. A smirk appeared on Yazukov's lips.

He strode toward her.

She backed toward the portico and dove into the dark of the pillars. Scrambling around a column she circled behind him, repeating her tactic. Emerging at his back, she picked up a bayoneted rifle and crept close to the alcove where she saw Yazukov standing over Moshe Gimmel, his sword on Moshe Gimmel's chest.

"Come out," he said. "Or he will die."

She emerged from the shadows.

"No Cossack to shield you now?" he asked.

She dropped the rifle.

"Dmitri will find you," she said.

"Step forward."

The blond Lieutenant's pistol lay next to his body behind Yazukov.

"Where is the princess?" Yazukov asked.

"I don't know."

"Perhaps she's no longer important," he said. "Princesses are like flies, and many would enjoy becoming an empress if they had the chance."

With a twisted smile his saber pointed to the jewel.

The diamond at the end of the chain dangled outside Usell's blouse.

With a step forward, Yazukov flicked the tip of his blade, hooking the chain around Usell's neck.

"And it appears that you are no longer necessary."

He lifted his elbow aiming the point at her heart.

From the shadows beside her a shashka chopped down on Yazukov's saber. Rotovak stepped in front of her, his sword stalking the retreating man's neck.

Yazukov banged his steel at the shashka, but Rotovak pressed forward with an unyielding wrist.

Yazukov's back hit the stone wall of the ministry.

"Drop it," Rotovak said.

The saber hit the stone.

"I heard a loud foreign weapon," Rotovak said.

"Dmitri," she said.

"She doesn't care about you," Yazukov said through his teeth.

"So, Yevgeny, a coin is tossed," Rotovak said.

He pressed the point of his shashka to Yazukov's windpipe. Yazukov turned his jaw, straining against stone for space. A blood line crossed the width of the blade.

"She's with slime." Yazukov pointed at Moshe Gimmel. "She has stolen the jewel. Obey our masters. Dispatch her. Dispatch them all before they spread their poison to us all."

Usell picked up the dead lieutenant's pistol.

Rotovak met Usell's eyes.

"Tell me the truth about us, Usell," he said.

"What do you want from me?" she said.

231

"To make up your mind."

"I cannot walk away from myself," she said.

Rotovak's sharp nod was followed by a step back from Yazukov. He lowered his blade.

Yazukov lifted his saber from the patio, stood to his full height, and set himself.

"What are you doing?" Usell asked.

"Taking back my honor from a thief." He brushed his hand over his scalp.

With his straight saber in hand, Yazukov lunged—point of attack at Rotovak's chest.

Rotovak knocked the thrust aside, his motion mechanical, a slight lean avoiding the saber's tip.

Rotovak grabbed Yazukov by the throat and tossed him against the wall.

"She steals the empire's future," Yazukov said.

Rotovak circled Yazukov, shashka low.

"Our empire has changed," Rotovak said. "It no longer represents its people."

Again Yazukov attacked with a fury. Round beating strokes, cross cuts meant to cut and maim, banging against the steel of the deflecting shashka that did not loosen under Rotovak's iron wrist.

Yazukov backed off. Took short breaths.

"Your benefactors," Rotovak said, "serve themselves."

"Without them there's only chaos," Yazukov said. "There is no good, no commerce." He slapped at Rotovak's blade.

"With them there's only greed," Rotovak said.

"Loyalty first," Yazukov said.

"Blindness serves only evil," Rotovak said.

And then Rotovak attacked. Slamming against the saber his blows beat Yazukov to the wall. The saber broke in half. Still holding the broken hilt of his fragmented weapon, he lifted both hands in surrender and crouched to his knees under the shashka.

"He does not deserve to live," Usell said. "I saw him in Oylaif. I recognize him." She uttered a small cry. "Zapora was my friend."

"You need to leave," Rotovak said. "More like him will come."

"Come with me," she said.

He turned his head, looked into her eyes.

"I do not fit in your world," he said.

And then his body stiffened. His head turned to face Yazukov. Half a saber pressed under Rotovak's ribs to the hilt.

"Die, Judas," Yazukov said.

Usell fired the pistol. Walking toward Yazukov, she kept squeezing the trigger until there was only the hollow click of metal on metal and splatterings of Yazukov melting down the wall.

Rotovak buckled to the pavement.

On his back with her kneeling next to him, blood pumped from the wound in his chest. He opened his eyes. They swam in black swirls. Gripping the diamond hanging from her neck, he said, "Don't let her take it from you."

"Who?"

"Mother Russia," he whispered.

And then his eyes looked between the pillars at the moon glowing gold and saw nothing.

51 . . .

Light shimmered from the opera house, its haloes rising above the dome. The chorus echoed into the street as Marguerite was saved with everlasting life. *Sauvée! Christ est resuscité.* Moshe Gimmel was unconscious. Yazukov was dead. Rotovak was dead. Between them Usell sat and clutched her knees.

Her head swirled with her father's words. *Time,* he said, *has a heartbeat that fades like the mist with the dawning of the sun.* But there was no sun. There was only night, dark night. With her forehead resting on her knees and the music in the background, she wanted to surrender to it, let it take hold of her, do nothing, let it carry her away. She brushed her fingers across Rotovak's cheek.

"Why should anyone care?" she said.

Somewhere far away the rattle of gunfire mixed with the crackle of burning buildings and the distant roar of mobs. Hatred without reason. What did it mean? Meaningless. Where was Rudd? Moshe Gimmel lay on his side. His neck was cold. And then footsteps splashed through the puddles on the plaza.

"Help me," someone outside the ministry cried. "If God is in there, you must help me." The voice was high-pitched, a shadow outside the columns.

"Emma, where are you? Emma. Come help me."

Ludivica. Usell touched Moshe Gimmel's cheek. "Do not give up yet," she said.

Scrambling to her feet, Usell scurried out of the alcove where the princess prayed on her knees before the Ministry of Religion.

"Ludivica," Usell said. She showed herself.

Running to her, Ludivica wrapped her arms around Usell.

"I'm saved," she said.

"What are you doing here?" Usell asked.

"My guards and I were trying to liberate the empire from the Jews, but I don't know what happened to my army. They're gone. Citizens threw rocks at me. They knew who I was. There is war in the streets. Soldiers and guns, firing and firing, and the people, the people are looting, beating each other, burning everything."

At the corner a dozen riders on horseback stuttered to a halt. Usell pulled Ludivica behind the pillar. The riders' walked their horses onto Catherine Street,

A gust of sea wind blew the head rider's short hair to a crown about her head. Nikolayevna kicked the stallion in its haunches and Rotovak's black walked with short nods before turning its head toward the pillars.

Nikolayevna's jaw was set.

"Who is that?" Ludivica whispered.

Pushing Ludivica deeper into the shadows of the pillars, Usell put her hand over Ludivica's mouth.

"Be quiet," Usell whispered. "These rebels wish you dead."

Nikolayevna drew the restless stallion ahead. She searched the empty space to the sea. The aria from the opera house reached a high note. Rudd's gun rattled in the distance and the rebel horses galloped away from Catherine Street.

"I know her," Ludivica said. "I have seen her."

"Adrianna said she was your mother's friend."

"My mother?" Ludivica said.

"We don't have time for this," Usell said.

Releasing Ludivica, Usell headed back to the alcove. The princess chased behind.

"Where are you going? They said you betrayed me. Dmitri is the traitor."

"You shot him, remember?" Usell said.

"He defied me. He deserved to be shot. When he found me in the city, he hid me in a sewer. I could not stay there."

Usell sidestepped one of the dead men in black and silver.

The princess seemed not to notice.

"He saved your life, Ludivica. Doesn't that mean anything to you?"

"He did his duty. I will order him to protect us, now."

"Ludivica. Either he is a traitor that can't be trusted or he is your savior. You pit ideas against each other as if you don't see the paradox. Black is not white and white is not black."

"My words are law. I merely have to say them."

"Dmitri is dead," Usell said. She pointed. "Raise him from the dead if your word is law."

Covering her eyes, Ludivica said, "Who will save us from the Jews?"

At the alcove Usell knelt next to Moshe Gimmel.

"I do not have time to argue," Usell said. "Look at me. Understand this. I am a Jew."

"No, you are not. You are well-born."

"A lie," Usell said.

"Dmitri said . . ."

"A lie."

"I don't understand. Jews are evil."

"Lies. I tell you I am a Jew, but you cannot believe it. You cannot define me the way you define my people because you know me, you've touched me, you've listened to my words. I am real to you, not what the lies say I am."

"It's not possible."

"You'd rather believe a lie than face the truth?" Usell asked.

"You do not look like a Jew," Ludivica said.

Usell grabbed her arm and yanked her down to look at Moshe Gimmel, who did not move. "He is a Jew," she said. "He doesn't wish to hide. He doesn't wish to hurt you, either."

"A Jew." The princess reached for a rifle lying near, but Usell twisted it from her grasp.

"He is with me. He comes from my village. He is a good boy."

"I don't understand. How could he and you . . .."

"I am a Jew. Can't you hear me?" Usell said. "What do you care if my people study ideas 5,000 years old? It only strengthens their reason. It helps them learn. It teaches values. What does that matter to you? Do you care any less for me because I am a Jew?"

"I must."

"Why? What do you gain? Your protectors are dead. Think, Ludivica. I am your friend. I care about you. Who else do you have?"

"I'm trying, but I don't understand," she said.

"Then understand this. I am leaving the Empire and I'm taking this boy with me. We are not safe here. Think. Ludivica. I am your friend. We are like sisters. We shared the same fate – we are chattel because we are women. We can do better than this. We can live our own lives."

Ludivica blinked twice.

"I don't want to marry that boy," she said. "He is ugly and he is cruel. Take me with you."

Moshe Gimmel moaned.

"Help me with him," Usell said. "We must not miss the tide."

Usell slung the strap of the rifle over her head and across her body.

"Help me lift the boy," she said. "We must get to the piers and find a boat."

Kneeling next to Moshe Gimmel, Usell slipped her empty shoulder beneath his arm and lifted him to his feet.

Ludivica pinched a wedge of cloth on Moshe Gimmel's shoulder and held it away from her body.

"Help me with the boy," Usell said.

"He is filthy."

"So am I," Usell said. "Put your weight under his other arm so we can get to the piers."

"What if the rebels find me?"

"Ludivica. Pick him up."

She bent under Moshe Gimmel's other arm and between the two of them they struggled out of the portico of the Ministry of Religion across the parvis toward the seawall and the herd of white caps rushing toward shore.

Behind the opera house close to the water, the vocalists sang their final chorus and in the splash of wave, a faraway gun rattled and was answered in kind.

The two stumbled with Moshe Gimmel onto the slick wooden wharf. The pier extended into deep water and the full moon broke cloud cover. They struggled on the rocking pier and white froth lifted off the slick wavering planks.

No boats. Swells and crashing waves lifted the planks and tossed them as they headed to the end of the pier. At rope tied to an iron cleat held a single dinghy riding the surface.

"There," Usell said. "Come on."

The dinghy stretched at the end of a rope and bobbed. Two oars set in the iron locks flopped at its sides.

Moshe Gimmel's skin was cold but vapors fogged about his nose.

"Calm down, I order you," Ludivica shreiked at the sea.

In the trough of a long swell the pier settled. The planks leveled. Ludivica smiled, but when she loosened her grip on Moshe Gimmel, she slipped and fell.

Unbalanced, a heel of Usell's boot caught between the planks and she toppled. Moshe Gimmel fell in a heap. Unstrapping the rifle, Usell removed her boots and abandoned them to the sea. On naked feet she scrambled to the cleat rope tied to the dinghy and pulled it close.

"Ludivica, get in." she said.

The planks rose on the next swell. Ludivica pulled herself up and spread her arms and legs for balance. With a catlike spring she grabbed the bayoneted rifle and set the stock to her shoulder. She opened the breech, glanced inside, and slammed the bolt closed before lifting the barrel and aiming it back at the wharf. A rider on a black stallion stood at the end of the pier.

A wave heaved the dock and Ludivica pitched forward. The bayonet stabbed into a tarred plank. Resurrecting herself, she tried to jerk it free.

"It's the rebel." she cried.

At the end of the pier Rotovak's black stallion stomped a front hoof. Nikolayevna stretched in her stirrups, looking at them. A roar of voices tumbled from the plaza onto the wharf. A mob with torches chased those dressed for the opera toward the city.

Usell jumped into the dinghy. She crouched and balanced.

"Ludivica, forget the gun. Help me with the boy."

Nikolayevna beat the stallion with a whip and the beast leaped onto the pier.

Ludivica, leaving the rifle bayoneted at an angle, knelt and shoved Moshe Gimmel off the dock into Usell's arms. His weight felled her to the bottom of the dinghy. She laid Moshe Gimmel in the hull and stood with her legs spread.

"Untie the cleat, Ludivica," Usell said.

But Ludivica steadied herself on the planks and stared at Usell.

"What are you doing? Come on."

"My jewel," Ludivica said. "You have my jewel."

The diamond hung outside the frilled blouse.

"Now I remember," Ludivica said. "I gave it to you to ransom my father."

"It wasn't necessary. Come on."

"You kept it."

"Yes. Call it a dowry for our new lives. The rope. Get the rope."

"But the jewel will unify the Empire. Make us invincible."

"Yes," Nikolayevna said. The stallion's hooves stamped to a halt over them. She pointed her pistol at Usell.

"What are you going to do now, Nikolayevna. Shoot me? Shoot your own daughter?"

Nikolayevna leaned forward. "You think you're my child?"

"Yes, *Mother*. It makes sense. You are Vera Figner."

Ludivica tilted her head, stared at Nikolayevna.

"So, you are the daughter she abandoned. One of the Jews she said she could no longer tolerate."

The words struck Usell like a blow.

"Your mother is dead," Nikolayevna said. "I threw her from the parapet and took her identity, changed my name."

"Emma," Ludivica said. "She is my mother. I recognize her. I remember her now. She is not dead. She has come back to life."

Nikolayevna turned the pistol to Ludivica.

"Why don't you just die," Nikolayevna said. "This alliance will just strengthen the corruption." She cocked the hammer.

"You would kill your own daughter, Nikolayevna?" Usell said.

"The death of the princess will send a message to our enemies."

Ludivica slipped her hand around the forestock of her rifle and tugged. The bayonet point did not release the plank.

"Both of you," Nikolayevna said. "Don't move."

"Who are you going to kill first, Nikolayevna?" Usell asked. "Your own daughter? Me? This is deep water. If you shoot, the jewel will be lost."

"Very clever. Now get on the dock," Nikolayevna said. "With the jewel I will unify the proletariet and lead us all to a better life."

"No," Usell said.

Ludivica yanked at the rifle.

"Give me the jewel, you traitorous bitch," Nikolayevna said.

The rifle jerked loose and unbalanced Ludivica.

"You leave my friend alone," she said and lifted the barrel.

The stallion pawed the planks of the dock. A swell lifted both dinghy and pier. Usell steadied herself and faced the snout of Rotovak's stallion. Girding her legs, she threw up her arms in the face of the stallion.

Rotovak's horse reared as Nikolayevna fired. She tumbled backwards off the saddle as the pier heaved.

Ludivica dropped the rifle and clutched her chest. She staggered to the edge of the pier and with her eyes and her mouth wide open she reached for Usell. And then her gazeless body fell like a chopped tree. She hit the bulwark, flipped an oar into Usell's temple and they all tumbled into the wild sea.

52 . . .

Usell sank beneath the surface. Dropping into darkness, her weightless body floated without control. She was suspended without destination. Faint light above telescoped away. Stillness whispered in shades of green and black with nothing substantial, no light, no shadow, and no form filling the void.

In her cold garret, she struggled to warm beneath cold blankets where winter stayed too long, her father called. *You must come down.* She would do her lessons and fix her father breakfast and her father would tell her she was to marry Moshe Gimmel and she would thank him for choosing a man of character who would treat her with love and respect, but she would explain to her father that Emma Bovary chose her life and though it was ruined, it was hers to choose, hers to feel the pounding of her own heart and hers to suffer for it, even though it was wrong to do so. What Usell must do was up to her. If she chose a husband who loved her he could not be innocent of her failures and that was his choice.

In this cocoon she life was real.

But in the silence of a blur, a current swarmed over the last of the light, a thing that might help or do harm and in it she must also choose. The voice that called for her, called for her to swim. *Swim to me, my child. Swim to your mother.*

She reached for the formless mass, reached for the darkness and kicked her feet. Movement swarmed in eddies of cold. Her arm reached out and pulled at the black. A shade in a shape of a princess's split gown drifted by, a glissade in a ballet.

Light hovered in a glow and a course of a thousand days of repetition ordered her movement until she burst through the surface, and filled her lungs with cold salty air.

Wavelets splashed her cheeks, blurred in her eyes. There were stars. A black night. The dinghy was gone. The princess gone. Nikolayevna gone. The empty pier tossed and twisted in the spray of wild sea. The current beneath her feet pulled her to a shape buoyed on the surface. Moshe Gimmel. She grabbed him. He did not move. He floated and opened his eyes.

"Save yourself," he coughed.

"I have you, Moshe Gimmel," she said. "I have you."

The current pulled faster and rushed them along the surface.

"Lock your fingers around my neck," she said.

He didn't move.

"Around my neck," she ordered.

With his fingers entwined below her chin, she clamped down on his hands and swam with the current pulling them out to sea. She angled across the flow, buried her face in the water, kicked and stroked until the current let them go and lifted them on a swell.

On the surface was a light. She swam toward the vague notion of it. Her strokes grew heavy, sluggish. Her kick slowed. Moshe

Gimmel's body slackened. A shadowed moon hid behind barges of clouds. Treading water, she rolled Moshe Gimmel over.

"Float," Usell said.

"Save yourself," Moshe Gimmel whispered. "Let me go."

And then Moshe Gimmel folded like a pocket comb and sank. She took a deep breath and dove after him. He descended and she kicked, she grabbed at water, grabbed at his torn rekel, grabbed for his hair, and tightened her grip on a twirl of rising pais.

Reversing up, she pulled his head above water. A light passed close by her.

With barely enough time for a breath, she gasped, "Help."

"Look," a voice said. "Over there." English. Not quite English.

She raised her hand, keeping herself as high out of the water as she could. Wavelets crashed against her face.

The light turned away, a candle on a menorah blinked out.

Her fingers stiffened, loosening their grip. Her legs stopped kicking and she closed her eyes just as a shadow passed in front of a light.

The shadow – like a black giant cloth hung on a scarecrow – reached down from above.

It wrestled Moshe Gimmel away and she grabbed at him as she began to sink.

"I got her," the voice said.

Two circles of light hovered above. The shadow blotted out the light. Water surrounded her face. Claw hooks pulled at her jacket as a vice gripped her wrist and it all turned to a wet cold black.

53 . . .

Rusted paint flaked where flanges compressed metal to metal with fist-sized nuts bolting walls to floors, seats to cabinets, bunks to the inside bowels of the ship. Usell's back pressed against the interior wall of the cabin as she shivered on a bunk adjacent to a larger bunk. A rough wool blanket with hairy pumice wrapped her.

Her hair stank of brine. Moshe Gimmel lay on the larger bunk, curled up, facing the flaking paint, taking only half the space.

An older man with receding white hair, and his sleeves rolled up, scissored strips of cloth and laid them beside Moshe Gimmel. The man worked methodically, sewing Moshe Gimmel's skin like he was linen. He didn't cry out, though with each stitch, he flinched. Dabbing with cotton swabs and a bottle of spirits, the older man picked up the strips and tied them firmly around Moshe Gimmel's wounds.

What hair the older man had wrapped like a white laurel around his balding dome. He pinched the bridge of his nose below round wire-frame glasses and inclined his head like a bird inspecting a plump frog. His pale, puffy-cheeked curiosity seemed at odds with the authority of his movements. He wiped his hands in a white towel.

"How is he?" she asked.

"*Drai mir nit kain kop,*" he said.

Yiddish. Don't bother me.

"Tell me," she said.

His stare narrowed down his sloped nose. "Broken, battered, hurt," he said.

"Will he be all right?"

The man didn't answer.

Usell swung her legs off the bunk and pushed at the man's shoulder until he faced her. "I asked you a question."

"Ask politely and you might receive answers," he said.

"I'm sorry. Tell me, please."

"He will live." His tone was calm.

"Who are you?"

"Doctor Mordecai Bloom," he said.

Doctor Bloom had unnecessary weight about his middle and he had the weathered skull of a man who lost his hair early in life and yet something vital stayed alive in his look.

"I am usually more polite," Usell said.

He reacted to her apology with a shrug. Rotating to a basin, he washed his hands up to his elbows. A bandage wrapped Moshe Gimmel's forehead and one eye.

"We took on beef at port," he said. "The galley has hot soup. I'll have them send you some."

"Kosher?" she asked.

The doctor stared at her. His eyelids fluttered as matured crow's feet dug into his squint. "I can instruct our cook. We are friends," he said. "But we have no rabbi."

"Not for me," Usell said. She nodded at Moshe Gimmel.

"You are his wife?"

"He's what's left of my people."

"There's you."

Moshe Gimmel's breathing halted for a moment.

"He's the last of what we were," she said.

Tugging the rough wool blanket around her shoulders, Usell settled back against the iron wall. Steam rose from the grate in the floor.

"Ach," Doctor Bloom said. "The engines have been turned on."

A subtle vibration stirred the walls. The cabin trembled. The yellow kerosene lamp hanging on a bronze cleat threw shadows side to side, out of time with the sway.

The physician laid the cloth on his tray of instruments.

"We aren't moving," she said.

"True," he said.

"Can they board us, the Tsar's soldiers? Are we out of their territory? Are we prisoners?"

"Calm down, *shaineh maidel*. You are guests. I'm sure it's nothing to worry about. Maybe the engines have begun their work. Maybe they're taking on supplies from another vessel. If there were any trouble, you'd hear bells and whistles and men clanking down the gangways yelling and making hell a mere nuisance."

Usell removed something black and green and slimy from her hair and pulled the blanket like a towel over her crown.

"Where am I?"

"You are on an American ship."

"Where is Rudd Cothman?" she asked.

"I cannot say."

"Why not?"

He shrugged. "I don't know him."

"How can you not know him? Isn't this his ship?"

The doctor laughed.

"This is a government ship," he said. "You should get some rest. You've had quite a time of it. Saving this boy is a *mitzvah*."

"We saved each other."

The doctor nodded and then said, "If I were you, I would hide that thing around your neck. Just because we are sworn to uphold our duty doesn't mean we aren't human."

The jewel dangled outside the blanket. She hid it beneath her blouse.

With a shrug and an amused smile, the doctor opened the squeaking metal door and closed it behind him with a clang.

She tried the handle. It wasn't locked.

Running her hand through the dampness of her hair, she rubbed a towel on it and looked at the basin and soap.

Water lapped against the hull of the ship. The vessel trembled and then moaned with a metallic annoyance. Pistons chugged and the ship's skin vibrated as it began to move. The steady hum shook the lantern so that the yellow shadows trembled into pockets of right angles.

Moshe Gimmel rolled over.

"I have to tell you something," he said.

His one eye was bloodshot.

"You are awake," she said.

"I cannot marry you," he said.

"These are your first words of conversation with me? You cannot marry me?"

His eye fluttered. "I have nothing to offer."

Wrapping the blanket tight about herself, she hopped to his bunk, scooted close. He did not retreat. His face was pale, and bruised.

"It is wrong for me to stare," he said. "You hair is uncovered."

"And it will stay that way if the weather permits."

"But our beliefs . . . It is not . . .." He stopped his words.

"Moshe Gimmel." she said. "This is the first time we can truly talk. You to me. Me to you. For now we have only each other. Must we discuss the rules of our religion?"

"I know nothing else," he said.

"And yet you refuse to marry me."

"You would marry me?"

"How am I to answer if you have not asked?" she said.

"It is not proper that I ask."

"Moshe Gimmel, there is nothing proper about drowning or being arrested or being beaten almost to death. There is nothing proper in killing and there is nothing proper or improper about being alone with an unmarried woman and yet all these things are part of here, right now, and I say to you that there are more things for us to speak about than there are grains of sand on the beach. I wish to hear them from you. Not right now. In our futures. But this you should know of me: I tire of restrictions on who I am supposed to be."

Moshe Gimmel did not speak. His eye glimmered with yellow kerosene light.

"You are very beautiful," he said. "You have always been beautiful. You smiled at me once and the boys all saw and when you did not smile at any of them they mocked me and they mocked you and I could not look at you again."

"You may stare all you wish now, Moshe Gimmel. I will smile at you again."

She wrapped his hand in hers.

"I am sorry," he said. "I cannot shift so easily as you."

"We will have time," she said. "We will make a new life in America where they have streets of gold."

He squinted at her, the skeptic arguing the meaning of the words of God.

"Would you consent?"

"Do you think of nothing else, my preening boy?" she asked.

"We must bear more children, replenish what was lost."

"And so we become machines to pump out people who will believe what we believe, carry on our lives so we can live forever."

"The Torah says . . ."

"I care more about what you say, Moshe Gimmel. I care more about what you think. I look forward to spending many hours arguing, Moshe Gimmel, and we are both very good at it."

Usell brushed the hair from Moshe Gimmel's cheek and slipped his pais behind his ear. "You are beautiful, too, Moshe Gimmel. You are smart, you are devout, and you are brave; and if I were to marry anyone, it would be you."

His eyes looked tired and troubled, and he struggled with his tangled blanket.

She kissed him gently on the mouth. His involuntary flinch relaxed as if the surprise of her brazen act was somehow less corrupting than he'd assumed. When she pulled away, he touched his lips. He said nothing more, but turned himself into the mattress and with a blink closed his eyes.

Reaching into the pocket of her trousers, Usell removed the mezuzah. She lifted the diamond around her neck. Golden rays danced about the cabin. Fitting the gold chain into the nail holes of the mezuzah and clipping it back around her neck, she nuzzled next to him.

54 . . .

Just before the noise jostled her upright, she dreamt of her attic garret. She needed to put down the ladder and see who was knocking on her father's door, but she did not want to wake, did not want to escape the dream that gave her warmth and comfort.

The wall vibrated against her back and the blond light in the kerosene lamp blurred the cabin's edge. Someone tapped on the metal bulkhead outside the room. Moshe Gimmel did not stir. Steady pistons deep in the belly of the ship compressed. She sat up.

"Who is it?" she asked.

The tapping stopped.

She wrapped the blanket around her neck and hopped down. Tying her sash around her wet pants, she reached for the door handle.

"Who's there?"

No answer.

Three taps more, lighter.

Opening the door she peeked out.

Nothing. No one.

The gangway was empty and silent. She stepped over the iron threshold onto the wooden slats. The door closed behind her. Lanterns lit the narrow hall and Rudd Cothman leaned against the wall, grinning.

He was shirtless and bandaged around the chest. His thigh was wrapped with strips of white gauze and tied with the same professional knots as on Moshe Gimmel.

"People on the ship have been spreading lies about you," he said. "They say you are a princess."

"You will have to stop telling them that," she said.

And then she dove at him, wrapped herself around his middle, and tightened her grip.

His body constricted, but he didn't pull away. His hand brushed her hair as she flattened herself against him and held on. When she could breathe again, she realized that he winced. Relaxing her grip, she removed her cheek from his chest.

"Sorry I'm late," he said. "Had my hands full for a while. A whole army showed up."

She wiped her eyes against a mix of bandage and skin.

"I put so much pressure on that damn machine, *Utto* blew up on me, tossed me into the harbor. Lucky I found a dinghy with one oar missing or you wouldn't see me here now."

"I lost one like that."

"I lost something far more valuable."

"The jewel you wanted?" she said.

She slipped her finger around the chain and pulled out the diamond. "You mean this?"

"You have it. How?"

"The princess gave it to me," she said.

"When?"

"I didn't want to tell you I had it. You can take if from me now if you want. I owe you."

He snorted hot breath on her cheek.

"Promise not to give it back to the Tsar?" he asked.

"Why would I do that?"

"Promise," he said.

"Okay, I promise."

"Then you can keep it."

"I don't understand."

"You don't need to know," he said.

The frown that wrinkled her brow for a moment smoothed away.

"You're a spy."

"I'd rather you think of me as an adventurer who has flexible moralities," he said. "That way I wouldn't have to kill you."

"You wouldn't do that."

"No?"

"Too pretty to kill, remember?"

The quiet reset her as she nuzzled against him.

With a lurch of the ship against a rising swell the hatch door creaked open.

Usell pushed it closed.

"Moshe Gimmel is asleep. I would like to see land once more. Can you make it onto the deck?"

"With your help," he said.

His arm rested around her shoulder.

Usell supported his weight up the stairwell's iron steps.

He favored his right leg and limped to the deck, where sea air smelled of salt and a brisk wind stung her cheeks with spray.

The blanket whipped about her shoulders and sea foam washed across the width of the ship.

At the railing Usell clasped one arm around Rudd, the other onto smooth wood. There they stood, saying nothing for a time. Vibrations at their feet halted as the engines stopped.

The rasp of leather yolks cranked up the masts as seamen raised leviathan sails on tall spires, one forward, one aft, two midship.

Usell slipped her hand in his. Balancing against the railing, he pushed against her.

"I have a question for you," he said.

She lifted her head and pushed back. "Ask."

"You'll answer?"

"I will not know until you ask," she said.

"The Cossack. What went on between you?"

Rubbing her head against his shoulder and holding his arm in hers, she said, "You do not need to know."

He smiled and shook his head.

"I think you'll find America fertile ground," he said.

"When we reach my new home," she said, "I will go to University. I will educate myself. And I will engage with you Americans."

"You are a very serious woman," he said.

"No longer a child?"

His smile reappeared, but he said nothing and put his arm around her.

The soft splash of waves hit the hull as it cut through black water. The masts creaked as the ship changed direction, its tilt angling from the vertical, steel fittings tightening the stays, straining the vibrating sails and picking up speed. With strings of clouds disguising the full moon, darkness covered the water and whatever light was left on the land blurred to faint shadows that, as far as she could see, left nothing separating heaven and earth.

###

About Joel Chafetz

Growing up in a home where stories about his Eastern European ancestors were served at every meal led Joel to write *The Chaff*. Joel is a novelist and prize-winning short story writer who lives with his wife and daughter in the suburbs of Seattle.